The Tenth Crusade

Christopher Hyde

Houghton Mifflin Company Boston
1983

Library of Congress Cataloging in Publication Data

Hyde, Christopher.
The Tenth Crusade.

I. Title.
PS3558.Y36T4   1983   813'.54   83-4335
ISBN 0-395-34404-2

Printed in the United States of America

S   10   9   8   7   6   5   4   3   2   1

This is a work of fiction. All characters and events that play a part in the story are
fictitious; any resemblance to persons living or dead is purely coincidental.

This one is for Barrie Jones and Stephen Raptis,
for all sorts of reasons, and as always,
for Mariea, with love.

Prologue

The *National Geographic* photographer had been tracking the wild horses for more than a week, wandering through the Gabbs Valley Range of southwestern Nevada with his camping and photographic equipment strapped to the pillion of his fat-wheeled Yamaha trail bike. He already had more than 500 exposures of the elusive mustangs, but the requirements and standards of the famous magazine meant he probably needed at least that many again.

Not that he minded. The parched, corrugated landscape was fascinating and he had shot another fifteen rolls on his own, concentrating on insect and animal life, of which there was a surprising amount considering the dusty wasteland he had been traveling through. Trees were rare, the occasional juniper providing a morsel of welcome shade, but sagebrush grew everywhere, and there was enough of it to support an entire, virtually invisible, food chain.

But the subject now focused in the 500mm lens of his Nikon was neither the wild horses he had been tracking nor the insect and animal life that lived among the sagebrush. The photographer's subject was Man.

There were a dozen of them, all in military uniform. From his vantage point at the top of a high, rock-strewn hill, the photographer had a clear view of what they were doing. The soldiers were gathered around a small camp stove, drinking from mugs, and chatting. One of the men stood sentry with what appeared to be an AR15 assault rifle looped over his shoulder. As far as he could tell from the neatly piled packs

7

and other equipment, the men had been on some kind of overnight exercise. He automatically took a few exposures, his motor drive whirring softly. He frowned, his eye still pressed to the viewfinder. He moved the camera fractionally, running it over the figure of a tall, dark-haired man who appeared to be in command.

It was odd. The photographer had been in the business for a long time and had spent two years with UPI in Viet Nam. He'd done stories on a thousand different aspects of the military and in all that time he'd never seen soldiers like these.

For one thing they *were* soldiers and that in itself was strange, since the closest military base was Fallon, more than a hundred miles away, and it was an Air Force station. The uniforms were definitely army though, combat fatigues. But where the patch over the pocket should have said U.S. Army, there was nothing, not even a dark spot where a patch might once have been. The only rank insignia seemed to be a shield-shaped arm patch — a silver sword on a jet-black background. The tall man was the only one who had it; the others had a shoulder flash, once again shield shaped, but instead of a sword the flash depicted a white cross, piped in black on a red field. Behind the cross, and running through its center, was a white X, and it too was piped in black.

More jarring than the strange uniform insignia was the weaponry the men carried. All carried sidearms, which once again was strange, unless all the men were officers, and the pistols were not the standard U.S. Army issue .45 automatics. They were Colt Pythons, the custom MK3 version with the eight-inch barrels; monstrous weapons that weighed almost four pounds each, and completely incongruous both as infantry sidearms and as weapons with any purpose on the Nevada desert. A nickel-jacketed bullet from such a pistol was capable of passing through an automobile engine block and still being lethal on the far side.

The weapon cradled in the arms of the man with the silver and black sword patch was even more sinister in its implications. The photographer had seen such a rifle only once before — in a pile of captured material from a Viet Cong base in

Lang Vei. It was an SVD, or Dragunov, the standard Soviet sniper rifle. Just who were these people? Whoever they were the photographer was certain that his presence on the hill would not be welcome. He took a dozen more exposures, paying careful attention to the identifying patches and the skeleton shape of the Dragunov, and then he began to inch backwards, on his belly, the sweat in his armpits and crotch as much from fear as the early-morning sun. He had hoped to catch the small herd of mustangs unawares and he had left the Yamaha almost two miles away, making his approach on foot. He was sure it was far enough away that the noise of its engine wouldn't alert the squad of men in the bowl-shaped wash below him.

As far as he was concerned, his wild horse story was finished. By his reckoning earlier that morning, he was about thirty miles from Highway 95. From there it would be a three-hour drive to Hawthorne and his rented pick-up. If he kept up a good pace he could be in Reno by late afternoon and back in Los Angeles by the evening. He wanted to get the photographs developed. He wanted to show them to some friends who were most definitely not with *National Geographic.* He'd been a news photographer long enough to know he had walked into the middle of a big story. And a scary one.

He backed off the crest of the hill, and when he was sure its bulk was between him and the squad on the other side he stood up and began to walk quickly along the wide, winding gully that led back to his bike.

Suddenly and without warning the air was filled with the hammering thunder of a helicopter. Startled, the photographer turned and looked behind him, just in time to see the green and brown camouflaged shape of a twin-rotored C47 Chinook sweeping over the brow of the hill.

The photographer stood, open mouthed, camera slung around his neck, as the helicopter dropped down into a neat landing less than fifty yards from him, the rotors throwing up a stinging cloud of dust. The sound of the engines began to fade and the whine of the rotors began to wind down. A door in the side of the machine slid open, and seconds later the photographer found himself surrounded by half a dozen men in uniforms like those worn by the squad he had seen. All of them were armed with AR15s.

A slim, immaculately uniformed man wearing mirror sunglasses and a long-billed baseball cap, stepped out of the helicopter. The peak of the cap bore the insignia of a silver sword on a black ground that the photographer had seen on the man with the Dragunov. The man approached the photographer slowly and stopped a few feet away. The half-dozen others shifted slightly to keep the man out of their line of fire.

"Name!" snapped the man in the cap. He let one hand rest on the butt of the holstered Python at his waist.

"Curtis," said the photographer, swallowing. There was no thought of giving the man any trouble. "Mel Curtis."

"Why are you here?" the man's voice was like iron.

Curtis responded in a stuttering rush. "I'm—I'm—a photographer. *National Geographic.* I was doing a—story on the horses. The wild horses."

"Do you have a vehicle?"

Curtis nodded. "Trail bike. A mile or so back," he answered, and turned to one of the men behind him.

"Squire," the slim man said, pointing. "Fetch it."

The man nodded and began to jog off down the gully.

"Where is your home base?" asked the man in the cap.

"Home base?" asked Curtis, confused. "I don't—"

"You didn't ride here from Reno on a trail bike!" said the man angrily.

"Oh, right," mumbled Curtis. "I see. Uh. I've got a truck in Hawthorne."

"Inform the State Troopers you were going out here?"

Curtis, too afraid to bluff, shook his head. "No. I figured I could take care of myself. I've been in the desert before."

"You were wrong," said the man in the cap, a wide smile creasing his face. "Dead wrong." He barked an order. "Squire! The box."

Curtis frowned, understanding neither the reference to the box, nor the fact that the man had used the same name for two different people.

One of the soldiers turned and trotted back to the helicopter, reappearing a moment later carrying a metal box about a foot square with a dangling sleeve attached to one end. It looked like a portable darkroom box the photographer had once used.

"Take off your jacket," instructed the man.

Curtis did as he was told, completely confused now.

The soldier carrying the box stepped forward.

"I don't ..." began Curtis.

"Roll up your sleeve," said the man, his voice harsh.

Once again Curtis obeyed. He stood, one sleeve rolled up, and waited. "Look," he began again, "if I've broken any—"

"Shut up!" said the man. "Put your arm in the box, please."

The use of the word "please" seemed incongruous under the circumstances, and for a brief moment the photographer's fear began to lessen. The soldier with the box took another step forward, turning the contraption so that the sleeve faced Curtis. Curtis slipped his hand into the sleeve. It had suddenly occurred to him that he had inadvertently walked onto the Nellis nuclear testing site somehow, and that these men were checking him for radiation, although he couldn't see how he'd managed to wander that far off course. By his calculations Nellis was a good seventy-five or a hundred miles to the south.

The sound he heard as he pushed his arm into the box was neither mechanical nor electronic, as he had expected, and in the split second before the pain struck he was able to identify it.

Rattlesnake. Then the fangs of the three adult reptiles ripped into his palm and forearm. Curtis screamed and reared back, tearing his arm out of the box and sleeve. He fell to his knees, clutching his arm. Already the deadly venom was at work, his hand and arm were swelling as he watched. The pain was agonizing and he began to moan.

The man in the cap ignored the sound. He spoke to the young soldier holding the gruesome box. "Wait until he's unconscious, then put him onto the helicopter. When we have the trail bike we'll head back to the base. I'm going to pay my respects to the Recon Squad over the hill there."

"Yes, sir," said the soldier with the box.

"Come and get me when you're ready to go." The man looked down at Curtis. He had fallen face forward into the gritty earth and he lay twitching and writhing in horrifying pain. Then the man turned away and began walking slowly up the hill.

Behind him the soldiers stood around the photographer and watched him die.

PART ONE
Genesis

*Woe unto them that call evil good
and good evil.*

Isaiah, 5:20

Chapter One

Nguyen Ngoc Loan, Police Chief of Saigon, stood in the middle of the roadway, smoke from a burning house down the block swirling around him. His reptilian head was thrust angrily out of the protective carapace of his sweat-stained flak jacket and his thin right arm was outstretched. He snapped off a single shot from the nickel-plated ladies' gun. Two inches from the end of the barrel the captured Viet Cong officer had his eyes squeezed shut, a thin arc of blood spurting into the air as his brains were blown out the other side of his head.

Yawning, and stark naked, Philip Kirkland slipped the spatula under the perfect pair of butter-fried eggs, then slid them deftly onto his waiting plate. He glanced at the photograph hanging over the stove and smiled. It was the single most reproduced shot to come out of the Viet Nam war and, even now, after almost fifteen years it was still making him money.

He cut a thick slice of freshly baked whole wheat bread from the loaf on the counter and then walked across the cluttered expanse of the huge room. He sat down on the ledge of one of the dozen waist-to-ceiling windows that filled the whole south wall of the loft and began to eat, alternating bites of egg with pieces of the chewy bread.

Philip Kirkland was thirty-four years old, and except for the lines on his forehead and the look in his eyes he could have passed for a man ten years younger. His body was lean, the light olive skin offset by the thick arrow of body hair that flared up from the dark tangle of his groin. His face had the hard line of chin and jaw that was his father's, the black eyes and high cheekbones of his mother, topped by a thick, curly mass of jet black hair that could have come from either parent. His mother was Italian, his father Irish, and Philip was an archetype for both nationalities, flawed only by a missing baby finger on his right hand; lost in a childhood accident. It had never interfered with his work, but it had kept him out of the draft.

It hadn't kept him out of Viet Nam. At seventeen he was a highschool dropout with a flair for action photography, and armed with that and his natural charm he managed to get himself hired by the L.A. office of Associated Press. By his eighteenth birthday he was in Saigon and by his twentieth he had weathered the '68 Tet Offensive and traveled the Dog's Face into Cambodia, documenting South Vietnamese and U.S. search-and-destroy missions.

By the time he was twenty-five he had traveled around the world a dozen times and lived in every major world capital, establishing himself as a daredevil with a camera who was willing to do anything to get the necessary shots. Eventually he'd settled in New York, buying himself 1800 square feet in Lower Manhattan, south of Houston Street—a loft.

Philip picked up a crumpled package of Chesterfields from the window ledge and lit a cigarette with a kitchen match. He dropped the spent match into the tobacco-tin lid he used as a breakfast ashtray and looked down on Lispenard Street, three floors below.

SoHo was beginning to wake up. A sandy-haired man wearing an ancient leather jacket and driving a battered VW pick-up truck was haranguing a garbageman at a dumpster while up the street the owner of a natural food snack bar was cleaning the previous night's litter off the sidewalk in front of his establishment. On the corner by the AT&T long line terminal building two Puerto Ricans were screaming at each other while a wino, propped up against the traffic light pole, watched them.

Philip smiled, dragging on the cigarette, pulling the smoke deeply into his lungs. The only thing better than traveling was living here, he thought. By the evening Lispenard and the rest of SoHo would have turned into a nightmare or a carnival, depending on what you were used to. Transvestites would be tripping by on high heels, PRs would be shooting craps, and maybe each other in dark doorways, bottles would break and women would scream. Throughout it all, daylight and dark, the Mercedes and the Jags and the BMWs would roll in and out, sometimes buying what the SoHo artists had to sell—in galleries like Leo Castelli's, Sonnabends, O.K. Harris, and Paula Cooper—or taking in the scene at the Ballroom or the Spring Street Natural Restaurant.

He turned away from the window and surveyed the high-ceilinged expanse of the loft. Counterclockwise from the windows the four corners of the 30' x 60' room were taken up by kitchen, bathroom, darkroom, and bedroom, and all of these areas were relatively neat. The central portion of the room, however, was a sea of changes, a slowly circulating mass of equipment, cutting tables, racks of backdrops, props for ad shots, and the collected personal possessions of the last ten years. The neatly mounted and framed photographs on the whitewashed walls, spotlit by tracks in the ceiling, made the mess look even more chaotic than it was. Prospective clients or buyers, seeing his studio for the first time, were generally appalled by the disorder, but there was no denying that the end result of his work was as close to perfection as anyone could want. In the four years that he had been living in the Lispenard loft he had managed to create three one-man shows, hundreds of advertising assignments, and *Split Seconds*, the only book of photographs to hit the *New York Times* best-seller list in the past ten years.

It was the book that had made him famous as a photographer. It was a collection of his best work, all but one photograph focusing on his private obsession—the instants of time in people's lives that change them forever. The Saigon execution figured prominently, but there were others of equal impact, including a shot taken with a hidden camera of a murderer receiving his sentence of death, a father holding his newborn child for the first time, an old woman being wheeled into surgery, and the arch-necked heads of a couple in orgasm.

But of all the photographs, the one that critics found most

haunting was a simple, almost amateur, black and white of a young girl, no more than eighteen or nineteen, walking down an airport concourse, her head turned back to look where she had been. Her hair was blonde and frizzy, shoulder length, framing an oval face, the large eyes and wide mouth set in an expression of almost impossible emotion that combined sadness, longing, relief, and some hidden, brooding terror. He had known she would turn, and he had been waiting with the camera ready, knowing too that the photograph would be his final and only sure memory of her. The title of the shot, "Heather/Orly/1971," told the critics nothing, and when interviewed Philip always refused to talk about it.

What people who saw the photograph never knew and never guessed was that "Heather" portrayed the split second that changed Philip's life forever in the last glance of a love which had stayed with him for over a decade, and which he doubted would ever completely fade.

Philip butted his cigarette and stood up, stretching. It was almost noon, but over the past few months he'd been living in the timeless vacuum between assignments. It was one of the disadvantages of being a success; he wasn't hungry any more. He could pick and choose his assignments and if he wanted to he could beg off working for six months or more and not have it make a dent in his bank balance. It was exactly the position he'd wanted for years to be in, but now he was finding it boring, and more than a little frustrating. What I need, he thought wryly to himself, is a good war somewhere.

He padded along the long line of windows to his bedroom platform and slipped on a pair of worn jeans and a T-shirt. From the look of the street it was going to be another sweltering day. It had been uncommonly hot for June and he found himself almost wishing for the windy bluster of fall.

He threaded his way through the clutter to the kitchen, poured himself a cup of coffee from the machine beside the stove, and went back to his vantage point at the window. He lit another cigarette and leaned back against the window frame, wondering what to do with his day.

Without any work in hand he had a number of choices that ranged from snapping the tourists on Broadway on the off-chance he might get something good, to updating his negative files, a chore that should have been done months ago. Neither option was particularly appealing, nor were any of the others in between. He crushed out his cigarette and frowned.

The telephone on the upended milk crate beside his bed rang, the thin, anxious sound echoing off the patterned tinplate tiles of the ceiling. Philip looked over at the phone and wondered whether he should answer it before the answering machine cut in on the third ring. He shrugged. Good news or bad, it was better than nothing at all. He dropped down off the window ledge and sprinted down the relatively clutter-free alley between the windows and his work area. He made it to the bed as the phone began its third burst, hooked the receiver, and fell against the headboard bolster all in one motion.

"Hello. Philip Kirkland. Are you prying or buying?"

There was nothing but silence and breathing. In the background he could hear the wail of a siren, and suddenly he heard the same siren come muffled through his own windows. Whoever the silent type on the line was, he was close by.

"I don't have time for screwing around; if you're not talking in three seconds, I hang up," said Philip. The strange stereo effect of the siren dopplered into silence as the vehicle went by. Then the person spoke and Philip felt his palms go clammy.

"Philip?" she said. "Do you know who it is?"

His heart was racing. "I know who it is," he said softly. Oh Jesus! After all this time and her voice was almost killing him. "Your voice hasn't changed."

"I'm at the little restaurant a few doors down from you. I wanted to make sure that you were there. I'd like to see you. I *have* to see you."

"I'd like that," said Philip, not knowing if it was true, fearing it as much as wanting it. "Just ring and I'll buzz the door for you. I'm on the third floor."

"I'll see you in a minute, then," she said, and hung up.

I'll see you in a minute, after twelve years; a lifetime. "Heather/Orly/1971" turned fully from that final glance and stepped out of the past to haunt him in the flesh instead of from the safe, shining pages of a book.

Chapter Two

Nineteen-seventy was the end of the world for a lot of people. The war in Southeast Asia was a nightmare that threatened to turn into madness, Watergate was in the wings, and the children of the sixties saw their dreams dissolve in apathy and paranoia as the tribes dispersed in the face of the harsh reality that no one cared much any more.

For Philip Kirkland, 1970 was Paris; civilization after a year and a half in the rice paddy schizophrenia of Viet Nam. At first he hadn't wanted to leave, but his section head in Saigon told him that the war was like being underwater too long — you began to suffer from delusions, the worst being that the only reality was one of punji sticks and bicycle bombs. Officially Philip had been assigned to cover the peace talks, but in fact he was given *carte blanche* to shoot whatever he could find; even at that early stage in his career the people he worked for had recognized his talent and were willing to give it free rein.

Twenty months in Viet Nam had given him a good knowledge of French and he took to Paris easily. He rented a cold-water flat above a café on the Left Bank and roamed through the streets armed with a matched pair of battered Nikons and a jean jacket, taking roll after roll of film as he tried to capture the gently decaying soul of the ancient city.

He'd been in Paris less than a month when he met her. It was winter and Philip was taking a break from the damp, bone-chilling cold of the streets, sipping from a bowl-sized cup of the thin, bitter hot chocolate that Parisians favor. He was sitting in a café, at a corner table in the rear that gave him a good view of the gray, slightly hazy street outside.

She came in like a whirlwind, wearing a long purple coat, her hair flying in every direction, her mouth in a broad smile as she threw a flurry of conversation at the taller, less striking young woman with her. The two sat down a few tables away, and when they ordered *café-crème* and *tarte aux pommes* he could tell by the accent that neither one was French.

Philip watched, enthralled, as the wild-haired girl talked to her friend, leaning over the narrow table, speaking in a whisper and gesturing with her hands. The other girl, dark haired and dressed much more conservatively in a brown cloth coat, listened and nodded, rarely getting in more than a few words. Not that she seemed to care; the blonde with the huge silver-gray eyes was obviously in control. As subtly as he could Philip took a reading and set the F stop and speed on his camera. When he was sure that neither of the two young women was looking his way, he raised the camera and focused quickly, hoping to catch the blonde's intensity. A fraction of a second before his finger hit the shutter release, as though by telepathy, she turned and stared into the lens.

"*Qu-est-ce-que vous faites?*" she demanded, a touch of anger in her voice. He shrugged and smiled.

"*Une photographe,*" he said, explaining the obvious.

She caught the slight hesitancy in his French and frowned. "*Bâtard!*" she snarled under her breath. He grinned.

"*Bon phuc toy,*" he replied, raising his cup in a mock salute. Her mouth gaped.

"I beg your pardon," she said. Even the one sentence had Boston written all over it.

"It's Viet pidgin for 'screw you too honey,'" he answered, smiling.

She flushed. "You're American."

"Right."

Her frown turned into a sneer. She looked him up and down. "Your hair's too long for you to be a soldier," she said.

He nodded and held up his maimed right hand. "I take pictures." Before she could move he lifted the camera and got off another shot, catching her outrage.

"Prick," she said.

"I repeat, *bon phuc toy*. I'm just doing my job."

"Do you speak much Vietnamese?"

He shrugged. "Enough to get by."

"You were there?" she asked, the sneer gone. The other girl was beginning to look a bit nervous, as though she'd been with her friend in situations like this before and knew what to expect.

"Year and a half," he said. He lifted his cup and gave her his most charming smile. "Buy me another one of these and I'll tell you all about it."

"You're on," she said.

And that's how it had begun.

Their relationship was almost unbearably intense right from the start. He quickly learned that she was Heather Foxcroft and the other, quieter, girl was Janet Margolis. The two were roommates. Janet was studying fine art at the Sorbonne and Heather was dancing in the French production of *Hair* in the chorus as well as taking dance classes from several different schools. They lived together at Cité Universitaire in the Maison des Etudiants Etats Unis and they were chronically short of funds. Both of them were Beacon Hill, Boston. Heather's father was a general and Janet's was a top tax lawyer. They both smoked grass and hash when they could get it, loved Bob Dylan and Hermann Hesse, and hated their families and their backgrounds with a rebellious passion.

Much later Philip had asked Heather what she had been thinking while they had talked in the café, and she admitted that the only thing in her mind was the vision of him making love with her, and that the vision was made all the more excruciating by the intuitive knowledge that they both *knew* that sex between them was inevitable. After two hours in the café Janet had finally gotten the message and bowed out, pleading a class and a tour of the Louvre.

Heather went with Philip to his small apartment; they smoked a pair of smuggled Thai sticks, and then made love. Philip, used to the casual sex of the sixties and the even more casual sex of Saigon, was expecting a simple, pleasant liaison and was in no way prepared for the passion she unleashed.

There was something almost masculine about the way she

made love and more than once in the furious hours they spent together, Philip sensed that this was the way men had sex together; there was a dense, muscular feeling to it, a deep-rooted power he had never experienced before.

By nightfall they were sated, the sheets twisted at the bottom of the bed, both their bodies tangy with sweat. And even then it didn't end. They talked halfway through the night and when hunger struck they roamed the back alleys looking for a place to eat. Then, finding it, they talked more until the weak sun rose behind the ever present overcast of the Paris winter.

It went on like that for weeks. Except for her classes and performances, they were never apart. Janet faded into the background, still Heather's friend, but no more than an onlooker to the helter skelter love affair.

Philip and Heather fought constantly, two strong minds trying to dominate and neither one succeeding. Heather remained the impassioned optimist and banner carrier of sixties celebration, always seeking some kind of perfect peace and harmony, almost desperate in her desire for a world where everyone was equal. She read Hesse and Hegel, the Bible and Brecht, searching for some magic talisman, arguing for humanity, while Philip shook his head and told her stories of eighteen-year-old boys in the sweltering jungles who hacked off the testicles of the enemy and fire-bombed villages to the tortured armageddon wail of "Electric Ladyland." Philip saw himself as a documenter of a world that had always been insane while Heather screamed that mankind was essentially good and only needed a direction. Their love for each other was total, all-consuming, perfect, and doomed.

In a year and a half the intensity of their feelings never wavered and in the end it exhausted them both. By the spring of 1971, it seemed as though they had eaten each other alive. Heather had turned within herself, becoming moody and withdrawn, and Philip had allowed himself to harden, seeing the world only through the lens of his camera and despising it all. Bangladesh was born and had died a hideous death, Laos was invaded, and Idi Amin took power in Uganda. They went to see "Clockwork Orange" at a theater on the Champs Elysées and then, arguing over it in the Métro, they came apart at last. Almost before either of them knew what had happened, Heather decided to cut her studies short and hitchhike to India with Janet, and Philip took an assignment in Northern Ireland. He took "Heather/Orly/1971" just before stepping through the gate to board his flight to Dublin. He never saw her again.

Until now.

Seeing her again was almost enough to break his heart, as twelve years fled.

"You look fine," he said.

She stood, looking out one of the windows, everything about her taut with nervousness. She did look fine. She wore a simple skirt and blouse that did nothing for her, but he could see that her body had changed little. Her hair was shorter, the color slightly darker, and there was age in her eyes now. But she was still the same woman, though the fire and the passion had dampened by time, or experience, or both.

She turned away from the window, her arms crossed over her chest protectively. She smiled, a small sound rising, then dying in her throat. "So do you," she answered. The silence between them was like a rusty nail on slate.

Philip gestured toward the kitchen area of the loft.

"We could have coffee. There's a table and chairs," he suggested.

She shook her head. "No, I'm fine, really. I'd like to stand, to walk around a bit, you know?"

"Sure, whatever," said Philip. He lit a cigarette and levered himself up onto one of the window ledges. Heather walked down the bare floor alleyway to the end and stared at his photos hung on the stark wall. He watched her walk, the tautness of her thighs and back, the swing of her hips, and felt himself harden beneath his jeans. He shut his eyes and willed the feeling to pass.

She turned and walked back to him. "You haven't changed, Philip. Still taking pictures of death and dying."

"Not just that," he said, and tried to smile back at her. "Other things once in a while."

She nodded and let one hand fall to the wood of the sill a

few inches from his bare foot. Her finger caressed the thickly painted surface for a moment and then withdrew. "I know," she said. "I saw your book when I was in Mexico City. It made me cry a little bit. The picture of me, I mean. Leaving you."

"We left each other," said Philip.

She nodded. "I suppose that's true," she answered. Her hand fell back to the wood and they both watched the movement of her fingers.

"What were you doing in Mexico City?" asked Philip.

She looked away from her hand and into his eyes. "You wouldn't believe it." She smiled broadly and for a small moment the fire was back.

He grinned. "Try me," he said. "I think I've heard just about everything over the past twelve years or so."

"I was getting ready to take my final vows."

"Vows?" asked Philip.

She nodded. "I was going to be a nun. I spent eight years with the Sisters of Charity, as a volunteer and then as a novice."

"So what happened?" asked Philip, desperate to keep the conversation going so he would have time to deal with what she was saying.

"I couldn't go through with it. I didn't have the faith. I lost it, you know."

"Go on," he said.

She moved away from the window slightly, half turning away, her face shadowed by the wooden bars dividing the panes of glass. "I wanted to come home, wanted to join the world again, but everything had changed. I talked to my father and he said he wanted me to come back, but I didn't believe him, so I went to see Janet."

"Janet Margolis?" said Philip.

She nodded. "She lives in Canada now. Toronto. And she has a child. I went there and stayed for a while. I made some friends, or it seemed as though they were friends. They told me not to see my father, or you, but I had to."

"Did you see your dad?" he asked.

"Yesterday," she said. "He lives in Washington now. Still the

General. Even bigger now. Four stars instead of three and he's one of the Joint Chiefs."

"And now you're here," he said.

She smiled at him. "My friends won't be happy about that at all," she said, a dreaminess in her voice. "They said you were the most dangerous of all."

"Some friends," said Philip, wondering what kind of bunch she'd fallen in with.

There was a long silence and then the sound of her laughter, no louder than a whisper.

"Do you know," she said softly, "it's been more than eight years since I've kissed anyone other than a child. Eight years." She stared at him. "Eight, ten, twelve years, and I've been locked away inside myself, waiting for you again, as though you were some kind of Prince Charming who could wake me up." She began to cry, the tears running down her cheeks to the corners of her mouth. "I don't believe in Prince Charming, Philip," she said weakly. "I just don't believe it any more." She laughed, the sound faint and hollow. "It's like the Africans used to think. You took that photograph twelve years ago and you stole my soul."

Philip dropped down from the window and stepped forward, taking her in his arms.

"You can have it back any time," he whispered, and then he kissed her, the smell of her the same, the taste of her the same, except for the tears.

Much later, with the sun falling into dusk he asked her if she wanted coffee or something to eat.

"Herb tea?" she asked, and laughed. "I'm still a hippie."

"I can get it at the restaurant down the street," he said.

He dressed quickly and went to the door. "Back in a minute," he called. She didn't answer. He opened the door and stepped out into the dark stairwell. Something hit him on the back of the head so swiftly that he had no time for thought before consciousness faded. When he woke and stumbled back to his loft it was almost dark outside, but there was enough light left to see that the place had been demolished. The only sign of Heather was a long red streak, head-high on the wall behind the bed.

Chapter Three

Philip took a shuttle flight from New York the following day, arriving at Washington National in the middle of the afternoon. He passed through the terminal, picked up a cab, and settled back in his seat for the short drive to General Foxcroft's home in Alexandria. The Saturday traffic was heavy on the Memorial Parkway, but the driver knew his way around and soon had them out of the mainstream. The man behind the wheel was silent, and that was just the way Philip wanted it. His head still hurt from the day before and he needed time to get his thoughts together before meeting with Heather's father.

He was still furious at the way he'd been treated by the police. Since there was no body, Homicide had refused to take on the case and after half an hour of being passed around the local precinct house he'd wound up with a short, grizzled-looking detective from Burglary. Nothing Philip said seemed to interest the man at all.

"Nothing taken?" asked the man, whose name was Rabinovitch. He carried a small pad and pencil but made no notes beyond jotting down Philip's name.

"Not that I can see," said Philip.

Rabinovitch raised a thin eyebrow and looked around the loft. "Would you know if something was missing?" he asked.

Philip gritted his teeth. "Look," he said angrily. "I called the police because I think someone has been hurt, maybe even killed, then taken away. You understand?"

"Sure," nodded Rabinovitch, pursing his lips, and idly checking out the mounted photographs on the walls. "You said an old girlfriend came by. You hadn't seen her in ten years or something. You went out to get something at the restaurant and someone hit you over the head. When you woke up the broad was gone."

"And there was a streak of blood on the wall," added Philip.

The detective shrugged. "You say it's blood. Maybe it is. Maybe it's chicken blood, how the hell should I know? Maybe you fell and hit your head and the broad took a powder. Maybe there was no broad and you hit *yourself* over the head. All I know is you says there's nothing missing, so there's no burglary, so what am I doing here?"

"I'm reporting a crime," snapped Philip, his head throbbing.

"What crime?" asked Rabinovitch. "There's no body, so we can count homicide out. There's nothing missing, so forget burglary. The door's not busted open so there's no B&E. What crime?"

"Kidnapping," said Philip.

Rabinovitch grinned, thin lips almost disappearing. "That's a federal offense," he said. "Call the FBI."

"I give up," said Philip. He sank down onto the bed and lit a cigarette.

Rabinovitch looked down at him. "Good," he said. "I'm glad you give up. We got enough fucking crimes *with* bodies and *with* things missing. We don't need this kind of crap."

"Fuck you," said Philip.

Rabinovitch grinned again and dropped his pencil and notebook into the side pocket of his crumpled suit jacket. "You got it," he said. "Find something missing, give me a call." He waved a hand and left.

Philip, stunned by the rapidly unfolding train of events, had sat smoking in his loft until evening, trying to piece it all together. Foremost in his mind was the incredible knowledge that whatever it was that had made him and Heather so strong together was still there within him. Call it love, or call it obsession, he knew that the only way he would ever live and be at peace with himself was to find Heather and see if the few strange hours they had spent with each other was nothing more than a desperate grasping at the past, or a signal that what they had been together had never truly ended.

Beyond that there was fear. Fear that something had happened to her. The blood on the wall was real, and so was the rising lump on the back of his head. Someone had mugged him, then taken Heather by force. There were two obvious questions to be answered: who and why. Heather had said that she'd spent some time with her father in Washington, and then with Janet Margolis in Toronto. According to her it was in Toronto that she'd met these strange "friends." Friends who would not have approved of her meeting with him. Disapproved enough to knock him over the head and kidnap her? It didn't seem likely, but he had nothing else to go on. It was also clear that the police were not going to be any help. If he was going to find her, it was going to be on his own. He'd decided to find out what he could from Heather's father, and then pay a visit to Janet Margolis.

Twenty-five minutes after leaving the airport the taxi turned into South Lee Street and stopped in front of General Foxcroft's residence. It was a brick-wall enclosed "flounder," one of the strange half-gabled houses with the windowless side wall that is standard in Alexandria. Philip grabbed his flight bag, paid the driver, and slid out of the car.

The shoulder-high brick wall screening the front of the house had an old-fashioned swinging-door gate, painted black, and from the thickness of the paint and the scarring of the wood it looked as though it was as old as the house. Beyond the gate the large lot was heavily planted with apple trees, magnolias, and dozens of wild rose bushes. It seemed an oddly pretty setting for a general. Philip pushed through the gate, walked up the zig-zag brick pathway, and climbed three stairs up to the ornately carved front door. He hit the cherub's head knocker twice and waited. Half a minute later the door swung open and Philip found himself looking at a stooped black man dressed in a dark suit, white shirt and bow tie. The butler. The gray-haired man looked Philip up and down, taking in the tan leather bomber jacket, checked shirt, and bluejeans.

"Yes?" said the man coolly.

"I'd like to see General Foxcroft," said Philip.

The butler looked him over again and made his decision. "The General is not receiving guests," he said.

Philip shifted his bag to his other hand and took a deep breath. "Tell him my name is Kirkland and that I'd like to talk to him about Heather."

At the mention of her name the butler's eyes narrowed. He frowned. "Just a minute," he said, and he closed the door in Philip's face.

Enough time passed to make Philip think he'd been forgotten when the door swung open. It was the butler again.

"The General will see you," said the man, obviously not agreeing with Foxcroft's decision. "He is in the rear garden." The butler took a step forward onto the portico and pointed to the right. "Follow the path to the back of the house."

"Thanks," said Philip.

"You're quite welcome, sir," said the man. He stepped back into the house and shut the door silently. Philip turned and followed the man's directions.

The rear portion of the lot was small compared to the front and side gardens, but it was just as carefully planted. There was a small wrought-iron table painted white, and four chairs on a raised brick patio that looked out over a grouping of flower and shrub beds. The neighbors beyond were screened off by the brick wall and by a thick planting of white and purple lilacs. The General liked his privacy.

Heather's father was seated at the table, a silver tea service in front of him. Philip had never seen him except in head and shoulder shots in *Time* and *Newsweek*, and seeing him out of uniform was a shock. He was dressed in a short-sleeved print shirt and wore a battered straw hat to keep off the mid-afternoon sun that blazed down over the garden. Without the rows of ribbons and the peaked cap, he was somehow demeaned, the scrawny liver-spotted hands and the tired face not those of a man who was Chief of Staff of the United States Army.

The General made no attempt to stand as Philip approached. Instead he waved him to one of the other chairs at the table.

"Tea?" he asked. His voice was thin and reedy, as though sleep had eluded him for a long time.

Philip shook his head. "No, thank you," he said.

"Something hard then?" persisted the General. "I can ring for Otis." Foxcroft put his hand on a small silver bell but Philip shook his head again.

"Nothing, thank you, General. I'm fine."

The older man nodded curtly and reached for the large teapot, as though pouring himself a cup would demonstrate his independence from Philip's refusal. "Suit yourself," he muttered.

Philip noticed that his hand shook slightly as he grasped the teapot and wondered if it was from anxiety or old age. He waited until Foxcroft had finished the ritual, then spoke. "I'd like to talk to you about Heather," he said.

"I can't see what there'd be to say," replied Foxcroft, his voice taut with Boston Back Bay frost. "And if there was, why should I talk to you?"

"She saw you recently," said Philip.

"You know that?" asked the General coldly.

"She told me herself," said Philip.

The man looked startled but recovered quickly. "And when was this?" He sipped at his tea, watching Philip over the thin fluted rim of the cup.

"Yesterday, in New York. Before she disappeared."

"That's impossible," said Foxcroft, placing his cup deliberately down on his saucer. "Heather has been in Canada ever since she ... left Mexico."

"Dropped out of the convent," corrected Philip. "She told me all about it."

There was a long silence. A hummingbird whirled a few feet away, streaking across the jade green grass to one of the magnolias. In the distance Philip could hear the high-tension-wire hum of a cicada. He waited. Foxcroft ran a long arthritic finger around the edge of his teacup.

"You said after she disappeared," murmured the General, not looking at Philip.

"That's right. Someone hit me on the head. When I came to, Heather was gone. There was some blood."

The old man's head snapped up and his eyes blazed for an instant. For the first time Philip could see Heather in him.

"Blood?" he asked.

"Right. Blood. As though someone banged her around a little bit before they grabbed her."

"You're saying she was kidnapped?" asked the General.

"Yes," said Philip. "The cop I talked to suggested that I get in touch with the FBI. Maybe he was right."

"I don't think she was kidnapped," said Foxcroft.

"You weren't there," said Philip. "She was taken by force. I call that kidnapping."

"Why did you come to me?" said the old man.

It was Philip's turn to blaze. "Because she's your daughter, for christsake! She comes to see me out of the blue after a dozen years, she tells me she saw you two days ago, but you tell me that she's been in Canada ever since she left Mexico. Somebody's lying."

"She is not my daughter," said Foxcroft.

"What the hell is that supposed to mean?" asked Philip.

The man lifted his shoulders wearily. "It means what I said. I last saw my daughter in 1970, Mr. Kirkland. I last had a letter from her in 1972. She wrote me in response to the telegram I sent to her at the Mother House in Calcutta telling her that her mother had died. The letter I received was little more than a sermon concerning the mysterious ways of the Lord. My daughter was raised a Baptist, Mr. Kirkland. I forgave her when she stopped going to church, I even forgave her when she became a Catholic, Mr. Kirkland. I could not forgive her for not coming to her mother's funeral. At the end of her letter she told me that she felt she could better use her time by serving the living rather than mourning the dead. And God knows why I'm telling you all of this."

"Maybe it's because I loved her too, General Foxcroft. I still do."

"Yes," said Foxcroft. "You lived with her in Paris, didn't you? She wrote me about you, flaunted the fact that she was sharing her bed with you."

"It was more than that, General. It was always more than that. Do you honestly think I'd be here now if all there was between me and Heather was sex?"

"I don't care what there was, or is, between you. I no longer wish to discuss it."

"She said she'd met some friends in Toronto," said Philip insistently. "She also said that these friends told her not to visit you, and especially not me. Do you know anything about that, General?"

"Mr. Kirkland, Heather phoned me four months ago to tell me that she was leaving the convent house in Mexico City and was going to see Janet Margolis in Toronto. Up until that time I had no idea that Heather was even on this continent. She telephoned me once more from Toronto two months ago, asking me for money. I sent it to her, care of Miss Margolis. I haven't heard from her since, and she certainly never undertook to tell me about any friends she had made."

"These seem like fairly negative friends," said Philip. "Maybe negative enough to pull her out of my place in New York and clout me over the head into the bargain."

"She never mentioned anyone," said Foxcroft. "She only asked for money."

"How much?"

"Ten thousand dollars."

Philip's eyebrows lifted.

"And you just sent it to her?"

"I had little choice in the matter," said the man. "The money is part of the accumulated interest from the trust fund that was set up for her by her grandmother. The money is legally hers."

"She didn't say what she wanted the money for?" asked Philip.

"No. She just named the figure and asked that it be sent to her. Which is exactly what I did."

"And you haven't seen her or heard from her since that time?" asked Philip.

The old man shook his head. "That's right."

Philip stood up. "Thank you," he said, extending a hand.

The General looked at it disdainfully. "Nothing to thank me for," he said.

"If I find her, is there any message?"

Foxcroft looked at Philip, squinting in the harsh sunlight. He shook his head. "No message," he said.

Philip nodded, then turned and left without a backward

glance. He frowned as he walked up the path that ran alongside the house. There was no doubt in his mind that the General was lying. He had seen Heather, just like she'd said. But why had the old man lied? And what was he afraid of? Philip checked his watch. If he found a taxi fast enough he could get out to Dulles International in time to catch an early-evening flight to Toronto.

*　　*　　*

He arrived in Toronto at dusk and passed quickly through the cursory customs and immigration check. Exhausted, and still nursing his headache, Philip checked into the Airport Hilton, reserved a car from Hertz, then looked up Janet Margolis in the telephone book. He called the number half a dozen times over the next hour but there was no answer. Finally he gave up, ordered a room service meal and ate, watching the late news on television. The day's top story was the same on both the Canadian and the American channels he flipped through. "International terrorism comes to the United States."

At 1:30 Central Time that morning a stretch of railway track on the Missouri-Pacific line between Bridge Junction and Memphis, Tennessee had been destroyed in a violent series of explosions. Thirty minutes later there was a second attack on a section of Southern Pacific line between Grosse Tete and Port Allen, Louisiana. Within minutes of the Louisiana explosions, and more than 1500 miles away, four lines of sight microwave towers in Oregon had been simultaneously destroyed. Two hours later a massive detonation ruptured a secondary natural gas transmission line a few miles outside Freeport, Texas.

By 8:00 A.M. Eastern Time responsibility for all the destruction had been taken by a group calling itself the Devil's Brigade. According to audio cassettes left at major radio and television stations in Tennessee, Louisiana, Oregon, and Texas, the explosions were the first strike of a nationwide campaign of terrorism designed to "bring capitalist America to her knees." Within an hour, State and FBI authorities had confirmed that the tapes had come from the same source and that the terrorist acts had been the work of a highly organized and well-equipped group of people.

The T.V. news footage was like something out of World War Two: twisted rail lines, the crumpled remains of demolished towers, and billows of smoke and spikes of flame from the sabotaged pipelines.

Philip watched until he'd eaten as much of the club sandwich as he could stomach and then turned off the television. He drained the last of his Canadian beer and then went to bed. Within a few minutes he had fallen into a deep and dreamless sleep.

Chapter Four

Janet Margolis lived just off Danforth Avenue in a predominantly Greek neighborhood that had always been close to the poverty line but was now being rejuvenated by a wave of renovators and restorers. From the looks of Janet's street, though, the wave hadn't quite reached her. The houses were large, Victorian, and shabby, each one carrying at least four electricity meters; hers had five.

Philip parked the rented Ford in front of the sleepy-looking clapboard building. The windows on all four floors were grimy with pollutant soot and a drain pipe on one side of the building hung drunkenly from its brackets. He climbed out of the car, locked it, and went up the narrow walk to a steep flight of veranda steps covered in fake-grass carpeting. There were five buttons tacked to the doorframe; number 4 had Janet's name on it in faltering script. He pressed and waited. A few seconds later there was a dull click and the lug bolt in the front door drew back.

Philip pushed it open and found himself in an almost totally dark vestibule that faced a long flight of stairs. He began to climb, careful of where he put his feet, until he reached a tiny landing on the third floor. There was a small door mat and a confused heap of running shoes and sandals. At least one pair seemed to belong to a child. There was a woven god's-eye nailed on the door above the painted number 4. Philip knocked.

A moment later the door opened and he found himself looking down at a boy of about ten or eleven. He was wearing a pair of shorts and nothing else. His hair was cropped almost to the scalp.

"I'm looking for Janet Margolis."

The boy gave him a long look, then called back over his shoulder. "MOM." There was no inflection or exclamation, it was just loud. He turned back to Philip and stepped away from the door. "Come in, please." Philip entered a short hallway and the boy squeezed past him to shut the door. "Go right in," said the boy politely. Philip did as he was told and walked the few steps into what was apparently the living room. He stood and stared for a moment. It was like going back in time.

The room breathed the sixties. There was a slab of foam, covered in an Indian bedspread, on the floor along the far wall below the window. The window itself was screened by a bamboo roller blind. There was an ancient-looking beanbag chair in one corner, two sets of brick and board bookcases, two shelves high, and a large flat-topped trunk covered in blue enameled tin which supported the stereo and tape deck. There was no other furniture in the room and the only thing on the wall was a large black and white poster of what was probably an Indian spiritual master.

The boy went past Philip and dropped into the beanbag chair. Philip, unwilling to drop down onto the four-inch-high slab of foam, remained standing. A few seconds later, Janet came into the room. Her dark hair was cut short, her oval face had hardened over the dozen years since Philip had seen her last. She was wearing a sari-like arrangement dyed a shade of brown that made it look as though it had been stained with coffee.

"Go outside and play now, Karalla," she said. The boy stood up and left the room. Janet smiled at Philip and he was amazed to see that she was wearing braces. It seemed incredible to him that anyone who lived and dressed the way she did would care about orthodonture, let alone afford it.

"You age well," she said. She sank down onto the floor in a single fluid motion and looked up at him, a hand on each knee. Philip sat down on the beanbag chair.

"I'll bet you quit smoking," he said, and smiled. She grinned back, the metal on her teeth glinting. She rose as gracefully as she had gone into the lotus and briefly left the room. When she came back she was carrying a plain unglazed dish. She placed it beside the beanbag chair and sat down again a few feet away. Philip lit a cigarette in the silence. Janet kept staring at him.

Finally he spoke. "I feel like I've got a fly on the end of my nose," he said.

She shook her head. "I'm sorry. It's just that it's been a very long time. It's like looking at a ghost. I suppose it must be the same for you."

He nodded. "You're the second so far."

"I gather that means you've seen Heather," said Janet.

"The day before yesterday. In New York."

"New York," said Janet thoughtfully. "I wonder if that means she's left them?"

"Left who?" asked Philip.

"The Crusade. It's a fundamentalist group here in Toronto. Other places too. They're into neighborhood defense groups, vigilante squads, that kind of thing. Born again Christians."

"Heather was into that?" asked Philip.

Janet nodded and lifted her hands. "It's a long story," she said.

"I'm in no rush," said Philip.

"You're looking for her, aren't you?"

"That's right. She disappeared under rather strange circumstances. I'm worried about her."

"Did her father send you?"

Philip laughed and stubbed out his cigarette. "That's a joke," he said. "I talked to him and he acted as though Heather wasn't even his daughter."

"He sent detectives around here, you know. After she left the Sisters in Mexico and came up here." She shook her head. "I couldn't believe it. I open the door one day and there are these goons in shiny suits. Very heavy."

The penny dropped and Philip suddenly realized what had been bothering him. He'd noticed the same thing with Heather two days before—the use of vernacular speech that was more than a decade out of date. It was as though both she and Janet had dropped out of time and then stepped back in again.

"Did you tell them anything?" asked Philip.

Janet shook her head. "No way. Heather's old man had always been laying his trip on her. I wasn't about to help him lay another one. Besides, I couldn't have told them much anyway. She'd gone by then."

"Into this Crusade thing?" asked Philip.

"That's right." She looked at Philip carefully. "I don't know if I should tell you anything more than that. I mean, maybe you want to lay a trip on her, too. Or am I being paranoid?"

"You're being paranoid," said Philip. "I think she's in trouble."

"I can't believe that it would mean anything to you after all this time."

"You've talked to her recently," countered Philip. "Did she still have strong feelings about me?"

"She called you her eternal burden," said Janet, smiling sadly. "She said she dreamed about you every night for twelve years. No matter where she was or what she was doing."

"So is it so strange I might feel the same way?" he asked.

Janet lifted her shoulders. "I suppose not. I've never felt that way about anyone," she said. "I used to watch the two of you in Paris, and I don't think I ever quite believed it. Then we hitched to India. Every so often she'd, uh, you know, get it on with someone, but she said it never lasted the way it did with you. She used to tell me how intense it had been with you. Maybe all the stories she told me were true."

"They were true," said Philip. "Maybe that's why I'm here, because she's unfinished business in my life."

Janet laughed. "That's not quite how she put it," she said smiling. "She said you were something she had to run away from. She did a pretty good job of it too, for a lot of years."

"Did she ever say why?" asked Philip, knowing that he was being led off the track, but wanting to know more about the missing years in Heather's life.

"Guilt," said Janet simply. "It was always guilt. When we were doing all the hitchhiking she was always into guilt. Guilt about the world, about her family, about leaving you and being unfaithful to you. Always guilty. I started getting into it after a while, too. When we were in Calcutta I almost wound up joining the Sisters as well. She almost had me convinced."

"What stopped you?" asked Philip.

Janet laughed, a distant look in her eyes as she went into the past. "We spent a little bit of time in Kathmandu before we went down to Calcutta. Heather found us a place on Freak Street; she was always good at getting us places to crash. Anyway, there was a guy there named Michael, who was doing about an ounce of hash a day and meditating. Try doing that at twenty-three thousand feet above sea level. I mean, it does things to you. Anyway, we started making it. It wasn't until we got to Calcutta that I realized I was pregnant. Mother Teresa is a far out lady, but she doesn't take pregnant women as novices. I wound up going to a place in Australia to have Karalla; Heather stayed on in Calcutta."

"And that was the last time you saw her until she came up here?" asked Philip.

Janet nodded. "Yes. And when she was here she seemed really disturbed."

"About what?" asked Philip.

"A lot of things. A Catholic would probably call it a crisis of faith. I don't know. She seemed unsure of herself. Unsure of the order. She was about to take her final vows and it was scaring her. It was like, I don't know, like she was waking up but she wanted to go back to sleep again."

"What does that mean?" asked Philip.

"Maybe you had to see her go through the changes to appreciate it," said Janet. "But it was as though she's used Mother Teresa as a crutch and for some reason she didn't need it anymore."

"So why didn't she just quit then and there?" asked Philip.

"Oh come on!" scoffed Janet. "She'd been with the Sisters for eight years then. She had a hard enough time dealing with reality then, let alone after being a nun for all that time. She was scared. Terrified might be a better word."

"So she came here."

Janet nodded. "I offered. Like a half-way house almost. I came back here, then about four or five months later, she arrived at my door. She said she was through with the Order, that she wanted to be involved in something other than breaking her back doing work that could just as easily be done by a mule. I even watched her take off the habit. She was through with them."

"And then?" asked Philip.

Janet looked at him carefully. "You're not going to report back to her father?" she asked.

"No."

"All right." She stood up and went to one of the bookcases. She pulled a small pamphlet out from between two paperback books on yoga and handed it to Philip. The pamphlet was a single oblong sheet, folded, the cover printed in four colors showing a photographic image of a gleaming sword being held aloft in a chain mail fist. The chain mail appeared to be made of stainless steel. Philip opened the pamphlet and read the brief message:

THE TENTH CRUSADE IS GOING ON
A JOURNEY AND WE WANT YOU TO
COME ALONG.

Historically there were nine
Crusades. We are the Tenth. The
Tenth Crusade will be the hardest
and the most dangerous. It is,
quite simply, the Greatest Ad-
venture of all.
And it is taking place here and
now. Drugs, alcohol, rape, broken
homes, crime in the streets and
immorality in government. We are
fighting them all, and with your
help we are going to win.
If you would like to find out more
about the Tenth Crusade, talk to
the person who gave you this pamphlet
or drop in to one of our community
Round Table discussions.

*If you think you are the type of person
to help us with the Final Battle, then
why not join us now!*

At the bottom there was a Toronto address and a telephone number. From the way it was printed Philip could see that the address and phone number had been added locally and that the pamphlet was probably being distributed on a national scale. He flipped it over. The small union seal was American.

"Seems relatively harmless," said Philip. "What exactly is the Tenth Crusade?"

"If you spend any time on the streets you're bound to run into them eventually. They hand out pamphlets and raise money for their centers. That kind of thing. Not to mention the groups they have on the subways and cruising the neighborhoods."

"New York has the same kind of thing. The Guardian Angels," said Philip. "But there's no religion involved."

"You don't get the religion until the second or third meeting with the Crusade," said Janet. "At least it seemed that way from Heather. They come off like a mixture of Born Agains and Jesus Freaks. They even wear uniforms."

"Blue pleated skirt and white blouse?" asked Philip, taking a guess based on what Heather had been wearing.

Janet nodded. "And blue pants and white shirts for the men. They've got windbreakers too, with their crest. A cross with an X through it. The X is supposed to be the Roman numeral ten."

"How many meetings did Heather go to?" asked Philip.

"Three, in town, that is. Then she went to one of the week-long seminars they have at some kind of retreat place near Lake Nipissing. After that she came back for her clothes and stayed a couple of days trying to convince me to join up."

"Her father said he sent her some money," said Philip.

"That's right. She waited for him to wire it."

"Did she say why she was joining?" asked Philip. "I mean, after all, didn't she quit the Sisters?"

Janet shrugged. "She said that the Tenth Crusade was actually doing something to change the world. According to her,

Mother Teresa was a Band-Aid; the Crusade was major surgery."

"Sounds a little crazy," murmured Philip, fingering the pamphlet.

"I know," said Janet. "That's the trouble. Heather was in pretty bad shape when she was here with me. She kept on wondering if she should go and see you, or her father. I asked her about that when she came back from the Crusade seminar. She said that the Crusade wanted you to cut all past ties, especially with loved ones; that they were dangerous. It was tearing her apart."

"You think she was cracking up?" asked Philip, remembering the strange fugue state she had gone in and out of in New York, as though she'd been wandering through some mist-shrouded dream.

Janet nodded. "She was pretty upset overall."

"How long ago did she leave for good?" asked Philip.

Janet thought for a moment. "Six weeks ago. Maybe two months. I'm not certain."

"And nothing since?" he asked.

She shook her head. "I tried calling the number on the pamphlet, but they said they'd never heard of her."

"I suppose the next step is to check these people out," said Philip, fluttering the pamphlet. "You mind if I take this?"

"Go ahead," she said. "But I don't think you're going to find her here."

"Why not?" asked Philip.

Janet got up and went back to the bookcase where she'd retrieved the pamphlet. She leafed through a rubber-band-wrapped bundle of bills and pulled one out. She brought it to Philip and handed it over. It was a telephone bill, with a listing of long distance calls. There were only three calls on it – two to a number in Boston and one to a place called Barrington, New York.

"It's the New York number," said Janet sitting again. "I got a collect call about two weeks after she left. She could barely talk. I tried to get her to come back to my place but she kept on babbling on about her need to follow Joshua, or something like that. She sounded pretty crazy."

"Do you have any idea why she'd be in this Barrington place?"

"I'd never even heard of it until I saw the name on my telephone bill."

"Maybe I should write the number down," said Philip studying the phone bill. Janet got to her feet again and he followed suit. She found a pencil and a piece of paper and Philip took down the number. He handed her back the pencil.

"I guess I should be on my way," he said.

Janet reached out and touched him softly on the chest. "I hope you find her. I know it sounds silly but I think we're all she has left."

"Except the Tenth Crusade," said Philip. He leaned forward and gently kissed her cheek. Then he turned and left, leaving her standing alone in the apartment, a single shaft of dusty morning sun covering her with light like some strange and troubled Madonna.

Chapter Five

Barrington, New York turned out to be a community of 3,800, five hours east of Buffalo in the Finger Lakes district. One of the area's eleven major bodies of water, Lake Conesus, was less than five miles from the town, invisible behind the curtain of heavily treed hills that surrounded the town.

Barrington was basically nothing more than the intersection of two state highways, one running north and south, connecting Rochester and Corning, home of the famous glassworks, the other going east and west between Buffalo and Syracuse. The buildings were mostly brick along the two main drags, the side streets thinly housed with clapboard residences whose peeling paint and missing shingles spoke of better times in the past. The focal point of the town appeared to be a small park in the town square which held a radio antenna type mast topped by a huge Stars and Stripes. A large metal sign half the size of a billboard was attached to the foot of the mast and announced that the flag had been erected during the Iranian hostage crisis, and that the flag had flown twenty-four hours a day during their incarceration, lit by twelve spotlights. Below the notice was the town's slogan, painted in alternating letters of red, white, and blue: BARRINGTON – SMALLTOWN AMERICA AND PROUD OF IT!

Philip cruised up and down the two main streets of the deserted town, and eventually found a place called Toby's Bar and Grill, apparently the only place that stayed open on Sundays in Barrington. An electric blue Genesee Beer sign flashed on and off in the front window. He parked the rented car and went into the dimly lit establishment.

There were nine booths receding into the darkness along one wall and a bar running along the other. The place was empty except for a chicken-necked man in a soiled white jacket who was sitting on a stool by the cash register reading a copy of *New York* magazine. Philip sat down on the stool at the bar closest to the cash. He had time to find his cigarettes and light one before the man looked up from his reading.

"Stupid magazine," he said by way of introduction. "Restaurants and the-aters. You'd think the world had nothing better to do with its time."

"It's a pretty crazy place," agreed Philip. The man frowned. "You from New York City?" he asked.

Philip shrugged. "By way of a lot of other places," he said, then dragged on his cigarette slowly. "I was born in Oregon, raised in Seattle, and went to school in San Diego. And that was before I started traveling."

"West Coast," grunted the man. He peered at Philip sharply. "You in the service ever?" he asked.

Philip, remembering the flag in the square, lifted his hand and waggled the stump of his missing finger. "Two years in Nam," he said.

The chicken-necked man nodded seriously. "You want some coffee? Kitchen's closed, but I can give you coffee."

"That would be fine," said Philip.

The man slid off the stool, poured two cups from a Corey machine, and set one down in front of Philip. He reached into the depths of his stained tunic and pulled out a single cigarette. He lit it with an old Zippo and stepped back up onto the stool, cranking open the drawer of the old-fashioned cash register to use it as a tray for his coffee. Philip peeled back the tab from the tiny cup of synthetic cream, and poured it into the dark coffee. He sipped and nodded appreciatively.

The chicken-necked man looked pleased. "You should have gone to Canada," he said after a moment.

Philip grimaced. "I don't get you," he said.

The man tucked his cigarette into the corner of his mouth and talked around it. "Dodged the draft," he explained. "You were either crazy or stupid to do two years over there."

"You don't sound like you belong in this town," said Philip, grinning. "Not if that flag out there is any indication of how people around here think."

"I don't give a shit how they think," said the man. "I'm as patriotic as anyone else. I fought in the Second World War *and* Korea. World War Two was worth fighting. Korea was edging toward being stupid. Viet Nam was just plain crazy. I lost two boys over there. Both my kids. Bang bang, one after the other. No more than a month between them. Two metal coffins and two parades down the main street of Barrington with everyone wearing their veterans' cap. Shit."

"I'm sorry," said Philip.

The man shrugged. He took the cigarette out of his mouth long enough to pull at his coffee, then put it back into the corner of his mouth again. "It was a long time ago. If I'd been smart, I would have told them to pack up their things and go to Toronto, but I didn't, and that's the way of the world, I suppose." There was a long silence, then the man spoke again. "So what brings you to Barrington on a Sunday? You don't look like a tourist."

"I'm not," said Philip. He paused, wondering how much he should say. "I'm looking for someone. The last I heard she was in Barrington."

The man smiled. "What's her name?" he asked. "We don't get many strangers here; maybe I know her."

"You wouldn't know her by name," said Philip, "but the last I heard she was wearing a blue pleated skirt and a white blouse, with a blue blazer to match the skirt. Pretty, blonde curly hair. About thirty."

"You a cop?" asked the man, dousing his cigarette into the dregs of his coffee. Philip shook his head.

"No."

"Private eye or something?" insisted the man.

"No. Why?" asked Philip.

The man sneered. "You wouldn't be the first," he said cryptically.

"I don't get you," said Philip.

The man shrugged expressively. "It's the skirt and blouse. The blue and the white. This woman you're looking for. She was probably up at the monastery."

"Monastery?" asked Philip.

The man smiled, his thin lips working into a lopsided grimace. "Used to be a monastery. Jesuits. Used it as a retreat, or whatever you call it. Sold it two years back to the Jesus Freaks up there."

"Jesus Freaks?" said Philip.

The man nodded. He dug around in his pocket for another cigarette and came up empty. Philip offered him one of his. "They call themselves the Tenth Crusade," said the man. "They're in and out of town all the time in those blue Econolines they have. Smart enough not to try any of their bullshit here, though."

"What kind of bullshit?" asked Philip.

The man laughed, squinting against the smoke from his cigarette. "Dunno. I told you, they don't try any of it around here. Asking for donations and like that." He shook his head. "That kind of thing doesn't go down too well in the lakes. There's been enough religious nuts around here over the past hundred or so years to last everybody. Goes right back to the Mormons. Brigham Young was born around here, you know."

"No, I didn't know that," said Philip. He wanted to get back onto the subject of the Crusade, but he knew the man was going to have his ramble, one way or the other.

"Yeah. Brigham Young, the Jemimakins, Horace Greeley. All that crap started up around here. And that was long before anyone started making wine, so you can't blame it on the liquor. Place seems to attract crazies. We even had the Moonies back here in the seventies but they moved on to Tarrytown."

"Are these Tenth Crusade people anything like the Moonies?" asked Philip.

"I dunno," said the man. "Maybe. Every once in a while we get a private cop coming around looking for some runaway. From what I can tell the Crusade people never make a fuss about it. I think you call it keeping a low profile. They use the old monastery about one week out of the month, and then everything's quiet the rest of the time. When the blue Econolines pull in for gas you know they're back for a while, though."

"Where is this monastery?" asked Philip.

The man sucked air through his teeth and looked thoughtful.

"East," he said finally. "Highway fifteen to Livonia. Just on the edge of town. Can't miss it. Big old brick place set back off the road a hundred yards or so. Give it to these people, they keep the lawn nicely cut."

Philip stood up. "Thanks," he said. "How much for the coffee?"

The man waved the question away. "Forget it," he said. "I don't get much chance to talk on a Sunday. The cigarette covers it."

Philip nodded and headed for the door. As he opened it the man's voice stopped him.

"Mister?" he called.

Philip turned around. "Yes?"

The man looked embarrassed. "These people. Some of them. They look kind of … I don't know how you'd put it … hard."

"You're telling me to be careful?" grinned Philip.

The man shrugged and settled back onto his stool. "Something like that."

Philip nodded his thanks again and went through the door, stepping out onto the empty street once more. The sun was already slipping quickly into the west, throwing a dull gold light over the blind-eyed storefronts on his side of the street. The far side was already deep in shadow. Beyond the town the thick green of the hills was dissolving into black. Philip checked his watch. It was 8:00. There was enough time to go out and take a look at the monastery before he went in search of a motel for the night.

He U-turned the car and headed east, the brick stores bleeding into bungalows and Chevron stations as he left town. He guided the car around the base of a low hill and the town disappeared completely at his back. He peered out the side windows, left and right, trying to spot the building. A moment later it appeared, a large Jeffersonian-style building on a sloping knoll with smooth lawns sweeping down to the highway. There was no wall of any kind around the grounds, and from what Philip could tell there were no lights on in the building.

Two hundred yards before the winding road that led through the grounds up to the building, Philip saw a gas station, its sign off, the only light coming from the illuminated interior of a telephone booth attached to its rear wall. The sight of the phone booth jogged his memory. He pulled off the highway into the gas station lot and switched off the engine. He climbed out of the car and went to the phone booth, digging into the pocket of his jeans for the slip of paper on which he'd jotted the Barrington number at Janet's place. He banged open the door and peered in at the number on the graffiti covered phone, then checked it against the one on the piece of paper. They were identical.

He turned and walked across to the closed pumps and stared down the road at the monastery, trying to put his few facts together. Heather had hooked up with the Crusade in Toronto, gone on a week-long seminar, and then disappeared. Janet had received a garbled call from a pay phone at this gas station, five hundred feet away from what appeared to be a major Crusade operation. Then Heather had dropped out of sight again, only to reappear a month or so later at his loft in Manhattan. And according to her, after having seen her father in Washington, although he denied it. Then he was hit on the head and she disappeared again, leaving a blood smear on his wall and a lot of unanswered questions.

As he stood watching the building, he noticed a small car moving slowly down the highway from the other direction. It was a TR7, dark green, and barely visible against the backdrop of trees. It was dark enough now for the car to be using its lights, yet they were still tucked into their streamlined cubbyholes above the snout of the wedge-shaped car. On top of that the driver was holding the powerful engine down to no more than ten miles an hour. Acting instinctively Philip crouched down beside his car and kept his eyes on the Triumph. As the sportscar reached the roadway leading up to the Crusade's monastery, it pulled off onto the shoulder. Philip peered into the semi-darkness, trying to make out what was going on. He noticed the shadowed bulk of four garbage cans lined up to one side of the entrance road.

The door of the small car opened and a short figure climbed out. The person ran across the highway, threw the lids off the cans and began hauling out the green plastic garbage bags within. With the cans emptied the person began dragging the bags back across the highway and then stuffed them into the car, two in the diminutive rear trunk, and two onto the passenger seat. Finally, the person ran back across the highway, replaced the lids on the cans, then raced back to the car. There was a brief pause and then Philip heard the sound of the Triumph's engine starting up. The sportscar did a quick U-turn and, still with its lights off, headed back the way it had come.

Philip stood up and blinked, watching the car disappear into the distance. For some unknown reason somebody in a British racing-green sportscar had just stolen the Tenth Crusade's garbage. Obviously he wasn't the only one interested in the Barrington monastery. He jumped in behind the wheel of his car and took off after the receding sportscar. He waited until the Triumph went around a curve before he switched on his own headlights to counter the growing darkness, and when he came out onto the straightaway he saw that the car ahead had done the same.

He followed the TR7 for an hour, trailing by a mile or more, through the sleeping town of Livonia, then south, still on Highway 15, heading for Conesus and the junction of Interstate 390. He prayed that the car ahead wasn't heading for the Interstate because he knew he'd lose it there. A Ford Fairmont was no match for a Triumph on a six-lane highway.

Thankfully the sportscar turned off the highway at Wayland, pulling into a slot in a motel parking lot. Philip guided the Ford off the road, gliding up to the motel office just in time to see which room his quarry had slipped into. Philip got out of the car and went to the cigarette machine beside the door to the office. He began feeding it quarters, keeping one eye on the parked sportscar down the row. A moment later the room door opened and the TR7's owner appeared. Philip pulled the handle on the cigarette machine and tried not to look as if he was staring.

There was no mistaking it; under the harsh light from the spots in the roof overhang he'd seen that the owner of the sportscar was a woman. From the brief glimpse he had of her as she began wrestling the garbage bags into her room, she looked to be in her late twenties with long dark hair pulled back in a twist and pushed under an old-fashioned deerstalker. She was wearing jeans and a bulky sweater to finish off the unflattering ensemble. Ignoring the first package of cigarettes that had dropped down onto the machine's lip, he kept on putting change into the slot. Out of the corner of his eye he saw her again, this time popping the narrow trunk lid and retrieving the two bags of garbage from it. She didn't give him a second look. She went back into her room and shut the door behind her. Philip pulled the handle on the machine again and picked up his cigarettes. Both of them were low tar and nicotine brands. He opened one of the packages, removed a cigarette, tore off its filter and lit up, wondering what to do next.

After three drags on the amputated cigarette he had decided on a course of action. He dropped the two low tar packs into a large waste receptacle on the other side of the office door, picked a shred of tobacco from his lower lip, and went down the narrow walkway to the young woman's room. He knocked firmly on the door and waited. He could almost sense her hesitancy, but after a few moments the door opened slightly and he found himself looking down at her. The deerstalker was off and her hair was down, and he realized that although far from beautiful, she wasn't unattractive.

"Hi," he said, as pleasantly as he could. "My name is Philip Kirkland. I saw you stealing garbage from the Tenth Crusade building outside of Barrington and I wanted to ask you why."

Chapter Six

Philip could barely stop himself from laughing. The woman's jaw dropped and he actually saw the blood drain from her face. She took a step backwards and Philip pushed open the door.

"Nobody could have seen me!" she whispered. "I planned it perfectly."

Philip stepped into the room and shut the door behind him. He tried to flash her a reassuring smile.

"I was at the gas station down the road," he explained. "It was just luck that I saw you. Don't worry, though, I'm one of the good guys." He looked around the room. Two single beds were arranged against the side wall, facing a bureau and mirror. There was a bedraggled-looking armchair in one corner next to a door that probably led to the bathroom. The garbage bags were piled in a heap at the foot of the nearest bed.

Philip went around the still gawking woman, stepped over the pile of garbage bags and sat down on the bed. He motioned toward the armchair. "Why don't you sit down and we'll talk."

Without taking her eyes off him she moved around the end of the bed to the chair. She sat down, still watching him. "Who are you?" she asked, her voice weak.

He smiled again. "I told you. My name is Philip Kirkland. You haven't told me your name."

"Sarah," she muttered almost as an aside. "Sarah Logan. Now look, how come you were spying on me?"

This time Philip did laugh. "I think that's a case of the pot calling the kettle black. If I'm a spy, then you're a thief."

The young woman flushed, her eyes flaring dangerously. "I am not a thief," she said, her tone precise. "There is nothing illegal about stealing garbage in New York State. I checked."

"Are you serious?" grinned Philip. "You actually checked?"

"I believe in being thorough," she snapped. "Now, I'd appreciate it if you would answer my question. Why were you spying on me?"

"I wasn't, not strictly speaking, anyway," said Philip easily. He pulled out his package of Chesterfields and lit one. Sarah wrinkled her nose but said nothing. "Actually, I was checking out the monastery."

"Why?" asked Sarah briskly, her self-control returning. She crossed her legs and looked at him expectantly.

She wasn't as cool as she looked, thought Philip, noticing that the fingers of one hand were working hard at the worn fabric of the chair arm.

"Why don't you tell me why you were stealing the garbage?" he countered.

"Someone has to go first. And this *is* my motel room."

"Fair enough." Philip nodded, and he told her his story, blurring the details slightly and omitting Heather's and her father's names, just on the off-chance that Sarah Logan turned out to be a reporter. She didn't bat an eye throughout, not even when Philip mentioned the blood on the wall, and this surprised him. Ten minutes later he had finished.

"All right," he said. "I've told you my whys and wherefores, now it's your turn." He lit another cigarette and waited.

She stood up and went to the only window in the room, which faced the parking lot outside. She opened it wide and took a few deep breaths through the screen. Then she turned back to Philip. "I want to ask you something first," she said.

"All right."

"You said you lived in a loft in Manhattan. Are you Philip Kirkland the photographer?"

"That's right."

"What was the title of your book?" she asked.

"Is this a quiz?" asked Philip, annoyed.

She shook her head. "I just want to make sure you are who you say you are."

"*Split Seconds*," he said curtly.

She nodded. "What was its ISBN number?" she shot back.

"Its what?" he asked.

"ISBN—International Standard Book Number," she answered crisply. He shook his head.

"I don't have the faintest idea," he said. "But I assure you I am Philip Kirkland, the photographer. I'll bet *you* don't know the ISBN or whatever number from my book." She grinned.

"Zero dash three zero three dash ten thousand and one dash five," she replied.

"I'm flattered," he said.

She shook her head. "Don't be. I only remember it because it was so euphonic. It stuck in my head along with the rest of the L double C PD."

"What the hell is *that*?" asked Philip.

"Library of Congress Catologuing in Publication Data," she answered.

"What are you, a librarian?"

"No," she answered, coming back from the window and seating herself again. "I'm a research historian for the Library of Congress."

"Now, what about stealing the garbage?"

"I'm gathering evidence," said Sarah, an emotional rasp rising in her voice. Anger and pain in equal measure.

"What kind of evidence?"

"Evidence of murder. Evidence I can use against the people who caused my father's death." She gritted her teeth.

Philip stared across at the small figure in the bulky sweater, her hair hanging down over her shoulders in a chestnut wave. She hardly looked the type to be involved in some kind of vendetta.

"Why don't you explain that?" said Philip softly. "And take it slow."

"Maybe you remember it," she began. "My father was the Democratic senator from Kentucky. About ten months ago they started a campaign against him."

"Who started a campaign?" asked Philip.

"ACCT," she replied. "The American Conservative Coalition for Truth. It's a huge lobby in Washington headed by a man named Jack Steenbaker. They came out with advertising campaigns that are as close to slander as you can get. But it didn't do any good. My father wouldn't budge. I think they were after him to vote against some abortion thing, or maybe they just wanted to make sure he didn't get in next election."

"But you said it didn't work," put in Philip.

She nodded. "He laughed it off. Said all was fair in love, war, and politics. But about three weeks later, after they started the ad campaign, he stopped laughing. They'd got to him somehow."

"What do you mean?" asked Philip.

Sarah shrugged. "I don't know. He never said. I'd go over there to his place at the Watergate for dinner, and he'd be half-drunk before the sun was down. A couple of times he started to tell me something, but he always cut himself off, managed to keep it a secret. But whenever I brought up the subject of ACCT and Steenbaker he'd hit the roof. After a while I stopped asking. Then, one day, about five months ago now, he killed himself. Stuck the barrel of his favorite shotgun in his mouth and pulled the trigger." Sarah squeezed her eyes shut and took a deep breath. Philip remained silent. She took a few seconds to gather herself together, then went on. "There was nothing—no note, no last message telling anyone why he did it. He just killed himself. And Steenbaker and all the others are responsible, I know it. The smear campaign with the radio and T.V. ads wasn't doing any good so they found some other way, and it ended up with Daddy killing himself." She let out a long rattling sigh.

Philip leaned back and butted his cigarette into the ashtray on the small night table between the beds. He looked back at her. "I don't see what this has to do with you being out in the middle of nowhere ripping off garbage from a monastery."

"Because they're all connected somehow," said Sarah wearily, a note of exasperation in her voice, as though Philip should have known the answer.

"Pretend I don't know what the hell you're talking about," he said lightly. "Fill in the blanks."

She smiled weakly. "I'm sorry. I've been working away at this for almost half a year, putting all the little bits and pieces together to make some kind of picture, something I could hit back at them with. I suppose I expect everyone to have gone over the same grounds."

"I'm just missing an old friend," said Philip. "You've got five months on me. Like I said, fill in the blanks."

"All right," she began, leaning forward, her voice tense. "I haven't got anything really hard yet, but I've connected them all. It's like a huge web from one end of the country to the other."

"Connected who?" prodded Philip gently. Sarah blinked at him and for the first time he noticed that her eyes were a strange silver color, the blue so light it almost faded into the whites. It was oddly attractive.

She gave him a lopsided grin. "Right," she said. "Okay. We start with ACCT—there's a direct link between ACCT and AAF, the America Awake Foundation."

"Isn't that the organization Billy Carstairs runs?" asked Philip. From what he could remember the AAF had sprung into public view soon after the election of Ronald Reagan, supposedly as the mouthpiece of Christian, wholesome America. Philip had never given either Carstairs or his group more than a passing thought.

"That's right," said Sarah. "Carstairs is chairman of AAF, but in actual fact it's run by a man named Andrew Douglas Kronen. He's an old-fashioned back-room type. From what I could find out he got his start as a minor actor in Nixon's Committee to Re-Elect the President. CREEP. Anyway, Kronen and Steenbaker go back years and ACCT does all the advertising work for the America Awake Foundation. Both Kronen and Steenbaker get their mailing lists, which translates into money, from Charles Todd, the big fundraiser, and Todd's computers are backed by Samuel Keller—"

Philip, glad to hear a name he recognized, interrupted. "Keller, the Howard Hughes type with the big pharmaceutical company?" Sarah frowned at his interruption, but nodded.

"That's him. He's also the founder of Eagle One, the big right-wing think tank in Nevada."

"So Keller is the kingpin of this whole 'web' as you call it?" asked Philip.

"No. In fact Keller keeps himself out of the limelight as much as possible. The real leading man is Senator James Harcourt Snow of Arkansas."

"You've got to be kidding!" laughed Philip. "Snow's a buffoon. He was standing next to George Wallace on the steps of that school in Little Rock back in the late fifties."

"Nineteen fifty-six," said Sarah. "The year I was born," she added primly. Philip did some quick calculations and came up with twenty-seven. She looked younger by a few years. "I assure you," Sarah went on, "Senator Snow is no buffoon. He struts his stuff like a good old boy, but he's been a senator for twenty-three years without a break. Even my father used to respect him for that. With this big wave of conservatism, he's finally coming into his own on Capitol Hill. People are paying attention to him now, and it scared my father half to death." She bit her lip at the choice of words but went on. "He's the Conservatives' conservative, and he's connected to everyone, including Keller. Keller Pharmaceuticals opened up its first plant fifteen miles from Snow's hometown."

"I still don't see what all of this has to do with the Tenth Crusade and you stealing garbage," Philip interjected. He'd smoked half a dozen cigarettes and had succeeded in becoming totally confused by her convoluted list of interwoven names and organizations.

"It goes back to Billy Carstairs," said Sarah. "The Tenth Crusade was his idea originally. I had to dig around to find that out, but I pulled an old copy of the *Saturday Evening Post* out of the files and there it was. A 1959 issue, just when Billy was making the transition from tent evangelism to T.V. He had a combination Sunday school-Boy Scout thing called the Tenth Crusade. Uniforms, marching, and Bible study."

"Kind of like the Hitler Youth," murmured Philip.

"Exactly," Sarah nodded. "And I think that must have been the problem, because the Tenth Crusade and the uniforms seem to fade out of the Billy Carstairs' picture once you hit the sixties. Anyway, I traced through all the companies that Billy is involved in, concentrating on the Gospel Way Evangelical Foundation which is the kind of flagship group that does his T.V. show, 'The Gospel Way Hour.' 'Gospel Way' wholly owns a group called the American Heritage Village Missionary Corporation. American Heritage in turn owns two of Carstairs' biggest money makers, Gateway Publishing and 21st Century Communications and Holdings. Twenty-first Century is the interesting one, because if you search through the land titles you find that 21st Century is the owner in trust of every piece of property run by the modern version of the Tenth Crusade."

"Complicated," said Philip.

Sarah lifted an eyebrow. "I'm just skimming for your benefit," she said. "Some of the ways Carstairs makes money from the 'giveaway books' he hands out on T.V. would curl your hair. But it doesn't matter. What matters is that I've got a link between Steenbaker and the Tenth Crusade."

"I hate to throw in a monkey wrench, but so what?"

"Because it's all I have," said Sarah. "After my father ... died, I went through his things, home and office. I found it in his wastebasket on the Hill."

"Found what?" asked Philip.

Sarah got up and went to the bureau. She took out a pad and a felt tip pen and began to draw.

"There were about twenty-five crumpled sheets of scratch paper. They were covered with this design; it's the symbol of the Tenth Crusade. They wear it on their blazers, their jackets, all over. Have you ever seen it?" She held up the pad.

"I've never actually seen it, but I've had it described to me," said Philip taking the pad from her. He studied the faintly sinister configuration. It reminded him of something, but he wasn't quite sure what.

"A swastika," said Sarah, watching him, her eyes burning. "You were wondering what it reminded you of," she said triumphantly. "Well, what it reminds you of is a swastika. And my father had drawn it a hundred times on those pieces of paper, sometimes so hard his pen tore the sheet. I asked one of the people on the Hill how often the wastebaskets were emptied and they said every day during the week. My father died on a Saturday at about ten in the evening. I went to his office the next day, looking for a note or some message. He must have done the doodles, those things ... a few hours before he died. My father had never said anything to me about the Tenth Crusade, and yet he drew their logo over and over again before he died. There has to be some connection."

"Pretty tenuous," said Philip, handing her back the pad.

She looked at him hotly. "Yes, it's tenuous," she snapped. "Just like the blood stain they left behind in your loft. We're after the same thing, Mr. Kirkland."

"Which brings us to the garbage," said Philip.

She nodded. "I studied history in university, Mr. Kirkland. For a while I even thought about being an archaeologist. One thing I found out was that over the centuries we've learned far more from people's garbage than from any other source. Ten thousand years from now the Library of Congress will probably be so much dust, but the junk yards will survive. I thought the same thing might apply to the Tenth Crusade's garbage. Barrington seems to be their East Coast headquarters, so I waited around until I figured out the routine, then stole it." She looked at him, a faintly hurt expression on her face. "And if you hadn't come along nobody ever would have known."

"Sorry," said Philip, smiling. "But now that I'm here, would you like some help going through the mess?"

She looked at him carefully. "Okay," she said slowly, "but first I think you'd better go out to the office and get yourself a room for the night, this could take a long time."

Philip nodded and stood up, smiling inwardly. She was quick to establish the perimeters. It was going to be a working relationship. He headed for the door.

"And could you get yourself a brand of cigarettes that doesn't smell quite as much?" she asked.

Chapter Seven

Philip rented the room next to Sarah Logan's. By the time he got back to Sarah's room she had already dumped out the first bag of garbage onto a large clear plastic drop-sheet.

"You really did have this all figured out," said Philip indicating the plastic.

She looked up at him from the floor and nodded. "I'm old-fashioned about that kind of thing. Neat and orderly. I suppose it suits the work I do."

"Garbage picking?" he grinned, dropping down onto his knees. She frowned and continued to paw through the detritus from the monastery. The bag she had opened contained almost no food garbage except for an empty box of milk powder and some slightly stale bread in a plastic wrapper. Philip was surprised and said so.

"It fits," said Sarah, poking through the litter. "The Barrington place is used for pretty advanced conditioning from what I've been able to find out. One of the methods they use is a minimal diet." She smoothed out a sheet of paper, glanced at it for a moment, then laid it aside.

"What do you mean, 'advanced conditioning'?" asked Philip.

She sat back on her heels and thought for a moment. "Okay," she began. "I've done a lot of digging and so far it seems as though the Tenth Crusade is a fairly straightforward Born Again movement. They concentrate on community activities, homing in on all the morality issues, from peeping toms to muggers and flashers. They round it off with a lot of

61

hard-hitting Fundamentalist teaching. They even have some so-called 'Christian Alternative' schools. They're also heavily involved in juvenile delinquency, and that's where things get interesting. They've set up at least fifty 'youth centers' in the East, all of them in large cities, all of them in depressed areas. They supposedly work to reform delinquents, but what they really are is recruiting organizations."

"Explain that," said Philip. He lit a cigarette and leaned back against the bed to listen.

"I was going to," said Sarah primly. "I went to one of the ones close to home, in Baltimore. It's on Pratt Street, down by the Inner Harbor; real Skid Row—lots of adult movies, that kind of thing."

"I get the picture," said Philip.

"I dressed the part, at least I thought so. I pretended to be down and out, looking for anyone who'd help. They gave me the full tour. On the outside the place looked really run down, but on the inside they'd spent a fortune. There was a fully equipped gym, a cafeteria, second-hand clothing bins, everything."

"Kind of like a combination YMCA and Salvation Army," put in Philip.

Sarah nodded. "Exactly. They had Kung Fu classes, reading classes, they even had some kind of marksmanship class that used an electronic rifle. A total recreation and adult education facility in one of the slummiest neighborhoods in the city, and without a nickel in government funding. It was mind-boggling."

"So where does the recruiting come in?" asked Philip.

"At night. I thanked them for the tour and then I went and sat in a twenty-four-hour restaurant across the street. I kept on buying cups of coffee and watching the place. Around seven o'clock it looked shut down, but then an hour later the lights came back on. A couple of vans pulled up and maybe a dozen people got into them. Most of them kids around eighteen or twenty. The lights went out again and the vans left."

"Blue Econolines, right?" asked Philip. She looked at him strangely.

"How did you know that?" she said.

Philip smiled. "I can play detective, too," he said. "But never mind that, go on with your story."

"It happened three nights in a row," said Sarah. "On the third night I had my car."

"A TR7 on Skid Row?" said Philip. "You must have stood out like a neon sign."

Sarah grimaced. "What do you think I am, an idiot? I borrowed a Datsun from a friend of mine at work. When the van left that night I followed. They drove out to a place near Elkton, just before you get to the New Jersey border. It was a farm, but it looked like they'd thrown up a bunch of barracks buildings. I couldn't see much from where I parked, but it looked like the kids in the bus were marched off to the barracks buildings."

"And from that you get recruiting centers and 'advanced conditioning,' as you call it?" scoffed Philip. "Come on, Sarah, that kind of circumstantial stuff isn't going to get you very far."

"You really do love to interrupt, don't you?" answered Sarah. "Of course it's not hard evidence of anything. But it's enough to get anyone suspicious. I worked on that line of thought for two weeks and I put a lot of pieces together."

"Condense it for me," said Philip. "You were the one who said we had a lot of work ahead of us with the garbage."

"All right," she said crisply. "The place in Elkton was where they winnowed out the people who weren't serious. I got the routine down pat after a few days. A dozen or so up every night, seven or eight back the next day. Another van, coming from the north, and with New York plates, took the kids that made the grade out of Maryland."

"And you followed one," said Philip.

"Yes. I followed one. It came here."

"And then what?" asked Philip.

"Nothing. Not for a couple of days. I bought a pair of binoculars in Barrington and parked the car way around the hill. Then I cut through the woods until I had a clear view of the building. They had curtains up on every window, day and night. There wasn't any light at all."

"So you went in for a closer look," supplied Philip, beginning to enjoy her James Bond-style adventures.

"I certainly did not," said Sarah. "I noticed that they had television cameras under the eaves of the building. Six cameras that I could see. Four of them stayed still, but two of them moved back and forth."

"Pretty sophisticated security for a religious group," said Philip.

Sarah nodded her agreement. "That's what I thought. I knew I couldn't get any closer, so that was when I decided to steal their garbage. They put it out when the place is going to be empty for a few days."

"It still doesn't add up to your advanced conditioning," said Philip. "I'm not nitpicking, I'm just playing devil's advocate."

Sarah shrugged. She plucked a damp piece of yellow paper out of the mess and put it on top of the small pile beside her.

"No," she said. "But after I got involved in this whole mess I started reading everything I could on fringe religions and how the whole cult system works. It fits, like the limited diet."

"Give me an example," said Philip.

"The Moonies. They use the same system. Find the disaffected, cut them off from their relatives and their friends, usually by taking them away from their home locale, and most often somewhere remote. The Moonies have two big places outside New York City, a secluded estate in Florida and a gigantic ranch in northern California.

"Once you have the raw recruits you start the whole behavior modification routine. In the case of Moon they teach the Divine Principle, which is his version of the Bible, and puts Moon himself on top of the pile. You hammer the doctrine into them day and night without any let up, and you keep the diet down to a lot of carbohydrates and very little protein. By the time you've had them for a week you either have dropouts or true believers. When Moon finishes the indoctrination he puts them out into fund-raising teams, shifting the people hundreds of miles away from any familiar territory. First you tempt them with something they want, then you brainwash them, then you put them to work. The Hare Krishnas do it, and so did the Children of God until they got chased out of the country."

"You've certainly done your homework," said Philip.

"It's what I'm trained for," answered Sarah.

"And you think that's what the Tenth Crusade has been doing?"

"The only difference is you never seem to see the people again. There's no fund-raising groups or anything. That's what's so scary. What happens to those people, and what about the connection to Billy Carstairs and the rest of them. *That* doesn't fit in."

"Have you come up with any guesses?" asked Philip.

She shook her head. "Nothing that makes any sense. The only overt tie between Carstairs and the others is the name. Carstairs makes his money by giving away his books and the America Awake Foundation solicits donations using Todd and his computer printouts."

"Well," muttered Philip, looking down at the heap of waste paper on the floor, "Heather certainly fits the bill as far as your recruiting theory is concerned. She was a prime target for them. Mentally confused, already indoctrinated religiously. Nobody to turn to. What does surprise me is how come the Tenth Crusade has a branch in Toronto. It seems like a totally American thing, somehow."

Sarah snorted. "Don't kid yourself," she said. "The Ku Klux Klan is an American institution, too, but they've got Klaverns all over Canada. Not to mention Nazis, John Birchers, and at least three T.V. evangelists directly tied in to Billy Carstairs' organization."

"More homework," said Philip.

Sarah grinned. "I told you," she said, "I believe in being thorough. Working at the L.C. makes it easier too; I can ask for just about anything ever printed and get it in twenty minutes. Even the Canadian stuff. Their national library uses the same computer we do and we're cross-referenced."

"You sound as though you work all the time," said Philip. "What do you do for fun?"

She looked up at him, a frown clouding her face. "I've suspended fun for a while. I've got more important things to do."

"What about your job?" asked Philip, trying to steer himself out of dangerous water. "What do they think about all the running around?"

"I took compassionate leave," she replied. "And then I went on an unpaid sabbatical. I can go back any time. And money is no problem. My father was wealthy and I have my own trust fund."

"No brothers or sisters?" asked Philip.

Sarah shook her head, a sudden sadness coming into her eyes.

"I had a brother. Daniel. My mother died giving birth to him when I was twelve. My mother was forty-four. Daniel was born massively retarded. I barely remember him, actually. He died when he was three. S.I.D.S."

"Pardon?" said Philip.

"Sudden Infant Death Syndrome," explained Sarah. "Crib death."

"I'm sorry," said Philip.

Sarah lifted her shoulders. "Like I said, I barely remember him. It was a long time ago." She sighed and looked down at the garbage again. "We'd better get to work. With all the talking we still haven't sorted through the first bag yet."

"Anything in particular that we should be looking for?"

"Information," said Sarah, digging in.

* * *

Philip worked away at the garbage with Sarah, his eyes scanning the crumpled pages for any reference to Heather. It was a long-shot, but Barrington was his only lead; everything dead-ended after that. He realized that Sarah's motivations were much more general; she was interested in revenge more than anything else, and any dirt she could find on the Tenth Crusade would be of use. On the other hand, the more he learned about the Crusade, the more likely he was to come up with a line on what had happened to Heather. If she *had* been picked up by the Crusade again it stood to reason that she was

66

being kept at one of the Crusade facilities – the question was, which one?

By midnight they'd culled through all four bags, winding up with a small pile of potentially useful material. Most of the papers salvaged were nothing more than shopping lists and schedules. The lists were for Bible texts and tract literature ordered from a jobbing firm in Virginia. Among the religious material were references neither Sarah nor Philip could make out.

"TM-31-210, TM-3100-1, FM 5-31 – they sound like reference numbers of some kind, but I've never seen them before," said Sarah, going over them. "And we have to assume they're books because they're in with all the others."

"Maybe it's some kind of coding within the jobbing company," suggested Philip.

Sarah shook her head.

"I don't know," she said, biting her lip. "Those numbers are familiar, but I just can't put my finger on it."

"Forget the numbers for now," said Philip. "We've got other things to deal with here."

The schedules were far more frightening than the lists. They'd managed to find daily routines for four days of the week, and since the sheets were mimeographed they assumed that the schedules were standard and handed out to each newly enlisted Crusader. The day began at five in the morning with reveille and a morning prayer in something called the "Freedom Shrine," followed by "rations," and then the first of seven "study sessions" that took place throughout the day. On Tuesdays the focus of the day's work seemed to be "spiritual authority" in the morning sessions, and Christ in America during the afternoon. By Wednesday, it seemed as though they had drifted from religion into politics. On that day the sessions were individually headed from one to seven: "1. Must Christians Obey the Law; 2. Liberty or Death; 3. Threats to Freedom; 4. God's Law; 5. Principle of Divine Authority; 6. Satan and Communism; 7. The Holy Fight." Friday and Saturday alternated between Wednesday's politics and a series of sessions on how the world had to be saved from the "child butchers," "pornographers," and "strutting sissies."

Philip felt his stomach lurch as he read through the topics. "Jesus," he muttered, "these people can't be serious!"

"They're perfectly serious," said Sarah. "Not only that, by the time those kids have been at Barrington for a week, they believe every word of it. I read about a twenty-three-year-old Rhodes Scholar who was at Yale. He wound up on a street corner selling flowers for Sun Myung Moon after two weeks of processing at their Tarrytown center."

"But this is hate literature!" breathed Philip.

Sarah shrugged and went back to sorting through the papers.

There were several dozen credit-card slips for gas in the pile, the imprint made out to 21st Century Communications on every one. At the top of the pile were a total of fifteen oblongs of yellow newsprint; tear sheet carbons from a Telex machine. Of all the material Philip found these the most intriguing.

Of the fifteen slips six originated from NSS/RENONEV, nine from CRUWEST/ASPCOL. The messages were all prefixed with a two-letter single-number listing, followed by a garbled string of letters that made no sense at all.

"Reno, Nevada," said Philip. "Didn't you say one of the Carstairs people operated out of Nevada?"

"Sam Keller. Eagle One, the big think tank, is in Reno."

"I wonder what NSS stands for?" he pondered. "You can't get Eagle One out of that.'"

"What about CRUWEST ASPCOL?" asked Sarah.

"Crusade West, Aspen, Colorado, I would assume," said Philip. "I also think it's going to be my next stop."

"What do you mean?" asked Sarah. Philip lit another in a long succession of cigarettes and shrugged his shoulders.

"I'm still looking for Heather," he said, "I'm not trying to research a book on the Tenth Crusade. My only lead was Barrington, and it's a sure bet she's long gone from there. The way I figure it she managed to sneak out of the place long enough to phone her friend in Toronto, and then she found some way to get to her father in Washington and to me in New York." He picked up one of the gas slips. "Maybe she ripped off one of the credit cards and used it," he suggested. "Anyway, Barrington is empty, so that means they've taken her somewhere else. If what you say is true they'll take her as far from her home turf as possible. Most of those Telexes are from Aspen, so that's where I go." He looked at Sarah carefully. "You're welcome to come with me if you've run out of information here."

She rubbed her forehead and yawned. "I'll sleep on it," she said. "It might not be a bad idea."

"I can take a hint," grinned Philip. He stood up, his joints creaking, and headed for the door. He turned as he reached it. "Goodnight," he said.

She smiled. "Goodnight, Mr. Kirkland. It's been a most interesting evening."

"Philip, please," he said. "And the pleasure was all mine."

"Goodnight, Mr. Kirkland," she repeated.

He grimaced and left the room, closing the door behind him. Outside the night air had turned cool. He took a long breath, then walked the few steps to his own room. He stripped off his clothes and fell onto the bed, but somehow sleep refused to come.

He lay on the too soft bed, staring up at the scalloped plaster ceiling. His brain went over the day's events, trying to sort out useful information from postulated fluff, but soon he found himself questioning his motives for being where he was. He was close to middle age; the time for this kind of thing was long over he thought to himself. Back in the sixties it was fine to get behind the barricades with the hippies and the Yippies, or make grandstand plays with a camera in the rice paddies of Viet Nam, but things had changed. Over and over he asked himself about Heather. Why did he care any more, and why did it seem to mean so much? He came to no firm conclusions, but when he finally fell into a lonely sleep he had the nagging sense that perhaps through trying to find Heather he was trying to find a part of himself long gone.

His sleep was filled with dreams of the past, spinning with a thousand different images of Heather; splinters of their life together in Paris, the harsh sounds of the Métro crowds, the damp-stained winter buildings as they shopped on the rue de

Rivoli, and the wildness of their lovemaking. Here and there the pictures shifted, and he turned and tossed on the bed as he dreamed of Heather only a few days past, her trembling nervousness as she slowly took off her clothes, then the face of Sarah Logan, then a striding knight, gray-armored, wielding a bloody pike and wading through a shifting desert of yellowed photographs, each one, as it skittered in his wake, showing the same thing: "Heather/Orly/1971." But where her head should have been there was nothing but a bleeding stump, and beside her stood the grinning figure of Nguyen Loan, Police Chief of Saigon.

Chapter Eight

After sleeping until almost noon, Philip and Sarah ate a late breakfast in the small motel dining room. They were the restaurant's only customers, and except for a tired-looking waitress dozing at a far table, they were alone in the low-ceilinged room.

"I thought it over," said Sarah, trying to use her fork to cut through a leathery fried egg. "And I decided that we might make a good team." She had her hair back in its twisted bun at her neck and Philip resisted the urge to lean over and take out the restraining hairpins. She'd also changed her outfit from the night before, but the new one was equally bad. The sweater had been exchanged for a loose lumberjack shirt tucked into a pair of jeans too wide-legged for her small frame. Her outfit offended Philip's photographer's eye, especially when he could see that beneath it all she was quite attractive. He wondered why she was trying to hide her looks but decided not to think about it long; he could sense his own attraction to her and he knew that the last thing he needed was any kind of involvement.

Philip chewed at a piece of toast, then washed it down with a slug of thick, bittersweet coffee. He dropped what was left of the toast back onto his plate and lit a cigarette.

"Does that mean you'll be coming to Colorado?" he asked. She looked at him for a moment and then went back to her egg. He blew a smoke ring, being careful not to waft it in her direction.

"Yes," she said, not looking up. She took a bite of egg and swallowed. "On one condition."

"What's that?" asked Philip.

She cleared her throat. "The condition is that you help me break into the Barrington monastery," she said, her voice barely audible.

"Are you nuts?" asked Philip, frowning. "What the hell do you want to do that for?"

"More information," said Sarah.

Philip shook his head. "Not a chance," he said. "Stealing garbage is one thing, breaking into that place is something else again. You're not in a fairy tale, you know. Places like that have dogs sometimes. Or people with guns. At the very least it's a crime that you could wind up in jail for. No. I'll go to Aspen by myself, thanks."

"You're chicken," said Sarah.

"I'm sensible," said Philip. "I was thinking just that very thing last night after we finished. I grew up a long time ago, sweetheart. I don't go taking pictures of people in war zones anymore, and I certainly don't break into buildings because some kid from the Library of Congress wants to prove that her father was driven to suicide. I'm looking for Heather, not a jail term."

"I'm no kid," said Sarah, flushing. She dropped her fork onto her plate angrily. "I'm twenty-seven. And I think my father was being blackmailed. That's just as much a crime as breaking and entering."

"I don't mean to sound like an old fogey, Sarah, but isn't that what you call taking the law into your own hands?"

"That's exactly what it is," she answered, her voice hard. "I'm taking the law into my own hands because no one else will. And you're in exactly the same situation. You went to Toronto, and then you came here, trying to find out what happened to your girlfriend, and you had to do it yourself because no one else would listen to you. Now you call it taking the law into your own hands."

"She's not my girlfriend," said Philip, bristling. "Not any more. She's somebody I care about who's in trouble. And to a certain extent you're right, I am working on my own. But that doesn't include breaking into a building, especially if she's not in it."

"Oh, for God's sake!" yelled Sarah, bringing the waitress out of her stupor at the far table. "Just what the hell *does* it include? Are you going to go up to their door and ask them if she's there and could she please come out and talk to you? You told me they hit you on the head and did God knows what to her. And what about me? Do you think I'm some kind of Pollyanna who does this kind of thing on a whim? I'm not Wonder Woman, damn it! I'm a mousy-haired little nobody at the Library of Congress who happens to believe that some people drove her father to the point where he killed himself. And I'm scared to death by it all, but that isn't going to stop me from finding out just what's going on."

"Can I get you anything else?" asked the waitress, who had appeared at their table.

"No, thank you," snapped Sarah. "We're finished." She glared across the table at Philip. The waitress went back to her position at the other end of the room. There was a long silence broken only by the muffled twanging of a country and western song coming from a radio in the kitchen.

"You're not mousy-haired," said Philip finally. Sarah was fuming. "And I take your point. Whatever it is we've gotten involved in is beyond the norm. Maybe you're right."

"Does that mean you'll help me?" asked Sarah.

Philip shrugged. "I guess it does," he said, and smiled. "But what about all those cameras you told me about?"

"I've already figured that out," said Sarah eagerly. She plucked a ball point out of the pocket of her shirt and reached for Philip's napkin. "Here," she said, drawing quickly. "Let me show you."

*   *   *

After breakfast Philip drove the rental car to an outlet in Dansville, with Sarah leading in the Triumph. Instead of returning the way they'd come, Sarah chose to go the long way around simply to avoid having to pass the monastery. They went up the turnpike to Mount Norris, then swung back along Interstate Alternate 20 until they reached the town of Barrington. This being Monday, the main streets were clogged with tourist traffic, most of it campers and cottagers stocking up on provisions after the weekend. Philip, who felt naked without at least one camera, had brought along a lightweight Canon F-1 with the motordrive removed. He bought several rolls of high-speed Ectachrome 160, knowing that he could have the exposure pushed in a lab, which would let him shoot inside the Barrington monastery without a telltale flash.

"I feel like a bit of an idiot," said Sarah, seeing the camera for the first time. "It never occurred to me that I should photograph the material I found."

"Makes the best kind of evidence," said Philip. "And I'll give you a deal on my day rate."

Philip also bought a dark pullover sweater and a pair of sneakers; he had almost no clothing with him, and certainly nothing that could be used for cat burglary. He kept on making jokes about the bizarreness of their situation, but as the daylight faded his humor soured even to his own ears. At 7:30 they went into Toby's for a meal and, when darkness had fully fallen they set out on the Livonia highway.

Thankfully, the gas station just before the entrance to the monastery grounds was closed again. They parked the Triumph at the rear of the station, then ran quickly back across the highway and up into the protective screen of trees to the right of the monastery grounds.

"Now what?" whispered Philip in the dark. Around them there were only night sounds; a faint creaking from the tree branches, sighing wind, and their own harsh breathing. The soft mossy earth was damp against his bare hand and Philip could feel the evening chill begin to creep through his sweater and the shirt below.

"We move up along this hill until we get behind the monastery," instructed Sarah, her voice low. "It's how I did it before, except I came in from the other side. Most of the windows are at the front of the building, not that anyone's going to be looking."

"You're really sure the place will be empty?" Philip asked, beginning to feel nervous.

"It should be," said Sarah from a few inches away. "The way I've figured it, they won't bring another van load up until to-morrow. Monday seems to be the day that gets lost in the shuffle. The sessions go from Tuesday to Sunday afternoon."

"Then why the cameras?" asked Philip, worried. "It sounds like they leave a guard on watch."

"No," said Sarah. "I would have seen something. There's no vehicle or anything. Maybe they set the machines on 'record' or something. After all, it's only empty the one night."

"I hope you're right," muttered Philip.

"Come on," said Sarah, "we're wasting time."

"Lead on," said Philip. "You're the one who knows the way."

Her body nothing more than a slightly darker shadow in the night, Sarah moved up the hill, Philip following close be-hind. It was an easy climb, and within a few minutes they'd reached the brow of the hill and began curving back along it, moving in toward the rear of the monastery. The trees began to thin and Philip could faintly see the building, outlined now by a weak half-moon overhead. Sarah stopped at the edge of the trees above the knoll on which the monastery stood, crouching low to the ground. She had brought them to a point about a hundred yards from the rear left corner of the building. For the first time Philip had a clear view of the prem-ises he was about to violate. The building was rectangular, four storeys high, and topped with a pale Jeffersonian dome. It looked for all the world like a slightly effeminate high school.

"There," whispered Sarah, pointing. "It's like I said. There are six cameras, but it's only the ones at the corners that we have to worry about. The one at the front corner must be out of order because it doesn't move, and I think it's one of the ones that should. The one at the corner closest to us goes through a one-hundred-and-eighty-degree sweep every thirty seconds. So with one camera out of order that leaves us about fifteen seconds to get from here to the corner of the building. That will be another blind spot."

"Unless the cameras have fish-eye lenses," put in Philip.

"I hadn't thought of that," said Sarah, clearly angry with herself. "It doesn't matter though. It'll probably be too dark anyway."

"Infrared," offered Philip. "I doubt they'd keep the cameras operational at night unless they can sense infrared; body heat."

"What are you trying to do?" she hissed at him. "Make me more scared than I already am?"

Philip shrugged. "You're the one who said there wasn't going to be anyone there anyway, so what are you worried about?" He looked out across the clipped expanse of lawn that separated them from the building. "The hundred in fifteen," he muttered to himself. Once upon a time he'd been able to do it in ten, but that had been in his teens.

"Any time you're ready," he said. She nodded, keeping her eyes glued to the binoculars.

"I've got it," she whispered. "There's a little glint of light, some kind of reflection off the camera when it's at the far end of its cycle. The next time we run. I'll say go."

"Fine," said Philip. He felt a brief surge of nausea, and recognized it as the sensation he'd had every time he'd gone out with the chopper crews in Nam. Terrible anticipation and an almost unbearable desire to begin. "Better Quickly Sickness" as a Private First Class, once English major, had called it, referring to Shakespeare's "If it were done when 'tis done, then 'twere well it were done quickly." The kid had died lifting the lid of a booby-trapped pot in an abandoned Viet Cong supply base.

"*Now!*" whispered Sarah loudly. She dropped the binoculars to the ground and raced forward across the grass, keeping herself in line with the corner of the building. Philip, caught unaware, followed, heart beating furiously as he tried desperately to cover the yawning space of ground before the searching eye swung back and spotted him. He kept a rough count going on his head, and at one thousand and thirteen he reached the corner in a swan dive, careening into Sarah who was already crouched beside the chiseled granite wall of the foundation.

76

"You didn't say 'go,'" whispered Philip. "You said 'now.'"

"Shut up," hissed Sarah.

"Where do we go from here?" asked Philip. His heart was slowing down but he could feel the acid sweat trickling down his armpits.

"I don't think you listened to a word I said before," said Sarah, her voice low and angry. "I told you, we use the windows."

"Right."

Sarah stood up, her back tight to the wall, and edged around to the short side of the building. Philip followed, keeping his head craned back. Above them, a row of windows ran five long to the far corner toward the building's front. Halfway along the side of the monastery Sarah stopped. It was the section of the wall in the deepest shadow.

"Give me a boost."

Philip locked his hands together and lowered them in a sling. She put her sneakered foot into the laced cradle of his fingers and he heaved up. He shifted as he straightened, twisting around so that he faced the wall, and took Sarah's weight on his shoulders, his arms upheld, supporting her legs as she reached for the window ledge. As he held her he couldn't help noticing the feel of her thighs and the taut hardness of her buttocks. Underneath the badly cut jeans she had a firm, strong body.

There was a small snapping sound in the darkness and a few seconds later the weight lifted from his shoulders. He turned and stared upward, peering up into the gloom in time to see her legs squirm through the window above. Then her face appeared, a pale oval in the surrounding charcoal of the night.

"There's a little ledge where the foundation meets the brick," she instructed. "Get your toes onto that and I'll pull you up." She stretched her arms out to him, waiting. He felt with his hands until he found the four-inch ridge between the granite and the brick wall. He moved away from the side of the building, took a short run and jumped, his toes catching and his hands flung upward. He felt Sarah's fingers on his wrists as he scrabbled for some purchase and then his hands

77

were on the window ledge. He grunted with effort as he hauled himself up and through the window.

He looked around. They were standing in what appeared to be some kind of classroom. Several rows of old-fashioned desks faced a blackboard that filled the entire front wall. The room was almost totally dark, the only light coming from the night-faint spill of illumination that came through the win dow Sarah had opened. Sarah rummaged around in her jeans and pulled out a penlight she'd bought in Barrington while Philip had been getting his film. She flicked it on, a small need-le of light flaring toward the floor.

"Come on," she whispered, "there's nothing here."

Philip followed the puddle of light as Sarah moved toward the door, his ears tuned to any sound that might announce the presence of a guard. There was nothing except the creaking of the old floorboards beneath their feet.

They left the room and moved out into a wide, half-paneled hall, narrow and long, seeming to run the length of the building. There were doors every few yards. Philip stopped.

"There's got to be fifteen rooms on this floor alone. How do we choose?" asked Philip. "We can't stay here all night."

"We're on the second floor," Sarah whispered back. "We should go down one flight and see if we can find some kind of an office."

It took them almost twenty minutes of fumbling around in the darkness to find what they were looking for. It was a large room on the main floor, close to the front entrance of the building and to one side of what was obviously the central staircase. The door was locked. A small hand painted sign read: SOAO/NY.

"I wonder what it means," muttered Sarah.

"I saw the same letter groupings on those coded messages," answered Philip. "It must be some kind of title. Sounds sort of military, like CINCPAC."

"Like what?" asked Sarah.

"Commander in Chief Pacific," explained Philip. "That SOAO sounds like some kind of military acronym."

"That's not important now," said Sarah. "The question is, how do we get the door open?"

"Give me the light," said Philip. Sarah handed it over and Philip bent low for a closer look at the door. There was nothing but an old-fashioned skeleton key lock. Philip had opened dozens like it in most of the places he had ever lived. He wondered at the anomaly. Expensive camera systems on the one hand and penny ante locks on the other. "Give me one of your bobby pins."

"You're kidding."

He shook his head and held up his hand. "Just give me one," he said. She reached up into her hair and extracted a pin. She handed it to him and he worked it into the lock. A few seconds later the door swung open and Philip stood up, feeling ridiculously proud of himself.

"That's terrific," said Sarah, peering at the open door and then at Philip as though he were Houdini.

"I live in Manhattan." He smiled. "It's a survival skill."

"Let's go in and see what we've unlocked," said Sarah. She pulled off the small, lightweight nylon carrying bag from her back and felt around inside, coming up with Philip's camera. She handed it to him and they went into the office. Sarah swung the penlight around the room. There was a large desk with a telephone and several ranks of filing cabinets. Other than that the room was empty.

"No windows," said Philip. "Shut the door and we can turn on a light." Philip pulled the door closed, careful not to let the lock spring back, and Sarah found a light switch. The room flooded with crackling light from a panel of overhead fluorescents and the two amateur burglars blinked in the sudden glare. When his eyes had adjusted Philip snapped off a couple of fast exposures with the Canon, just to establish their location. Sarah was checking the filing cabinets.

"There's no way we're going to get into these with a hairpin," she said. Philip joined her. The filing cabinets were new, with good quality bar and rachet locks.

"Do you have any objection to people knowing that we've been here?" asked Philip.

Sarah shook her head. "No," she said, "they'll probably find the window I opened anyway, unless we close it on the way out. Why?"

"In for a penny in for a pound," said Philip. He stepped back and rammed his foot into the bottom drawer of one of the cabinets. The metal creased deeply. "Try it now," said Philip. "The whole row should open."

Sarah pulled at the top drawer of the row and it slid back easily. "You're pretty good at this kind of thing," she said, impressed.

Philip shrugged. "I did a short haul back to Viet Nam in the last days of the war. I saw Marines doing that to the filing cabinets at the embassy while they were landing choppers on the roof. There was no time to fool around with keys then either."

"You make me feel like I've lived a sheltered life," said Sarah.

Philip laughed. "Not any more. Let's see what we've opened up." Each of them pulled out a handful of file folders and took them across to the desk.

"Dossiers," said Sarah after a few moments. "Personnel files. They must keep track of everyone they bring through here."

"Listen to this," said Philip, reading through one of his files. 'Martin, James Talbot, age twenty-four.' Blah, blah, blah, education, parents, etc. But down here on page six: 'On third day subject agreed to purging. Purging attended by Johnson, ALC, Baltimore. Subject admitted to homosexual encounter at university with roommate, Michael Lattimer. Encounter repeated several times during year, but not repeated during following year. N.A.V.'" He frowned. "I wonder what N.A.V. means."

"I know," said Sarah. "I see it on customs invoices all the time. It means 'no apparent value.'"

"These people sure do like their acronyms," said Philip. He went on to another file, taking occasional photographs as he worked through the papers.

"It's all potential blackmail material," said Sarah, looking across the desk at Philip. "These 'purging' sessions are confessionals without a priest, or in this case the priest is usually one of these mysterious 'A.L.s' or an 'L.G.L.' They get these people softened up, then have them confess to their sins; except there's no sanctity of the confessional here, it's all written down. God!"

"It's sick," said Philip softly. "They keep on banging away at the gay end of it, too, complete with names of the other people involved. And for every file here with a gay confession you've got material on the person the 'subject' got it on with. It's incredible."

Abruptly they both stiffened, their senses tuned. A noise, muffled, came from outside.

"What was that?" whispered Sarah.

Philip shook his head. "I'm not sure. Sounded like a car door closing or something. Hit the lights."

Sarah tiptoed quickly to the door and snapped the switch, throwing the room into utter darkness. She opened the door a crack and peered out, Philip at her shoulder. Directly in front of them, and down five steps to the main lobby, the front doors of the building were being opened. As the doors opened fully Philip could see out to the gravel drive in front of the building. There was a van parked. A man was silhouetted in the faint light, standing by the open doors while half a dozen people climbed down out of the van.

"Christ!" hissed Philip. "You said they weren't going to be here until tomorrow!"

"They changed the schedule!" Sarah whispered back faintly. Philip felt his mouth go cottonball dry. Then a voice echoed up the lobby toward them. The man at the doors was giving orders.

"Take them up to the dorm, Squire. I'll be in the office if you need me." The new recruits from the van were led to the stairs by a tall man wearing light-blue pants and a dark blazer. As they disappeared up the stairs the man at the doors, shorter than his colleague but identically dressed, walked toward the office. As gently as he could Philip pushed the door firmly shut.

"Oh my God!" whispered Sarah.

"Shhh." Philip pushed her back from the door and stood upright. There was a fumbling at the lock and then the door swung open. There was a momentary pause and then the lights came on again.

Philip raised his fist a foot from the floor, and caught the blinking figure directly on the chin. There was a sharp clicking sound as the man's jaws snapped shut and then a gush of blood as Philip's right fist hammered into the man's nose. The man's eyes fluttered for an instant, then closed as he sagged toward the floor. Philip caught him before he could fall and lowered him gently. Acting quickly he stripped off the man's jacket and slipped it on, barely noticing the small insignia at the chest, identical to the one Sarah had drawn for him the night before. He leaned over the huddled body on the floor and doused the lights again.

"We leave," said Philip. "Follow me." He opened the door slightly, checked to make sure that the coast was clear, then motioned Sarah forward. Together they stepped out into the main hall. They could faintly hear noises from above them. Philip put a finger to his lips and then moved toward the stairs that led to the main doors. Thirty seconds later they were out in the cool night air. Sarah started moving toward the side of the building to close their entry window but Philip stopped her, his hand on her arm.

"No time for that. We take the direct route." He pointed across the huge expanse of lawn that led down to the highway. He hoped like hell that the man upstairs wasn't armed because they'd be sitting ducks. He took time for one glance up at the blank, curtained windows, then ran forward to the truck. He opened the driver's side door, reached under the dashboard, and pulled, coming out of the cab with a handful of wires clutched in his fist. "That'll slow them down," he whispered. He took Sarah by the arm and shoved her forward. "Run like hell!" he whispered loudly. She ran, and he followed close behind, checking back over his shoulder every few seconds.

But there was no alarm. They reached the highway, lungs burning, then made it across to the gas station. They clambered into the Triumph, and for an agonizing moment Philip was sure that she'd lost the keys. She found them finally, switched on the ignition, and the engine roared to life. She reversed, twisted at the wheel, shifted gears again, then tore out onto the blacktop. Seconds later they were passing the dark bulk of the monastery, heading down the dark road to the relative safety of their motel.

Philip leaned back against the high-backed contour seat, heart racing, and gasping for breath.

"Well," he said, "that does it. Trespass, break and enter, and assault. We're up to our asses in it now, kiddo."

PART TWO
Prophesies

Chapter Nine

Sarah and Philip checked out of the motel, then drove into the night, the muffled thunder of the Triumph's engine sending back its dopplering echo from the low hills and scrubland and from the darkened houses of the small towns they raced through in the darkness. They moved steadily south, putting as much distance as possible between them and the monastery. Then, at Bath, they turned west and north, following the vacant Interstate up through Dansville and Geneseo. By dawn they were on the outskirts of Buffalo and they stopped there long enough to have something to eat at a truck stop and check on flight connections to Aspen. The first useful flight out of Buffalo didn't leave until almost noon, and rather than take the chance of waiting that long in one place they agreed to keep on the road, crossing into Canada at Niagara Falls, then following the shoreline of Lake Ontario up to Toronto. While in Buffalo Philip had checked the schedule and discovered that there was an American Airlines flight to Denver via Chicago leaving Toronto at 7:30 in the morning. They valet-parked the Triumph and they made the flight with ten minutes to spare. The 727 was due into Denver at 11:20 Mountain Time, and from there they could make a connecting flight to Aspen at noon.

Philip put the time spent on the long hopscotching journey to good use, questioning Sarah Logan and plumbing the depths of her seemingly inexhaustible supply of general knowledge, building up a background to the situation they had fallen into. An hour out of Denver the puzzle was as complete as it could be, the only blanks being spaces left for the forced suicide of Sarah's father and the sudden disappearance of Heather. Philip was exhausted after more than twelve hours of constant travel, but his mind was still clear enough to take in the implications of what Sarah told him.

Far from being the slightly ludicrous sidelight on the American way of life that he had once considered, he now realized that the entire Fundamentalist-neo-conservative groundswell in the United States was the result of a powerful and potentially dangerous psychology and philosophy that owed more to Adolf Hitler than it did to the founding fathers. He'd heard and been involved in dozens of conversations about evangelists, Bible thumpers, and fuzzy-brained right wingers before. But the focus of those conversations had always been the Elmer Gantry-like methods of fund raising and proselytizing that had been revealed by people like Marjoe Gortner. The long chain of fact, theory, and hypothesis presented to him by Sarah pointed to something much more sinister than the bilking of backwoods boobies out of their weekly egg money. As Sarah poured out the information she had collected a number of patterns began to appear.

Fundamental evangelism had existed in North America for decades, but in prosperous times it had few adherents outside the Southern Baptist Bible Belt. Its effects, if any, were bound to small, localized areas, invariably rural and poor. It was only with the advent of cheap and available mass communications systems that it took any kind of foothold. Even then there were few "stars" like Billy Graham and Reverend Ike. Of those two, Ike was definitely lunatic fringe and Graham, who has been a salesman of the first water, was selling a religion that studiously avoided any real interaction with politics beyond his friendship, usually somewhat one-sided, and based more on his golfing abilities than his philosophy. Even so, it was Graham, with his awareness of the need for organization, who set the stage for the swing to the Conservative right.

His board of directors was strong on attorneys, bankers, and presidents of large corporate bodies including Service-Master Corporation, State Street Investments of Boston,

First International Bancshares of Dallas, Texas, and the vice-chairman of Holiday Inns.

Graham had spent the fifties preaching anti-communism, and it was that stance which kept him afloat more than anything as abstract as an afterlife; it was only when the disillusionment of the sixties appeared and the economy began its downward slide that more and more people entered the religious field. As expectations declined and inflation grew, the Fundamentalist movement blossomed. Directly tied to its growth was the burgeoning of television as a cultural fact in America. Once again, the beginnings came from the South and the Midwest. Oral Roberts began to climb in the ratings and by the mid-sixties Oral Roberts University in Tulsa was firmly established. Jim Bakker was gaining a following on the 700 Club in Virginia, and within a few years he established the Praise The Lord television network and its flagship program, the PTL Club in Charlotte. Rex Humbard, a well-known tent evangelist from the fifties, also climbed on the bandwagon, and by the early seventies there were a dozen others. Unlike Graham, though, they quickly crossed the line from religion to politics, and for a lot of Americans, bloodied by Viet Nam and a creeping failure of their paychecks to keep up with the cost of living, their pill, coated with television-talk-show sugar, was an easy one to swallow.

Using sophisticated broadcasting techniques and a simple philosophy, they outlined the decadence of America, hammered at her failures, both economic and social, then laid the blame squarely on a common enemy, the liberal-intellectual minority who practised something they referred to as "secular humanism." Humanism became the catch word. If you agreed with Women's Liberation you were a humanist. If you were a Jew you were a humanist. If you believed in welfare you were a humanist. Humanism was socialism, communism, homosexuality, judaism, free sex, pornography, abortion, and any kind of sin, all rolled into a neat, easy-to-understand package. Even so, their messages were generally confined to obscure hours of the night and the early morning as well as the broadcast desert of Sunday mornings. It seemed as though television might have extended the preachers' reach somewhat, but the congregation remained much the same. The one-two-three punch of Nixon, Ford, and finally Jimmy Carter, changed all that.

Middle America watched as American prestige fell even further, and combined with rising unemployment, increased inflation, and a nationwide feeling of impotence, the elements fell into place and the stage was set. Jerry Falwell's Moral Majority came into being and, together with several other large and very well-funded lobbies in Washington, Ronald Reagan was elected to the presidency of the United States – the American version of Hindenburg. Here was an old man whose ideas were fifty years out of date, surrounded by an ever-growing group of hard-eyed men who saw America's only salvation as a ritual purification of her sins and a scourging of her enemies. Socially, economically, and psychologically the scenario was frighteningly close to that of Germany in 1933, the year Hitler took power. Strength, direction, focus, and a simple answer to a complex problem, were required. Billy Carstairs and his organization were there to fill the need.

Carstairs and his group, Gospel Way, based in Kansas City, had grown right along with all the rest of them, with one important difference. Very early on in his career Carstairs had seen the potential power in mixing God and government. Unlike the other evangelists, *his* board of directors was crammed with U.S. senators, congressmen, State senators, assemblymen, mayors, school board trustees, county supervisors, and sheriffs. He expanded quickly out of Kansas City, until by the early eighties he had offices of one kind or another in thirty States and a gross income from all sources of almost half a billion dollars a year – most of it tax free. While Falwell's Moral Majority made a lot of loud noises, Carstairs and his *éminence gris,* Senator Harcourt Snow, through the America Awake Foundation, pulled a lot of strings, quietly infiltrating organizations and government bodies from the county level right into the Executive Office.

From what Philip could tell the Tenth Crusade was another tool Carstairs and company were using to build themselves a strong power base. Sarah Logan was willing to take it one step further – she was positive that the Crusade forced her father's suicide and didn't doubt for an instant that they had kidnapped Heather as well, although like Philip, she couldn't come up with a logical explanation of why they'd want to take her.

"You're painting a pretty ugly picture," said Philip as the Fasten Your Seat Belt sign flashed on for the approach to Denver's Stapleton International Airport.

Sarah, raccoon-eyed from exhaustion and the long trip, shrugged her shoulders. "The early stages of Nazi Germany were ugly too."

"You've used the comparison before," said Philip. "Don't you think it's a little far fetched?"

"No," said Sarah bluntly, "I don't. It's the same thing. High inflation, high unemployment, loss of national pride, a weak, overextended government, poor world economic situation. Hitler gave the German people a vehicle to take out their aggressions—the stormtroopers of the SA, and later on the SS. Carstairs has given us the Tenth Crusade."

"I still think you're being melodramatic," said Philip.

"Of course. Melodrama is part of the whole thing. You're talking about a country that eats up Laverne and Shirley and the Beverly Hillbillies. Melodrama works. Just like the SA uniforms did. And remember, the SA in Germany started out with twenty unemployed beer drinkers in a tavern."

"I just want to find Heather," said Philip uncomfortably.

The jet began its descent and Philip caught a glimpse of the long jagged line of the Rockies to the west.

"Don't be surprised if you run into a few other things you didn't bargain for on the way," said Sarah, brooding beside him.

The jet landed without incident and a few minutes later the tired couple was boarding a battered American Airlines Convair that did the shuttle run between Denver and Aspen. After a brief, turbulent flight, which took them into the heart of the looming chain of mountains, they finally reached their destination. Philip rented a car, picked up a road map, and then they headed toward the town a few miles away, presided over by the towering bulk of Snowmass and Aspen Highlands. The giant mountain slopes were carpeted in a thick cover of trees, and the ski runs cut bright green scars a mile long.

Aspen, Colorado lies in a long, irregular valley 8,000 feet above sea level – high enough so that dogs don't have fleas. The town was founded in 1879, and was originally called Ute City. At that time, its future seemed secure, since the town sat on top of one of the richest silver lodes in the world. But the boom only lasted for fourteen years, ending abruptly when the United States went onto the gold standard in 1893. During its heyday, Aspen had streetcars, the first electric lights in the State, a dozen major hotels, an opera house, and a population of 12,000. By 1895, the boom over, Aspen's population had dropped to 600.

In 1945, the town was miraculously resurrected at the hands of a Chicago businessman, Walter Paepcke, a Goethe addict who somehow managed to convince the Goethe Society of Frankfurt to celebrate the writer's bicentennial in Aspen. From that point on it was roses all the way; slowly but surely the town revived, skiers began to trek in, followed by the Aspen Design Conference and the Aspen Music Festival. By the end of the seventies, more than 300,000 people a year were spending their dollars in Aspen, and the permanent population had risen to 6,000.

"Why would the Crusade pick a place like Aspen for their western headquarters?" said Philip, moving slowly through the bumper-to-bumper traffic on Main Street as they headed toward the Jerome Hotel. "Why not Denver or some place larger."

"It fits with the way that kind of organization operates," answered Sarah, cracking a gigantic yawn. "The people here are transient and they've all got money. The Moonies, Hare Krishnas, Children of God, they all use the same tactics. That's why you find them at airports and places like that. Guilt, too, maybe. The Moonies do a lot of business outside liquor stores, for instance. Aspen is for hedonists – lots of sex, drugs, and booze, so maybe the Crusade is skimming off a bit of money so that people can feel a little better about all the fun they're having."

"Is there anything you don't know about these people?" asked Philip. "You sound like an encyclopedia of loony religious groups."

"I don't know nearly enough," Sarah muttered. "The stuff we found at Barrington pretty well confirms what I thought all along—these people have been building files they can use as blackmail material—that's how they must have gotten to my father. But it's not proof, and I can't take guesses and theories into a courtroom. You've got it easy, all you want to do is find your friend. Anything else after that is a bonus; maybe a big photo spread in the *New York Times* magazine. Or a Pulitzer," she added sourly.

"You really think I'm that crass?"

"No," she sighed. "I think I'm just very, very tired."

They eventually reached the Jerome, one of Aspen's main tourist attractions, a massive, four-storey brick structure built at the height of the silver boom. Luckily it was late enough in the season to get rooms, and after checking in they headed for the hotel's San Francisco-style bar to plan their strategy for the rest of the day. The place was almost empty except for a single, shabbily dressed figure leaning against the far end of the bar nursing a can of Coors and staring moodily up at a baseball game on the large color television that sat on a narrow shelf high on the back wall.

They found a booth, sat down, and ordered beer. When the bored-looking waiter had come and gone, Sarah asked: "What are you going to do while I'm catching up on some well-deserved beauty sleep?"

"I'm going to find the Crusade. Or better yet, let them find me."

"Why don't you explain that," said Sarah. "I'm too tired to try and unravel your logic."

"You seem to think that the Crusade will have their people out panhandling. I'm going to fall for the touch if I can find one of them."

"They'll be working in pairs," put in Sarah. "But I still don't see what you're after."

"If Heather is in Aspen I'm not going to make much headway by knocking on the Crusade's door and telling them I'm there to take her back to her father. The only chance I have is to let myself get recruited. I can't see any other way of getting inside."

"You're taking a big risk," answered Sarah, frowning. "What if they find out who you are? Not to mention the possibility that you might get taken in by their brainwashing."

Philip laughed. "I think I can handle myself against a Bible-thumper's spell," he said.

"You're a fool if you think that's what this is all about," snapped Sarah. "These people use techniques that make the Manchurian Candidate look like a wallflower."

"Your concern is touching," said Philip. "But I think I'll be all right."

"It's your decision." She looked at him strangely, her expression a mixture of anger, concern, and exhaustion. "Just ... just be careful, okay?"

"Don't worry," soothed Philip. "I won't do anything rash." He reached across the table and patted her hand. She pulled it away quickly, and picked up her Coors.

Philip checked his watch, studiously ignoring her reaction. It was just past 2:00 Mountain Time. "We'll meet back here at six, how's that?" he said.

Sarah nodded. "Fine."

Philip slipped out of the booth, fished around in the pocket of his jeans, and laid a crumpled five-dollar bill on the table. He turned away and left the dimly lit bar.

* * *

Once outside, Philip stood on the wide sidewalk and looked around, trying to get his bearings. The sky overhead was a pale, watery blue, the deep-green, steep-sided mountains rearing up on all sides like an impenetrable wall. From what he could see the town made no attempt to compete with the jutting monoliths; there wasn't a building over four storeys, and most were only two. He found a sign informing him that he was on Cooper Street, and, from the volume of pedestrian traffic, and the mass of angle-parked cars, it was Aspen's main drag.

He made his way slowly down the sidewalk, pausing now and again to peer into the elaborately designed shop windows, trying to keep his expression as blank and mindless as possible, assuming the role of someone down on his luck with nothing better than a jailhouse meal and a vagrancy charge to look forward to. The character acting worked almost too well; a block from the hotel he reached a stop light and, waiting for it to flash green, he saw a blue Saab coming at him from the opposite direction. It took him a few seconds but he realized that the exotic vehicle was a police car. The officer driving, no older than he was, and sporting long hair and a drooping moustache, gave him the once over and Philip could almost see the wheels turning in the cop's head. Philip tensed, waiting for the car to pull over, but the light changed and the Saab went through the intersection. Philip crossed to the far side, and, breathing a sigh of relief, he noticed that his lungs were aching, probably a result of the high altitude. The rarefied air, his tiredness, and the single beer he'd had in the hotel, were combining to make him feel almost giddy, and he wondered if Sarah wasn't right after all—maybe he *wasn't* in any shape to take on the Crusade.

Ten minutes of ambling later, Philip found himself in front of a sixties-style restaurant called The Shaft and he stopped to read some of the notices pinned up on the bulletin board outside. Once again it seemed as though Sarah knew her stuff—to say that Aspen had a liberal lifestyle was an understatement.

Big party at Red Rory's.
Free booze, free spoons.
Bring your own snort.

Two girls heading for
Minneapolis end of August.
Need ride—will trade ass
for gas.

Ted—Carla wound up with
Herpes. Call me so I can
explain. Dana.

Philip turned away from the bulletin board and found himself staring into the bland face of an attractive young woman with huge blue eyes and a fall of blonde hair which swept down around her shoulders. She was wearing a white blouse topped by a navy-blue blazer and a pleated navy-blue skirt. The breast pocket of the blazer held a shield-shaped badge sewn onto it – the red, white, and black insignia of the Tenth Crusade. Beside her, equally blond and equally bland, was a tall man in his mid-twenties. He was also wearing the blue and white uniform of the Crusade.

"Looking for something, friend?" asked the man. He turned on a brief and, to Philip's mind, a totally insincere smile.

Philip shrugged, remembering his role. "Whatever," he muttered.

"New in town?" asked the girl. Her voice was smooth, almost without inflection.

"Yeah," answered Philip. The two were standing uncomfortably close to him. He backed off a few steps and found himself up against the bulletin board. "Look, I don't have any money, if that's what you're looking for. You some kind of Jesus Freaks, or what?"

Again the smile from the man. He shook his head. "Far from it," he said. "We're more like, um, social workers."

"Really?" said Philip. The lie had come out of the man's mouth as smooth as silk. "You look like Mormons or something."

"We're from the Tenth Crusade," said the woman, stepping closer to Philip again. This time he had no room to move. The girl smelled like soap. "We're sort of a social action group. It's our job to go around Aspen, looking for people who need help."

"Oh yeah?" said Philip, trying to put a note of suspicion into his voice. "What kind of help?"

"Money, food, clothes, a place to stay. Whatever you need," said the man. The girl nodded, looking at her partner happily.

"And what do you want back?" asked Philip. He figured that putting some kind of resistance to the spiel would be more convincing.

"Nothing at all," said the girl. "We've got a ranch out by Ragged Mountain where we have a series of three-day sessions. We take you out there, get some good food into you, give you a chance to put things into perspective, maybe get hold of a better outlook on life. It's a lot of fun, actually."

"Yeah, well I could use a bit of fun," said Philip, sounding as bitter as he could. "You're sure you people aren't a bunch of religious nuts?"

The man laughed. "The philosophy of the Tenth Crusade has a lot more to do with getting back to the good old American way of life and the U.S. Constitution than it does with heaven and hell."

"So when's your next session?" asked Philip. "Supposing I wanted to go, that is."

"They run continuously during the summer," said the girl quickly. "We have a van that picks people up every evening at seven. Then we go out to the ranch."

"Where exactly?" asked Philip.

"The van?" asked the girl. Philip nodded. "Right here in front of the restaurant. We usually park in the loading zone, but Aspen's men in blue usually turn a blind eye. They know we're doing good work." She paused and smiled broadly enough to show her teeth. "We'd love to have you come," she said.

"Give yourself a break," put in the man.

The girl smiled and reached out, placing her palm flat on Philip's chest. "Please," she said softly. The touch, and the warm, vulnerable look in her eyes were enough to arouse Philip even against his better judgment and despite Sarah's warnings.

"I'll think about it," he answered finally, his voice wavering.

The girl stepped back and the man turned on his machine-made smile for a second. "We can't ask for more than that," he said. "We'll be looking for you this evening."

Philip nodded and then turned away, heading back down Cooper Street. He walked for about a hundred feet and then stopped, looking into a store-window display of sports equipment. Out of the corner of his eye he saw that the two Crusaders had moved on, heading in the opposite direction. Philip watched, and when they'd gone another fifty feet or so, he turned and followed them. He watched as they slipped through the meandering tourists and then saw them approach a man in crisp tennis whites who was coming out of a liquor store with a single bagged bottle in his hand. The Crusade couple split and flanked the man as he turned onto the street. The girl reached out, touched the man's arm and he stopped. Philip paused in the shadow of an awning and watched.

The male Crusader talked earnestly for a moment, and then the girl spoke briefly. A few seconds later the man in the tennis outfit reached into his back pocket with his free hand, and then, tucking the liquor bag under his arm, took out a bill. He handed it to the girl Crusader, everyone nodded, and then the couple moved on. The man with the bottle watched them go, then crossed the sidewalk to a bright yellow MG convertible.

Philip frowned thoughtfully as the Crusaders disappeared into the crowd of pedestrians. It was obvious that they had two functions—recruiting, which was what they'd laid on him, and fund raising. He wondered what lie the man had told to the fellow with the bottle of booze. Not that it mattered; Philip had what he wanted—a foot in the Tenth Crusade's door.

He walked back up Cooper Street toward the Jerome. On the way he kept his eyes open for a photographic store. If he was going to make like a spy he decided to go the whole route. He still had the Canon he'd taken with him from New York, but he doubted that the Crusade gave guided tours for the curious. He was going to need something he could slip into his pocket. A block from the hotel he found a shop with a Kodak sticker in the window and went in. Five feet inside the door and he'd fallen in love with the place; it was a photographer's dream. The store was half brand-new equipment and half museum. The cases below the counter and on the walls were crammed with everything from the newest Japanese video-still cameras to a gigantic Petzval Monorail Camera from about 1860. There was even a Mick-a-Matic, a 126 camera in the shape of Mickey Mouse's head. It was the kind of eccentric store that could only exist in a place like New York, with 15,000,000 people to sell to, or a place like Aspen where the clientele were mostly rich and bored.

The owner, a man in his fifties, with a weathered-looking Stetson tipped back on his head and wire-rimmed glasses over a pair of small, twinkling eyes, rose from his stool behind the counter as Philip approached.

"Browsing?" he asked, giving Philip the same kind of once over the cop in the Saab had.

Philip shook his head and pointed to a strange-looking device on a shelf on the wall. It looked more like a battered washing machine motor than a camera. "Admiring your Periphote," said Philip, wanting to establish his credentials right off the bat. The Lumière Periphote was a camera made in France in the early 1900s for taking panoramic photographs.

The man raised an eyebrow. "There's not one person in a thousand comes into this place and knows the name of that camera," he said. "You a photographer?"

Philip nodded. "From New York."

"Help you with anything?" asked the man. "You a collector?"

"When I get the chance," he answered. "I'm most interested in concealed cameras. You know, the kind of joke thing they used to make back in the twenties and thirties?"

The owner of the store beamed. "Then you came to the right place," he said, and disappeared behind the counter for a moment. He came back with a large wooden tray, and set it down on the glass for Philip to look at.

There were twenty or more cameras on the tray, none of them larger than a package of cigarettes. There was a Presto from the late 1890s, a classic Minox from 1933, a circular Japanese Petal from 1948, and a 1944 Kodak MB, designed to fit into a box of matches. In among these was something that looked like a cheap imitation of an American Zippo lighter.

"What's that?" asked Philip.

The man reached down and picked up the dull metal device. He flicked open the top to reveal what appeared to be a lighter. Then he showed Philip the bottom. By sliding back a stud, a small lens and winder were revealed. "It's an Echo. Japanese-made in the mid-fifties."

"Could I get film for it?" asked Philip.

The man nodded. "You couldn't get the stuff that was originally made for it but I fooled around with some eight mil. black-and-white Kodak home movie film. The camera has little cassettes. I took a couple of rolls. Works like a charm."

"How many shots on a roll?" asked Philip.

"Sixteen. They're no hell to do any real photographs on, but the thing does work. Low light stuff, if you use the Kodak Tri-X."

"Can you load it for me?" asked Philip.

"Sure. Throw in an extra cassette too ... that is if you're serious about buying the thing."

"How much?" asked Philip.

The owner of the store pursed his lips and then shrugged. "Three hundred."

"You take American Express?" asked Philip.

The man gave out a little hooting laugh. "Are you kidding? Aspen would be a ghost town without Amex. This place is like getting the clap. Fun at the time, but it hurts like hell a month later."

"I'll endure the pain," smiled Philip. He took out his wallet and they went through the ritual of buying on time.

"Hang on for a second," said the owner, handing Philip his slip. "I'll load it up for you. You'll have to get fluid at a smoke shop or somewhere."

"You mean the lighter works as well?" asked Philip, amazed.

"Of course the lighter works. It's Japanese, remember?"

Five minutes later, the lighter-camera in his pocket, Philip went back to the hotel. Once in his room he thought about taking a shower, but decided against it in the interest of vagrant authenticity. He also decided to leave the entire contents of his wallet behind, with the exception of his driver's license. He spent twenty minutes prying up the insole of his right boot and inserting his American Express card. Checking his watch he found that it was only 3:30. He phoned down to the desk, asked for a wake-up call, and five minutes later he was asleep.

At 6:00 on the dot, groggy, and almost desperate for a long

hot bath or a shower, he made his way down to the Jerome bar. The place was packed. The length of the bar was covered with designer jeans and the stitched backs of Ralph Lauren shirts. Pina Coladas were flowing like water over Niagara and the dimly lit room was filled with laughter and an almost unbearable level of sexual tension. Philip scanned the room for Sarah, and finally picked her out at a small table in the far corner. She was dressed in jeans and another loose sweater, and looked wildly out of place. He threaded his way through the jungle of tables and dropped down into a chair opposite her.

"Hi," he said, raising his voice over the clamor.

Sarah looked at him owlishly through the smoky gloom. "You look awful," she said.

"Why, thank you. My disguise fooled you too."

"Disguise?" said Sarah.

"I'm supposed to be an indigent bum."

"You've succeeded," said Sarah crisply.

"Can the wit," said Philip. "It worked. I've got an appointment with the army of righteousness. I go off to fight the good fight in less than an hour."

"Tell me what happened," asked Sarah, leaning forward over the table.

"They hooked me like a fish. Two of them, just like you said, a guy and a girl. It was a straightforward recruiting. They've got a ranch or something near a place called Ragged Mountain. I'm supposed to meet them in front of The Shaft restaurant at seven."

"You're going?"

Philip nodded. "How else am I going to find out if Heather is here?"

"Did they tell you how long you'd be going for?" said Sarah.

"They called it a three-day session. Good food, a chance to get a better perspective on life, I think they said."

"Watch out for the food," muttered Sarah. "The Children of God have been known to use Henbane tea, and there was a group of religious loonies in Vancouver who spiked their food with Ritalin and probantheline bromide."

Philip stared at her blankly.

"Henbane is an herb, a member of the potato family. It causes visual hallucinations. It also causes nausea, diarrhea, confusion, blackouts, and dizziness. It can kill you in too large a dose. Ritalin is a kind of super wake-up pill they used to keep the fundraisers out working and probantheline bromide is an ulcer medicine that has a side effect of reducing sexual desire and also causes impotence in men."

"Jesus!" whispered Philip, horrified.

"I told you before," warned Sarah. "These people are playing for keeps."

"Okay, so I should assume the food has been drugged, then?"

Sarah shrugged. "It's possible, maybe even probable. There was a man named Ted Patrick, he was famous for deprogramming kids caught up in the cult groups. From his experience the speed with which the groups got the kids fully involved was phenomenal. Almost as though it was artificially induced. Maybe the drugs are being used as some kind of adjunct to the brainwashing techniques."

Philip shook his head. "I don't know," he said slowly. "It really does sound like fairy tale stuff."

"Really?" said Sarah, grimacing. "Then why does a sophomore majoring in psychology and Russian, well adjusted, on good terms with her family and her friends, an A student, suddenly turn over her whole life and convert to the Moonies after forty-eight hours? Two days."

"That actually happened?" said Philip.

Sarah nodded. "That actually happened. She was a student at the University of New Hampshire. Don't underestimate them."

"You've convinced me," said Philip. He lit a cigarette and drummed his fingers thoughtfully on the table. "All right," he said after a moment. "I'm supposed to be going to this place for a three-day session. I should know if Heather's there or not in less time than that. One way or the other I'll be out in two days, even if I have to crawl on my hands and knees."

"How are you going to get back?" asked Sarah. "That's one of the standard ways these people get at you—isolation."

"I'm only going in there to try and *find* Heather—I'm not going to try and play hero and get her out. If she's there I'll get out on my own and go for reinforcements. If they kidnapped her, that's a criminal offense. I'll go to the nearest police station."

"You've got a lot to learn about these people," said Sarah. "It's not going to be that easy."

"Can you think of anything better?"

"No. But what if she isn't there?"

"Then we'll rendezvous somewhere. You name the spot."

"Reno," said Sarah. "There's got to be a connection between Keller's think tank and that NSS thing we found in the Barrington garbage. I've already booked a room."

"What hotel?"

"The Holiday. And not the Inn. Just the Holiday."

"Okay. Book me a room as well. I'll either be there or get in touch with you somehow. I'll check out of here and leave my stuff with you if that's all right. I'll put it in the car."

"Okay," said Sarah.

Philip looked at his watch. It was 6:45. He stood up. "I've got to be going." He looked down at Sarah, wanting to say something, but not sure what. She stared back at him. There was a brief moment where the incessant din of the people crowding the room dropped enough for Philip to faintly pick out the sound of the basketball game commentary on the television over the bar.

"Good luck," said Sarah quietly.

Philip nodded. "Thanks. I'll see you or talk to you on Thursday or Friday."

"I hope so," said Sarah. Then the conversation in the room surged again. Philip turned and left the room, a sudden feeling of coldness wrapping around him and sending a shiver down his spine.

Chapter Ten

The van, predictably a blue Econoline, with seating for twelve, headed northwest along Route 82 out of Aspen. As well as Philip and the two in uniform he'd met earlier, there were seven people in the truck with him. The first ten minutes of the drive were spent introducing. Philip learned that the blond driver's name was Eric, his companion Wendy.

From what Philip could tell none of the others knew each other, but there was a sameness about them—they were all fairly young, none of them as old as he was, and they all looked a bit down on their luck.

After the introductions were made there was a long uncomfortable silence that lasted until they were past the airport. Then, turning back in her seat, Wendy started up a sing-song. It started half-heartedly, but after a while everyone began to join in, Philip included. There was nothing religious in the choice of songs. They started off with "America" and kept on with the patriotic theme, going through everything from the "Star Spangled Banner" to the "Battle Hymn of the Republic," and "Dixie." It reminded Philip of the time his parents had dumped him at a Republican Youth Rally when he was a kid. It was all Boy Scout stuff, but everyone knew the words and it helped to pass the time. They were obviously being eased into things gently.

They kept on Route 82 as it twisted back and forth, following the sinuous track of the Roaring Fork River, passing through the smaller resort town of Snowmass, and then Basalt and El Jebel. The singing had stopped. After a little less than an hour, and with the light starting to fade quickly, they turned off 82 onto 133 at Carbondale, heading almost due south between the dark sloped mountains and thickly wooded hills of the White River National Forest. By the time they reached the tiny one-street town of Redstone, it was completely dark and they continued along the winding highway with nothing to see except the yellow light from twin bores poking ahead of the van. Philip saw that everyone except Wendy and the driver was asleep.

"How much farther?" asked Philip, leaning forward and speaking over Wendy's shoulder.

She kept her eyes on the road ahead. "Not much," she murmured. "Just be patient."

"Do we go through Ragged Mountain?" he asked. "The town, I mean."

"No," said Eric. The tone in his voice was clear. Questions weren't appreciated.

The strange, cold feeling he'd had as he left the bar at the Jerome came back to him. Not fear, more a jagged anxiety, as though he'd neglected something important, or made some terrible error in judgment that had somehow slipped his mind. He began to appreciate what Sarah had said about isolation. The Crusade had him at their mercy, it was dark, and he had little or no idea of where he was. He'd committed himself, and was without any real means of bailing out. For the first time since the surreal afternoon when Heather had suddenly reappeared in his life he found himself wondering if he'd bitten off more than he could chew.

After traveling for slightly more than half an hour along the narrow highway, the van turned off onto an unpaved road that rose steeply and was bounded on either side by a screening veil of trees. As they headed upward Philip checked his watch again in the faint light. Ten minutes before he'd seen a sign pointing down a sideroad to a place called Bogan Flats so at least he had some idea of where he was, though he had no idea where Bogan Flats was in relation to the rest of the world.

The van slowed, and Philip caught a glimpse of a high chain-link fence as the headlights swung around a curve and then came out onto a large clearing in the forest. The road straightened as they approached the fence, and in the bright glare from the headlights Philip made out a gate with a guard posted. He was wearing a jumpsuit variation of the uniform worn by Eric. The guard dragged open the gate and they rolled slowly over the gravel road into the Tenth Crusade compound. The gravel road continued on for another hundred yards or so and, peering out the side window on his right, Philip could dimly make out the shapes of low, log cabin buildings. The road ended at a circular drive around a slightly mounded and barren-looking flowerbed with a tall flagpole at its center. To the right Philip could see the lights of a large ranch-style house, also made out of logs, and to the left he could faintly make out a warren of small cabins arranged in clusters. Directly in front of the van beyond the flagpole, and outlined starkly in the headlights, was a gigantic barn, its two main doors emblazoned with the Tenth Crusade crest.

Wendy turned, smiling. "This is it, friends, end of the line. All out for fresh air!" She opened her door, hopped out, and a few seconds later there was a click and a well-oiled rumble as she slid open the side panel of the van.

Philip waited for the others to drop down onto the ground and then followed. He felt as though he was trapped in a movie about a man's first introduction to a prison camp. He shivered in the cold night air and fell in beside his companions. Above him the clear sky was pricked by an infinity of unblinking stars. Around him, the only sound other than the recruits' breathing was the faint old-bone rustle of the forest outside the compound.

Eric came around to the front of the van and stared at the new recruits.

Philip remembered what the man in the Barrington restaurant had said; there was something cold about the people of the Tenth Crusade. Standing now in front of them, lit only by the stars overhead and the spill of light from the windows of the ranch house, Eric fit that description well enough; he looked as though he was carved out of pale marble, and his expression was just as lifeless. When he spoke his voice was hard, and strangely distant.

"First things first," he said. "All of you look tired, so we'd better assign you bunks." He turned to his companion. "Wendy?"

She nodded. "Okay," she said crisply. "Girls, come with me. The women's dorm is over there." She poked her thumb back over her shoulder at a long, barracks-like building to the right of the main house. She turned away from the group and the three girls obediently fell in behind her.

"Men over there," said Eric, pointing to a distant cluster of small cabins on the far side of the compound. He motioned with his hand and set off across the circular drive to the hard-packed earth beyond. Philip and the other two followed in a straggling line. It was feeling more and more like a prisoner-of-war film. Philip almost expected to see Steve McQueen bouncing a baseball against one of the cabins. Strange and sinister as it was, the whole thing seemed to Philip to have its ridiculous side, and he barely suppressed a grin. Kids playing at being in the army. Then he remembered the streak of blood on the wall of his loft in SoHo and the grin was stillborn. They played for keeps, Sarah had said. If they were children's games, maybe the fantasy had gotten out of hand.

Eric left two of the men at a cabin close to the large barn-like structure, promising that he'd be back in a few minutes, and then he led Philip and the remaining man up the gently inclined ground to a cabin close to the perimeter fence and the wall of trees beyond it. They passed seven or eight other cabins on the way, but they were dark, the windows carefully shuttered. If there was anyone inside they were asleep.

Eric swung open the door of the cabin he'd assigned to Philip and the other man and stepped aside, ushering them inside. The tall blond man followed, flipping a switch set by the door. A single bulb hanging from a long piece of flex in the ceiling came on. Philip guessed it was no more than forty watts—enough light to undress by, but useless for reading or anything else.

The room was decorated in early monastery—two sets of bunk beds, four foot lockers piled against the far wall, and a single folding chair. There were no washing facilities, no place other than the foot lockers for clothes, and no mirror. And, oddly, considering the austere decor, Philip saw that the cabin was heated electrically with baseboard fixtures.

"It's not much," said Eric, the words coming out as though he'd spoken them a hundred times before, "but it's clean and warm. Toilet and bathing facilities are located on the far side of the study hall – that's the barn building you saw. Breakfast is served in the study hall. In case you hadn't noticed we're even higher up here than Aspen, so don't be surprised if you find yourself getting tired more easily. I suggest you get some sleep now; you'll be having a busy day tomorrow."

"What's on the agenda?" asked Philip.

Eric turned to him, his eyes blank. "There's an orientation meeting in the study hall right after breakfast."

"When's that?" asked Philip's new bunkmate.

"Early," said Eric. "But don't worry, someone will be around to wake you up." He gave a little nod and then left the cabin, shutting the door behind him.

Philip had an urge to try the door to see if it was locked. He tried the knob and the door creaked open. He shrugged and turned back to his new companion. "Well at least we're not locked in for the night."

"You thought we might be?" asked the other man, a hint of nervousness in his voice.

Philip shrugged. "It had occurred to me." He held out his hand. "My name's Philip. Philip Kirkland."

"Dan Jackson," said the other man, shaking Philip's hand.

Philip guessed Jackson to be in his late twenties. The man had longish, straw-colored hair, a narrow, pinched face, and small eyes behind rimless glasses. He wore age-whitened jeans, a pale green T-shirt, and a stained U.S. Army fatigue jacket. All in all, he looked like a pale and myopic facsimile of a sixties runaway.

Jackson sat down on the lower bunk and the springs creaked. He tested the mattress with his palms and grimaced. "Too hard. I like something softer."

"I don't think this has all been laid on with our comfort in mind," said Philip, sitting down on the folding chair and pulling off his boots. He sat back wearily and lit a cigarette.

"What's that supposed to mean?" asked Jackson from the

bed. He twisted around and flopped back against the single pillow, hands clasped behind his head.

"Do you know anything about these people?" asked Philip, ignoring Jackson's question.

"Only what they told me."

"And what was that?"

"They said they ran some kind of social work camp. Free food, free bed, a place to rest up. I didn't ask too many questions. I mean us beggars can't be choosers, can we?"

"They didn't give you any kind of religious spiel?"

"No," answered Jackson. "Why? You think they're into that kind of thing?"

"Maybe," said Philip. "Did you catch the little crest they wear on their blazers, and the big symbol on the barn doors?"

"Kind of a cross thing, right?" said Jackson. "Shit, maybe they are a bunch of freakos." He squinted up at the bottom of the upper bunk and then turned his head toward Philip. The light from the dim, single bulb hanging from the bare rafters reflected off the lenses, hiding the man's eyes. "But so what? Like I said, we don't have a lot of choice. I've got maybe ten bucks to my name and not much chance of getting more."

"Where are you from?" asked Philip. He stood up and began stripping off his clothes.

"You've never heard of it," answered Jackson, sighing.

"Try me," said Philip.

"The Pines," said the small-faced man. "A town called Chatsworth."

"The Pines?" said Philip, now down to his Jockeys.

"The Gold Pine Barrens. A thousand square miles of swamp in New Jersey," said Jackson. "It's between Phillie and the ocean just south of New York. Chatsworth is the big deal. You sit outside Buzby's General Store and watch the weeds grow."

"Pretty exotic name for a swamp," said Philip. He padded across the room, flipped off the light, and boosted himself up onto the upper bunk.

"Third largest producer of cranberries in the U.S.," said Jackson wryly, out of the darkness. "You work the berries, or you pull sphagnum moss out of the spongs and cripples for a living." He pronounced "spong" to rhyme with "tongue."

"What's a spong and what's a cripple?" asked Philip.

"A spong's a swamp with dead oak trees rotting in it. A cripple's exactly the same thing except the dead trees are white cedars. Real exciting place to grow up. My big decision after I got out of high school was whether I'd work for one of the big cranberry farms or pull sphagnum moss. My brothers all worked the berries and my Daddy worked the spongs. I didn't want to do either, so I took off. That was six years ago and I haven't been back since. Now I'm on my ass in a forest in Colorado. Come a long way in six years, haven't I?"

"How old are you?" asked Philip.

"Twenty-four."

"I thought you were older than that," said Philip.

"You tend to look older if you come from the Pines."

There was a long, empty silence. Outside, the wind scraped across the shingles of the cabin roof sending faint creakings through the wood, making it sound like a ship rocking on the sea. Eventually the creaking was counterpointed by small ratcheting snores from the lower bunk and Philip knew that Jackson was asleep, dreaming perhaps of Buzby's General Store and a thousand square miles of swamp between Philadelphia and the Atlantic shore.

Lying on the hard, thin mattress, the dark beams of the cabin roof only a few feet above his head, Philip suddenly saw how perfect it was. It was people like Jackson, from the forgotten places in America, who gave the Crusade their army. Places that bred people with no futures, either out of poverty, like Jackson, or neglect. The Barrens of the United States were fertile recruiting grounds for people like Billy Carstairs and the Tenth Crusade. Find people with nothing, give them some elusive hope, and they would gladly mortgage their hearts and minds and souls. It had been that way with Heather. Her dream of being a famous dancer had met with the reality that although she was very very good she would never be good enough, and rather than face that fact, she had given herself up to another dream, one that made her a charter member in a strange elite of martyrs, people with hurt hearts who were more than willing to exchange their individuality for a mind-less ordered life and a strong mother love. Mother Teresa, Mother Superior.

Philip remembered something that Sarah had talked about on the flight from Chicago to Denver; in almost every case, cults and religious groups relied heavily on a parental structure of some kind. The 3HO organization of Yogi Bhajan in California usually referred to Bhajan as "Father"; Sun Myung Moon of the Unification Church was hailed as "Father" and the "True Parent"; Claire Prophet of the Universal Church was called "Guru Ma" by her followers; Ron Hubbard of the Scientologists liked to be called "Father"; Eleanor Dairies of the Faith Tabernacle was called "Mother Dairies"; and Jim Jones, leader of the Peoples Temple and orchestrator of the mass suicide in Georgetown, Guyana, was often referred to as "Dad."

"They treated Hitler the same way," Sarah had said.

"You've got Hitler on the brain," replied Philip, smiling.

"'Fuhrer, my father, by God given to me, defend and protect me as long as may be.' That was the opening prayer in German day nurseries in the thirties," she had answered.

As he lay in the darkness, listening to the rising wind in the pines, Philip still couldn't quite bring himself to believe it all. It seemed almost childish. Uniforms, pamphlets, simplistic dogma. On the other hand, perhaps it was the simplicity that was the key to it. In a world of complex problems the simple answer might seem attractive, especially to the lonely, the disenfranchised, and the frustrated. Easy for people like him to forget that revolutions are started, and wars are fought, by ordinary men, and led by others shouting simple slogans.

"Sieg Heil," whispered Philip up into the darkness. "And Jesus saves."

* * *

Philip was awakened by the sound of an unfamiliar voice. He opened his eyes and found himself staring at the low watt bulb on its strand of flex.

"Clothes in the big bag, personal stuff in the small one. Remember your number. It's fifty-six. Forget it and we'll never be able to keep track. 'Kay?"

"Sure, but ...."

"Wake up your friend. Chow's in ten minutes. And don't forget to tell him his number's eighty-eight."

"Uh...." Jackson's voice again.

Philip turned his head to see a short, overweight man with pale, almost fishbelly skin, and a bad case of late adolescent acne, was going out the door. He had two duffle bags slung over his shoulder and he was clutching two smaller bags in his free hand. He was wearing what appeared to be a loose fitting surgical outfit—light green drawstring pants and a pullover shirt of the same color with short sleeves.

"Who the hell was that?" asked Philip, groggily, as the door slammed shut. Jackson stood up. Philip blinked. Jackson was wearing the same type of surgical greens.

"Said he was the laundry detail," answered Jackson. "Took all our clothes to be cleaned as well as our personal stuff. They keep it in a safe at the main house until you go. Something to do with insurance, he said."

"He took *my* clothes as well?" Philip burst out.

"Uh-huh. Left you a set of threads like mine. You're eighty-eight, by the way."

"Shit!" breathed Philip. He slid around in the bunk bed and dropped onto the bare wood floor. It was cold. Dressed only in his briefs he crossed the small room to the folding chair. Even his boots were gone. In their place was a neatly folded uniform like Jackson was wearing, complete with thick wool socks and a pair of tired-looking combat boots.

Behind him Jackson yawned. "You got the time?" he asked.

Philip checked his watch, then checked it again. Four-thirty in the morning. He turned to his bunkmate. "You actually let that kid take your clothes and mine?" he said angrily.

Jackson shrugged, his thin body looking absurd in the outfit that was at least two sizes too big for him. "What's the harm? All he's doing is washing them."

"Right," muttered Philip, teeth clenched. He stared down at the loose fitting clothes. In his conversations with Sarah she'd referred to it as "separation." It was the same thing the army did to you—a uniform to promote sameness, a number rather than a name—loss of identity. They even had his cigarettes and the Japanese lighter. That worried him; if they looked too closely they'd find the camera mechanism and that would be the end of him. He picked up the clothes and began putting them on—he had no choice.

"You never told me the time," said Jackson, a defensive whine in his voice.

"It's four-thirty," said Philip, his voice becoming muffled as he drew the shirt over his head.

"Jeez," muttered the pinched-face man. "Breakfast at four-thirty in the morning? I'm not even hungry."

Philip sat down on the folding chair, slid his feet into the socks and rammed them into the combat boots. He bent and began lacing them. "I think you'd better eat while you can," said Philip. "I'll lay you five to one the meals here are few and far between."

"I wish you wouldn't talk like that," said Jackson. "It makes me nervous."

"Me too," said Philip.

*　*　*

By the time Philip and Jackson reached the barn the cavernous interior was already filled almost to overflowing with people dressed in the pale-green uniforms. Simple tables made from sheets of plywood on trestles had been set up with long, plain wood benches for seating. At some point the barn had been stripped down to the bones and refinished. The walls had been insulated, then covered with wallboard. The hayloft had been glassed in to provide an office, complete with a wrought-iron spiral staircase. To the left, above a low riser, another of the Tenth Crusade emblems had been placed on the wall, and just above it Philip could see a valance that hid a large, drop-down projection screen. Somebody had spent a lot of money renovating the old building.

A young girl, who looked to be in her late teens, had greeted them just inside the doors, asked for their numbers and led them to their assigned spots. Jackson was taken to a table well in the rear while Philip found himself seated directly in front of the slightly raised head table.

If his level was a sea of pale green, the head table was an island of color, mostly blue. He spotted Eric and Wendy, among the dozen others, all of whom were dressed identically in the blue blazer and white shirt uniform. At the center of the table, with an empty place between them, sat two men. Both of them lean, tanned, and extremely fit-looking, and they wore tight-fitting black leather bomber jackets over black turtleneck sweaters. On the table in front of them were two black berets, each one bearing a small silver pin. From where Philip sat it looked like the insignia was a raised broadsword. He'd once done a photo-series on the Black Beret Special Forces squad used for anti-terrorist work by the U.S. Army, and the men at the head table could have been cloned from the same stock. Any doubts he might have had concerning Sarah Logan's estimation of the Tenth Crusade vanished. These two in black had been trained to kill.

As casually as he could, he turned and looked around the room, hoping for a glimpse of Heather. There was no immediate sign of her, but the green fatigues seemed to melt together, and at least half of the people in the room had their backs to him. Even if she wasn't in the dining room it wouldn't prove anything. If they'd gone to so much trouble to get her back it stood to reason that the Crusade might not let her mingle with the others so openly. It suddenly occurred to him that Sarah had been right, he did have a lot to learn about these people, and coming to the Ragged Mountain installation was beginning to look like a mistake—a dangerous one. Heather was obviously important to the Crusade for some reason and except for its relative isolation Ragged Mountain didn't seem like the kind of place you kept important people.

The low-voiced babble of conversation in the large room dropped to a whisper and then to total silence. Heads turned to look towards the open doors of the barn and Philip did likewise.

A tall, balding, dark-haired man entered the barn. He had a

114

round, almost cherubic face, its smooth-cheeked innocent appearance only slightly diminished by a pair of smoke lensed glasses that partially hid his eyes. He stood silently for a moment, his head swiveling to look around the room, then he moved slowly up between the tables to the platform. He climbed up the two steps and moved behind the table to take his place between the two black-jacketed men. As he did so the other people at the head table, with the exception of the men in black, rose and the rest of the room followed suit. Philip stood, his eyes on the newcomer.

The tall man waited until the room was silent again, then bowed his head and began to speak. It was the Lord's Prayer, and within seconds the words were being echoed throughout the barn, the litany reverberating darkly from the high roofbeams. Philip repeated the words along with everyone else, head bowed, eyes closed to slits. Through his lashes he saw that the two black-jacketed men had risen at the first words of the prayer.

The prayer over, the tall man at the center of the table looked up, surveying the room again. He gave a little nod, then sat down. As he did so, uniformed attendants, all women, appeared with heavy laden trays. They worked up and down the long lines of tables, placing a single plate in front of each person. It was porridge, thick and glutinous, surrounded by a moat of watery milk. Philip reached for the spoon on the table in front of him, but stopped, seeing that the people on either side of him hadn't moved.

Then he noticed that Eric was standing at his place, looking out across the expanse of the barn.

"Good morning, friends!" he called out, his voice firm and clear.

"GOOD MORNING, FRIEND!" came back the automatic response from the people below him.

"And why is it good?" chanted Eric.

"BECAUSE WE'RE FREE!"

"And why are we free?"

"BECAUSE WE BELIEVE!"

"And what do we believe?"

"WE BELIEVE IN TRUTH!"

"And?"

"WE BELIEVE IN JUSTICE FOR ALL!"

"And?"

"THE UNITED STATES OF AMERICA!"

"Whose truth?"

"GOD'S TRUTH!"

"Whose justice?"

"GOD'S JUSTICE!"

"Whose America?"

"GOD'S AMERICA!"

There was a rousing cheer that slowly faded into silence. Eric waited until he had everyone's attention, then spoke again. "I'd like to take this opportunity to welcome a number of new people and introduce them to the leader of the Ragged Mountain Compound, Dr. Gerald Lacey." Eric nodded his head to the man in the smoked glasses, who returned the gesture. "And I'd like to introduce everyone here to our guests. Commander Hal Bennett from the Denver Area Headquarters, and Commander John Holmes from national HQ in Reno. They're here to observe us for a couple of days, so let's make them feel welcome."

There was another cheer, not quite as enthusiastic as the first. When it had died Eric raised his right arm and flashed his patented smile. "Okay, friends, chow down!"

Although he was famished, Philip ignored the food on his battered tin plate, shoving the gray mass around with his spoon while the people around him wolfed theirs down. No one payed the slightest attention to him and he was left alone with his thoughts.

With breakfast over the crowd jammed into the barn dispersed rapidly. Philip lagged behind at the doors, trying to see if he could spot Heather among the streams of people leaving, but the identical uniforms made it almost impossible to pick out individuals. Within minutes everyone had disappeared into the pre-dawn darkness. The young girls who had been waiters immediately began breaking down the tables, replacing them with circular groups of folding chairs. As he watched, the brightly lit interior of the barn was transformed into its daytime function of study hall.

"Eighty-eight!" boomed a foghorn voice. It was Eric, speaking through a hand-held megaphone. "Are you going to stand there daydreaming, or are you going to join us?" The blond man was standing with a small group on the circular rise of tamped down earth below the barren flagpole.

Philip crossed over to them, suddenly aware of the early morning chill. As he approached he saw that the group was made up of the male members of the bunch he'd traveled up from Aspen with and one other person, a burly man with the thick slab chest and the bulging arms of a weight lifter. He was dressed in the same uniform as the rest of the group with the addition of a Tenth Crusade armband and a black felt beret.

"This is Bob," said Eric as Philip joined the group. "You might call him the Ragged Mountain compound's recreational director. He'll give you a bit of a workout to clean out your lungs, and then we'll meet back here for your orientation meeting in the study hall."

"Can I ask a question?" asked Philip.

"Shoot," said Eric.

"Our personal possessions. Is there any way we can get hold of them?"

"You won't be needing them," the blue-blazered man answered crisply. "We'll provide everything you need."

"How about my cigarettes?" asked Philip.

"No smoking here. Bad for your health." He frowned. "And I see you're wearing a watch. The orderly must have slipped up. Hand it over." He held out his hand.

"I prefer to keep it," said Philip.

The frown on Eric's face deepened. "No exceptions, I'm afraid. We've had too much trouble with our insurance people. You wouldn't want it stolen, would you?" He kept his hand out. Philip stared at him, then reluctantly unbuckled the worn Seiko diver's watch and handed it over.

"Okay," said Eric, turning his smile on briefly. "Now that we've got that out of the way, perhaps you people can get to it." He turned toward the weight lifter. "They're all yours, Bob."

And the day began.

The "bit of a workout" turned out to be a five-mile jog up the wooded slope of Ragged Mountain, following a trail that could only barely be made out in the gray half-light of the growing dawn. Bob never wavered, keeping up a steady grinding pace that soon had the four men behind him, Philip included, gasping for breath.

Without his watch, Philip had no accurate way of judging time, but from the increasing light he guessed that at least an hour had passed before the chain-link fence of the compound came into view again. By then his thin uniform was soaked with sweat and every muscle in his legs was on fire.

Returning to the compound they were taken immediately in hand by Eric once again and their "orientation" began. Within the first few minutes Philip realized that what was really going on was indoctrination. They sat in the study hall and listened to Eric deliver a long, rambling monologue about the present ills of the United States. Philip heard quotes that ranged from Socrates to Thomas Jefferson to the Bible, as the blue-blazered man hammered the same message home again and again. The United States was in trouble and the root cause of that trouble was an increase in sin and a decline in morality as the country was wooed by a small minority of "liberals" and humanists whose only desire was to destroy the nation, leaving its belly open to a gutting thrust by the waiting forces of godless communism. The convoluted theories presented by the Crusader were absurd, but looking at the others in his small group Philip could see that the man's words were having an effect.

Abortion was murder, homosexuals were "perverts" and "strutting sissies," the ERA was madness, since by their morality women shouldn't have equal rights, they should have more rights than men because they were blessed by God. Welfare was evil, since it destroyed the American Dream of getting ahead by dint of hard work and individual action, and unions had been corrupted by communist infiltration and by the Mafia. Pornography caused rape, foreign investment caused unemployment, and arms reduction made the country impotent. Through each subject the same note was struck: there was only one law, the Law of God. And if, by following the tenets laid down in the Bible, an individual or a group broke the laws of the country, then they were innocent of transgression by right of the fact that God's Court was the only truly supreme center of absolute justice. If local laws could be superseded by State and federal laws, then the word of God could overrule them all.

A hundred times during the lecture Philip spotted logical holes big enough to drive a truck through, but he was too tired and too listless to make any comment; from the looks in the eyes of his companions the thought of trying to object never occurred to them.

Throughout the morning other groups filtered into the study hall, and by the time the sun was well up in the clear mountain sky there were at least a hundred people in the barn, sitting in small clusters and listening with rapt attention to their leaders, the cavernous room echoing with the strident lectures, voices mixing into a bizarre kaleidoscope of sound that had Philip's head spinning.

Philip scanned the other groups for some sign of Heather, but there was nothing. If she *was* at Ragged Mountain she wasn't openly mingling with the others.

But even if he had spotted Heather that day it wouldn't have done him much good – the lectures were continuous and there was never a moment when he wasn't accompanied by some member of the Crusade, even when he went to the bathroom. He began to see that what was going on was less brainwashing than brain *stunning*. It was like the shot they gave you before general anesthetic, something to dull your mind before the greater trauma; and it worked. Philip could feel himself becoming more and more lethargic, mentally. It wasn't that he was taken in by what he heard, but by simply allowing it to seep into his brain, his rational thoughts were being steadily overwhelmed. Bizarrely, there seemed to be one beneficial side effect – chainsmoker that he was, the stuporous flow of words seemed to have robbed him of any desire to smoke.

There was no break for lunch. Instead they were served sandwiches at their chairs, followed by mugs of what Eric said was lime Kool-Aid. The sandwiches were peanut butter on white bread. Philip wolfed his down hungrily, rationalizing that it was unlikely that anyone would go to the trouble of spiking the peanut butter. The Kool-Aid was something else again. It had been a vat of the same sugary drink that Jim Jones had used in the mass suicide in Guyana.

By early afternoon, Eric had gone, replaced by another leader, a woman who called herself Rina. She picked up where Eric had left off, going from the general to the particular. Her subject was sins of the flesh, and she taught it with zeal, her pale, pasty face gleaming with sweat, her eyes glowing as she talked about temptation, fornication, sodomy, and incest.

Late afternoon brought on a third teacher, a lank-haired, and pipe-stem-thin man named Josh, who lectured on the creeping horror of government growth and the loss of personal freedom. By the time he'd finished Philip was no longer capable of coherent thought. He was dead tired, his brain spinning with the incessant babble of the teachers.

As the sun lowered, the study hall was transformed into a dining room again and the evening meal was served—a glutinous stew of unknown origin, chased with skim milk made from powder. By then Philip didn't care if the food or drink was drugged or not and he ate along with everyone else as Eric, standing to one side of the head table, read verses from the Bible in a loud, ringing voice.

After the meal, Dr. Lacey, the compound leader, delivered a set speech on the purposes of the Tenth Crusade. According to him the members of the Crusade had a sacred duty to save their country from the rising tide of sin, greed, lust, perversion, and communism that was threatening to drown the nation. They were "God's soldiers" and they were fighting on the "front lines of desperation and hopelessness," and in "the trenches of degradation and immortality." No price was too high, in the war to save America from herself, and, according to Lacey, the time was drawing near when the Crusade's mettle would be tested on "the battlefield of truth."

With his mind dulled into a half-hypnotized stupor, Philip found himself nodding as Lacey spoke, a part of him believing it, taking it all in. Ultimately he knew it was all a lie, but the pattern, the rhythms of speech were like a siren's call, slowly but surely dragging him down.

With dinner over the crowd in the barn trooped out into the compound for the flag lowering ceremony, which was followed in turn by an outdoor study session that lasted until the sun had fully set. Finally, with darkness fallen, they were all ordered back to their cabins.

Philip stumbled gratefully across the compound, Jackson at his heels. The rat-faced man had utterly transformed since the morning. His eyes were bright and eager, and there was no trace of a whine in his voice as he chattered on and on about how great it was to have found the Tenth Crusade, and how all his problems seemed to have faded away into nothing. He'd found a place where he was important. Philip, almost comatose by that point, ignored Jackson and climbed up into his bunk without even taking off his wrinkled, sweat-stained uniform.

The chances of finding Heather at Ragged Mountain were beginning to seem slim, and a much greater incentive was taking precedence—he had to get out of Ragged Mountain himself, before it was too late and he wound up like Jackson, a mindless convert.

Thirty seconds after hitting the mattress he was asleep.

Chapter Eleven

Philip's second day at Ragged Mountain began much as the first had; at 4:30 the laundry orderly appeared with fresh uniforms and instructions that they were to head to the study hall for breakfast. According to the orderly there would be no workout for them. In its place there would be a church service.

Somehow the night's sleep had left Philip feeling even worse, but he managed to drag himself to the barn along with the others. Jackson was ebullient, eager to begin another day, and even through the haze of tiredness Philip found himself wondering at the transformation. In the space of twenty-four hours the man from the Gold Pine Barrens had changed from a slightly disgruntled vagrant into a full-fledged zealot, happily parroting the phrases, theories, and slogans he'd heard the day before.

For the first time in his life Philip understood what the term "brainwashing" meant, and he also realized why it was so effective. Unlike the mind manipulation of the original "brainwashed" prisoners of war in Korea, there was no bulwark of mental defenses to be breached at Ragged Mountain. The people recruited by the Crusade were, for the most part, disaffected, alienated, and unhappy, for one reason or another—they actually *wanted* what the Crusade had to offer, and accepted the co-opting of their minds eagerly. Even for Philip, who considered himself a reasonably happy and successful human being, the previous day's mental hammering had taken its toll; it was only by force of will that he was able to ignore the crooning words of Dr. Lacey, as he worked his way through the church service in the barn, and to concentrate on a way of getting out of Ragged Mountain.

Whatever its administrators chose to call it, Ragged Mountain was in reality a subtle but effective prison camp. Philip wondered how many people had been brought here, realized their mistake in coming, and then had no way of leaving. From what he could recall of the ride up to the compound they were at least a dozen miles from the secondary road, and that much again from the main highway. And even if you did reach the main highway without being picked up by the Crusade, you'd be there without any identification, money, or clothes, except the thin green uniform, which would look to a passing motorist like something out of a mental hospital. And that meant he'd have to get back his clothes, his wallet, and his boots with the hidden credit card before he could even begin to make his way out of the camp. It was already early morning and he doubted he'd have a chance of getting his possessions back before that night.

These thoughts filtered through his mind as Lacey wrapped up his sermon with a resounding diatribe against a book Philip had never heard of called the *Humanist Manifesto*. According to Lacey, the book was on a philosophical par with *Mein Kampf* and was the blueprint for the takeover of the free world by the forces of the antichrist. Philip couldn't have cared less – he was mentally kicking himself for not having looked at a map before letting himself be driven out into the middle of nowhere.

The long and often venomous sermon finally ended and the brain-shriveling day of lectures began. As a seminar on the bizarre pseudo-scientific theories of "Doctor" Tim LaHaye started up, the heavens split and a thundering downpour hammered down on the compound.

Philip wasn't sure whether it was the rain, or the knowledge that he had to get himself out of Ragged Mountain, but he found himself much less responsive to the mental brow-beating of that day's lectures. At the same time he realized that he was taking the content of what was being said much more seriously. The theories being promulgated ranged from the ridiculous to the absurd, but they were also tremendously powerful by virtue of their simplicity.

LaHaye's style was a perfect example. The man, whose doctorate it turned out had been earned at the Western Conservative Baptist Seminary, set things out simply. There were good guys and bad guys. The good guys believed in God and the Bible and the bad guys didn't. The battlefield was the United States and, as in any war, all weapons were proper and correct as long as the cause was an honorable one. In basic terms, LaHaye believed that the means justified the end, that end being the Christianizing of the Western World. His means for achieving that end were various.

LaHaye, it seemed, was a great believer in the "Sixteen," as he called it. The Sixteen was an ascending ladder of authority from county sheriffs up through local, State, and federal governments, ending with the President of the United States. According to LaHaye, it was the duty of all right-thinking Christians to watch all these authorities carefully, and when they saw something immoral, amoral, or even vaguely humanist, they were supposed to do everything possible to oust the particular sinner. "Everything" went from relatively harmless petitions up to full-fledged smear campaigns.

After an hour or more of the world according to Tim La-Haye, Philip found himself enthralled—not by the lecture, but by the horrible, convoluted logic of the man's theories. Now, the lecturer from the previous day, Rina, used a blackboard to demonstrate the theory that the United States was ruled by a small, vicious cadre of slavering humanists, and according to her the chart was derived "directly from Dr. LaHaye's book, *Battle for the Mind*," as though that gave it instant credibility. The chart showed that while Christianity was based on the wisdom of God, humanism, Confucianism, Buddhism, and Muhammedanism were pagan and based on the wisdom of man. The chart also showed that while there were only 275,000 humanists in the United States, they controlled T.V., radio, newspapers, the motion picture industry, magazines, most of the major foundations, unions, public education, the Civil Liberties Union, the National Organization of Women, and the Supreme Court. It went on to show, by a series of connected lines, that humanists were obsessed with sex, pornography, and marijuana.

At that point Philip almost burst out laughing, the image of Earl Warren with a joint in his mouth reading a copy of *Rubber World* almost too much to bear. It ceased to be funny when Rina went on to say that LaHaye's theories about humanism were backed by the Southern Baptist Convention, Jerry Falwell and the Moral Majority lobby in Washington, as well as by the 54,000 active members of the Tenth Crusade.

It was the first time Philip had heard anything about the group's size, and even if Rina was exaggerating by a hundred per cent it meant there were 25,000 others across the country like her. He did some quick calculating in his head and the results were staggering. Sarah had told him that the average amount of money brought in by a member of Sun Myung Moon's Unification Church, and its one hundred front organizations, was $200 per day. If only one-quarter of the Tenth Crusade membership was involved in fund raising that meant the Crusade was bringing in at least $1.25 million dollars a day, all of it tax free and untraceable. The implications of an organization like the Tenth Crusade with the power of a $400,000,000-a-year slush fund was horrifying. No wonder they could afford places like the Ragged Mountain compound, the New York headquarters, and the "club" Sarah had discovered in Baltimore.

Ironically, the next lecture, this one given by Eric, was on the subject of fund raising for the Crusade.

"We're not fooling around here," he began, his voice tense, his eyes scanning the group. "And we're not kidding ourselves either. We're in a war ... a war against everything rotten, depraved, and immoral in this country. And our war is no different than any other ... it costs money. When Richard the Lionheart went out on his crusade to recapture Jerusalem and the Holy Land, the people of England impoverished themselves for his noble cause. Well, things are different now. We have to educate, or maybe you might say we have to re-educate the American people, and show them that this country's greatness is rooted in the scriptures. We have to tell them about the things we're doing, and we have to make them see how important that work is, and how important their contributions are. But we don't want to waste time either. You don't have to work out on the streets, fund raising, for very long before you recognize people who simply won't believe. When you do see people like that, move on quickly ... you can't get blood from a stone, and you don't want to be tempted by them. If the person isn't willing to donate, find someone else. We're running out of time, and that makes *your* time valuable, so don't throw it away. You're not out there to convert people... that's not your job. Your job is to win us the time and the money so that we can continue to work towards an America that is truly free ... free of the influences of humanism, communism, and immorality.

"I'm not going to beat around the bush. We're committed, and if you can't come up to that standard of commitment we don't want you. And I'll tell you right now, it's not going to be easy, friends. There are going to be times when people will laugh at you, or call you names, and there will be times when you're so tired you'll barely be able to stand up, but don't worry. You've got God on your side, and God's truth to give you strength. And you've got us. We'll stand behind you a hundred per cent. We're your family now, your brothers and sisters, and we'll give you all the help you need."

He went on for what seemed like hours, flirting with the whole question of money and fund raising; veering away, then coming back to it, over and over again, drumming it into the group that the money they raised was for God's work. Every now and again Philip glanced at the small circle of people around him, amazed and appalled at how easily the man's sophomoric diatribes seemed to be taking root. The others were nodding when agreement was required, frowning and smiling on cue. Eric had them, lock, stock and barrel—there was no more indoctrination because it wasn't necessary; in the space of a single day they had been converted and Eric was talking to them as though their joining the Crusade was a *fait accompli.*

As the rain continued to pound down onto the compound, turning it into a sea of mud, the day slipped past, the hours filled with the repetitious lectures, seminars, and workshops.

It wasn't until the study hall was broken up for the evening meal that Philip realized how much time had passed. It seemed as though he'd fallen into some kind of trance that filtered out the endless stream of garbage assaulting his brain.

By the time he'd finished a repeat of the thick stew he'd been served the night before, the rain had slowed to a drizzle, and as Philip slogged through the mud to the cabin with Jackson at lights out, it stopped completely. Thankfully Jackson's eager babble had ceased, replaced by a beatific expression and the humble, head-bowed walk of a penitent.

As they climbed into their bunks Jackson said into the darkness: "The enlistment ceremony is tomorrow."

"I know," answered Philip. "I heard the announcement too."

"Are you going to enlist?" asked the man.

"I think so," answered Philip. He wasn't about to tell Jackson his plans.

"You don't seem very sure."

"Are *you* going to enlist?" asked Philip, knowing the answer. He could almost see the look on Jackson's face.

"Yes," Jackson said. "For the first time in my life I have a reason and a purpose. A soldier for God and America."

One of Eric's catch phrases. "Right," said Philip. There was a long silence, and then from the bottom bunk Philip could hear the whispered words of the Lord's Prayer. He lay above Jackson, forcing himself to stay awake, and waited for the mumbled litany to turn into the softer cadences of sleep.

* * *

The sky was clear when Philip stepped out of the cabin and softly closed the door behind him. On his left was the jet-black bulk of Ragged Mountain itself, the immense splinter of granite looking like a gigantic ancient curtain, blotting out a million stars. The compound was silent, empty, and dark, the barn and the other buildings almost invisible; slightly darker shadows against the night.

Philip decided that there was only one place his clothes and possessions could be, in the large windowless extension on the main house. The extension had been added to the rear of the low, ranch-style building and it could only be seen from the bath house and toilets between it and the barn.

Philip stood close to the wall of the cabin, waiting for his eyes to adjust. There were only two ways to get to the extension; he could either walk directly across the compound beyond the flagpole to the house, or skirt the open space and go in behind the barn and then the bath house. The route straight across was the shortest, but it also offered the least cover if someone were to step out onto the porch of the main house. On the other hand, the low brush behind the barn and the bath house was unknown territory; for all he knew it might be a maze of ankle-catching roots and bracken.

Finally, realizing that every moment he spent in front of the cabin made him more vulnerable, he chose his route and moved quickly through the still wet mud to the far side of the barn, and slipped in behind it. He soon saw that the ground was relatively clear. There was a rough pathway curving behind the barn, probably beaten down by people going the short way to the toilets from the cabins further up the slope. Philip silently prayed that there were no Crusaders around with small nocturnal bladders.

Stopping every few seconds to listen, he eventually reached the edge of the barn, where he waited for a moment, and then, breath held, ran the dozen yards that separated the larger building from the toilet facilities. He crouched at the base of the rough log wall and waited. Still nothing. He rose halfway and proceeded. At the far end of the bath house he stopped again and waited. Fifteen feet away was the blank end wall of the extension. He closed his eyes and tried to remember what he'd seen in daylight. If his memory served, the only door was on the long side, facing the barn. Once there, he would be utterly exposed to the entire compound, but he had no choice. He listened, ears straining for the slightest human sound, but there was nothing except the ever present rustle of the wind in the trees. He bit his lip, his better judgment telling him to give up on the whole thing and return to the cabin. He could wait it out and not come forward at the enlistment ceremony. They'd have to let him go then. Or would they? Sarah had told him a story about that too. A Moonie had once decided to leave the cult and had been given a session with a dozen of his peers. They grilled and harassed the young man for half a day, and when it was over the defector wandered away from the Tarrytown, New York headquarters and put his head across a railway track. His remains were found spread out over half a mile of New York Central roadbed.

Steeling himself he stood up and raced across the soggy ground, his Crusade issue combat boots like lead around his ankles as the mud pulled and sucked at his every running step. Coming around the side of the building he slowed, his eyes scanning the dark area around the flagpole. Deserted. He kept on going and reached the door into the extension, his heart pounding wildly.

And found the door locked. Of course it would be locked he told himself. If he'd had the sense to think about it earlier for more than five seconds he would have realized that of course the door would be secured. It was a cheap padlock on a hasp, hinged on the outside. He dug his fingers into the soft, wet wood, and tugged. The screws gave slightly and he pulled harder. There was a tearing sound that brought his heart into his throat and he stopped, the hair on the nape of his neck prickling. Even though the evening was cool, sweat was forming at his hairline and in the creases around his eyes, stinging. His hands had gone clammy as well. He listened, but no one seemed to have heard. He wiped his palms on the thin material of his pants and tried the hasp again, hooking both forefingers around the metal and tugging until he felt his knuckles pop. With a claw hammer or even a screwdriver he could have had the hasp off in a few seconds. He flexed his fingers, wincing at the sting of his torn skin, then tried again. The hasp gave so suddenly that Philip almost fell over backwards. He regained his balance, and, letting the hasp dangle from the lock, he gently pried open the door and slipped inside. The interior of the long, windowless room was pitch dark. He closed the door carefully, then fumbled around on the wall until he found a light switch. He flipped it and suddenly the room was filled with light; a dozen overhead pans coming to life instantly.

The room was laid out in rows of floor-to-ceiling roughwood racks partitioned off into small cubbyholes. A square of cardboard was tacked over each small space with a stenciled number on it. It looked like the baggage room at a train station. Tense as he was, Philip grinned, remembering how he and Heather, after a trip to London had stopped off in Calais and left their luggage in a place much like the room he was standing in. There had been a sign on the door of the room announcing that it was a *consignée,* and the attendant, after looking at their tickets for the next Paris train, had nodded and taken the bags. Both he and Heather had assumed that the bags would be put onto the train for them, and it was only when they arrived in Paris that they were informed that a *consignée* was the equivalent of a North American locker room, and that their luggage was still in Calais.

The memory of Heather, a memory from more than a decade ago, tugged at him, and he closed his eyes for a second. A fresher memory, almost like a dream, took the place of the long past remembrance. Making love to a woman who was almost a stranger to him, yet whom he knew as well as he might know a twin. Blood on the wall. Reality cracked like a whip.

He leaned back against the door, confusion, exhaustion, and a nauseating anxiety twisting up his spine like snakes on a tree limb. Strangling. Time, distance, and memory stretched and contracted, bringing the hot taste of bile up into his mouth. Night terrors of a bivouac on the road to Quang Tri as nineteen-year-old soldiers in the furious dark beside him touched themselves and thought of home; like now, too insane to be real, yet so real it brought on madness.

He fought it off. Using his palms to push himself off the door, he straightened, refusing to think of anything but the present. There was no time to let the ten thousand shards of event and coincidence that had brought him here rise up and overwhelm him. That was a luxury for later if he could manage to get himself out of Ragged Mountain intact.

The numbers on the cubbyholes. He went down the narrow aisles, checking, leaving a muddy trail behind. Each small space had its own bag, each bag the same. Philip wondered how many young people who were brought to the compound

130

ever saw their personal belongings again. There had been a whole lecture earlier in the day about giving up the past and dedicating themselves to a perfect future of a Christian America. Contact with family or old friends was taboo, tantamount to temptation by the devil. The Crusade was a world apart, providing all. Paranoia planted like some terrible blight, hell bent to sweep across the nation.

He found his number, eighty-eight, and opened up the bag. He stripped where he stood, replacing the pale green with his own clothes. The watch was gone, probably into Eric's pocket, but the camera-lighter and his cigarettes were there. It had been two days since he'd smoked, but he resisted the temptation to light up on the spot. That was a luxury for later. He walked back through the stacks on his way to the door; it was past time to be gone.

As he tiptoed up the aisle he almost tripped headlong as his foot caught on something. He looked down and noticed an inset ring on the floor, the trap door half-heartedly disguised in the pattern of the gray linoleum tile. He bent down and, hooking his hand into it, he pulled. The 3 x 3 square of flooring came up and he could dimly see a sharply angled stairway. Furnace room? Boiler for the main house? He bit his lip, thinking hard, and then, tempting borrowed time, he flicked on the lighter and went down the stairs. At the foot of the steps he found another light switch. The overheads came on in the hidden room, harsh, crackling fluorescents that threw everything into sharp relief.

It was identical to the room above, except that instead of wooden racks and cubbyholes, the shelves and supports were made of welded steel. What the shelves contained was different too. There were no duffle bags filled with the flotsam and jetsam of Crusade recruits; instead this was an arsenal. The fifty or more shelves that went from the concrete floor up to the bare joists above contained at least five thousand weapons, of assorted types, and the ammunition to make them useful. From what Philip could tell at first glance most of the armaments looked out of date, but that made them no less deadly. Dumbstruck by the sight before him Philip wandered up and down the rows, taking a closer look.

Lanchester Mark Ones from the forties; Thompson M1s; stub-barrelled M3 "Grease Guns"; WW2 MP40 Shmeissers; Heckler and Koch model 33s; Soviet AK47s; piles of old Mannlicher-Carcanos, like the one supposedly used to assassinate John Kennedy; boxes of lightweight Colt Cobra pistols; Canadian-made Browning .45-caliber automatics; slender-nosed HK parabellums; Rugers; Radoms; Mausers; nickel-plated Ivor Johnson revolvers from the late thirties; the list could have gone on and on.

Philip stopped, brought out the camera-lighter and checked the light by eye. The film the man at the Aspen camera store had loaded with was a fast black and white—400 ASA. The exposures would be grainy, especially given the small size of the film, but they'd be better than nothing. He hauled out half a dozen weapons and laid them out on the floor directly under one of the lights. He made three exposures, then took out some more of the guns. Five minutes later he'd used up the roll. There was no point putting the weapons back—he'd left a trail of broken locks and muddy clothes a blind man could follow. Instead he picked out a pistol and rummaged around until he found ammunition to load it. According to the etched name on the slide action of the palm-sized automatic it was South African, a Pretoria Arms Factory "Junior." He put the camera into the pocket of his jacket, and keeping the gun in his hand he crossed to the stairs. He listened for a second, then hit the lights and began to climb.

The upstairs room was as he'd left it. He let out his breath, slipped across to the door and killed the lights. He cracked open the door a fraction of an inch and peered outside. The compound, at least what he could see of it, was quiet and empty. He waited, eyes adjusting to the darkness, and went over in his mind the next step in his escape plan.

During the two days he'd spent at Ragged Mountain he'd counted a total of five vehicles—three of the blue Econolines, a school bus painted in red, white, and black, that had its rear axle on blocks, and a late-model Ford station-wagon. The school bus was out in the open, parked beside the barrack-like women's dormitory on the far side of the main house, and the rest of the transport was kept in an open-fronted structure that might once have been a corn crib or a storage shed for drying wood. The garage was the building closest to the main gate at the bottom of the slope the compound was spread over.

As far as discretion was concerned his best course would be to simply slip through the gate and hoof it down to the main road, but that would leave him with a long walk that would probably take him most of the night. If his break-in was discovered he'd have the Crusaders all over him within minutes. The other way was more dangerous—he could steal one of the vehicles after somehow disabling the others, and make his escape in style. On the other hand, there weren't all that many places he could go, and the people at Ragged Mountain could alert their counterparts in Aspen and Denver, his logical destinations.

"Well," he murmured out loud, "I'll just have to be illogical." He retraced his steps back to the rear of the extension and then, running along behind the buildings, he made his way down the slope to the garage. As he passed he saw that the rear windows of the main house and the women's dormitory were dark and shuttered. It seemed as though the Tenth Crusade at Ragged Mountain depended on its isolation for security. Philip sent up a fervent prayer that the practice went as far as the guard at the gate; he was desperate to escape, but he wasn't sure his desperation would make him into a stunt driver. He had a sneaking suspicion that chain-link fences didn't burst open in real life as easily as they did in your average Clint Eastwood movie.

The sloped-roof shape of the garage jumped out of the darkness at him, the building looming up like the bones of some ancient monster. Through the slats Philip could make out the dim forms of the three vans and the station-wagon. Slipping in through a gap in the strutwork, his nostrils filled with the faintly nostalgic smell of gasoline and rotting wood. He went in behind the vans, keeping them between him and the open front of the shed. He reached the station-wagon and, crouching down, he worked his way around to the side of the car and popped open the driver's side door.

Miraculously, the keys were in the ignition. He let out a

long fluttering breath and backed out of the car. Five minutes on the vans and he would be ready. He worked quickly, dipping into the guts of each truck and ripping out the distributors and the generator wires. He wondered if the people in the compound would connect this to the job he'd done on the van in Barrington. He carried the dangling handful of parts back to the station-wagon and dumped them onto the long bench seat, keeping them in case one of the Crusaders happened to be an auto mechanic. Then he gently closed the door of the car and turned the key. The engine started easily, purring almost silently. He eased the shift lever into drive and with no pressure on the gas he let the wagon drift out into the compound. There was no sound except for the crunch of the tires on the gravel of the roadway. Peering through the windshield he looked ahead, trying to see if there was a guard at the gate. There was nobody; the gate, although closed, had no security on it at all. Philip slid out of the car and ran to the gate; there was nothing keeping it closed except a simple drop bar. He flipped it back, pushed on the chain link and the gate swung back. He got back into the car, put the shift into neutral and coasted out through the opening, eyes on the dark road ahead, and often on the rear-view mirror. For a moment the compound was a ghost behind him and then it was gone, hidden by a turn. He coasted that way for more than a mile and then, unable to keep his fear in check, he threw the car into drive and stepped on the gas.

It took him half an hour to reach the main road, and every mile was agony. A thousand paranoias jumped and jarred — each tree had a green-uniformed Crusader behind it, and he expected a roadblock around every bend.

He relaxed slightly once he was on the highway, turning north, back toward Interstate 70. He remembered his cigarettes and lit one, taking in a long, marvelously raw lungful. The mind-curdling horrors of the Ragged Mountain compound began to fade, replaced by a savage anger that went far beyond what they'd done to Heather. If they wanted to play the role of a perverse Richard Coeur de Lion then he'd upstage them with his own version of Saladin the Infidel. He wondered how long it would take him to reach Reno if he drove non-stop.

PART THREE
Acts

Chapter Twelve

The city of Reno, Nevada lies in a desert valley between the Virginia Mountains and the nearby Sierra Nevadas just across the border in California. Reno and its sister city on the other side of the Truckee River have a local population that hovers around the 100,000 mark. The city has a history much the same as a hundred other towns of its size in the west. Originally a watering stop for wagons on the way to the promised land of California, Reno grew steadily if unspectacularly through the nineteenth century, developing a firm base of commerce that included meat packing, bricks and metal products, as well as a university, established in 1874. The real economy of Reno, however, is based on greed and marital discord, a multi-million-dollar industry for the city that came about as a result of the Nevada Gambling Act of 1933, and the State's liberal divorce laws.

Most of the action in Reno takes place in an area along ten blocks of Virginia Avenue in the city center, beginning at the overhead sign at the corner of Commercial Road that announces Reno as being "The Biggest Little City in the World" and continuing south across the Truckee to California Avenue in what passes as the city's business district. The mile-long stretch of pavement caters to the breaking of virtually every one of the Ten Commandments. Sex is available at the Topdeck Cabaret and the Hideaway Topless, as well as on every corner and in every bar. Jewelry can be pawned at a hundred places and the Palace Loan on Plaza Street will cash your checks twenty-four hours a day. They'll also sell you every-

137

thing from stereos to shotguns. Shrimp cocktails are sold for less than a dollar, whisky goes for fifty cents a shot, and there are casinos everywhere—big ones like Harold's, Harrah's, Mape's Money Tree, and the Cal-Neva, as well as small ones like the Eldorado, which offer you their Chinese-Italian-steakhouse cuisine. All day and all night the slot machines chatter in the open-front plazas, and when the money is all gone you can get married at the second floor Wee Kirk O' the Heather, with free music, candlelight and witnesses, or divorced at the One Stop next door. During the high-season months of summer and just before Christmas the streets are clogged day and night with tourists, gamblers, and divorcees. A local merchant, owner of Bobby's Nickel Slots, when asked to describe the atmosphere of Reno, proudly replied, "Sleazy."

Sarah Logan, brooding in her room at the Holiday Hotel, would have agreed wholeheartedly. She would have added "dump," "tasteless," and "obscenely garish" to the description.

She sat in one of the large air-conditioned room's two armchairs, staring out through the picture window across the narrow width of the Truckee a hundred yards away. Beyond it she could see the skyline of Reno, the jutting clusters of neon casino signs impotent in the mid-afternoon sun. She sighed, one hand coming up automatically to twine itself in a few loose tendrils of her loosely pulled back hair. She'd been in Reno since the previous evening, and in that time she'd learned absolutely nothing. She had already known Samuel Keller's Eagle One Foundation was based in Reno, and seeing the office address in the phone book was no justification for a lost day. Her only other clue, the "NSS" discovered in the Crusade garbage, had turned into what appeared to be a dead end. She assumed that the "N" stood for Nevada, and following that course she'd found no less than nine businesses and organizations that fit, from Nevada Steel Supply to Nevada Survival Skills.

Well, she had to begin somewhere. She began shuffling through the photocopies she'd made that morning at the Washoe County Library. Most of them were of local business records and directories for Reno and Washoe County, including as much as she could find about the personnel makeup of the companies in the phone book with the NSS initials.

It didn't take long to cull out the obvious. The chances of Keller, Eagle One, or the Tenth Crusade being involved with the Nevada Safety Supply company or Nevada Seed Sales was slim. Given Keller's industrial background, something like Nevada Steel Structures was far more likely. Except there was no connection. She already had the corporate structure of Eagle One and Keller Pharmaceuticals to check with, and none of the names seemed to match.

After an hour of reading the photocopies she was almost ready to give up again. Then she hit pay dirt.

Ironically, she came up trumps with a company she'd almost dismissed right at the beginning, and now, there it was, staring her in the face: "Nevada Survival Skills Inc." A casual eye would never have spotted it, but Sarah was trained to follow the complex snakes and ladders of corporate ownership.

The information on Nevada Survival Skills came from the Nevada Directory of Corporate Ownership and the Washoe County Business Guide. According to the NDCO, Nevada Survival Skills was headed by a man named William Radmore, and was a wholly owned subsidiary of CalNev Silicon, probably a company involved in the Silicon Valley electronics and microprocessor industry just across the border in California.

It was the CalNev Silicon entry that rang the bell. She checked her file on Eagle One and saw it immediately. The treasurer of the Eagle One Foundation was someone named Dickinson Burnett. Burnett was also listed as president of CalNev Silicon. Even more damning, and so obvious, was the address for Nevada Survival Skills. The Washoe County Business Guide listed Nevada Survival Skills at Suite 1280, 30 East Second Avenue. The Reno administrative offices of the Eagle One Foundation were listed as taking up the entire seventeenth floor at the same address. Not only were the two organizations connected, they shared space in the same building.

On a hunch, Sarah checked the Reno phone book, found the number for City Hall and dialed. Her fingers played with the loose strands of her hair, pulling so hard she could feel it at the roots.

"Reno City Hall, can I help you." The woman's voice on the other end didn't make it a question. She sounded as though she wouldn't have cared if it was the President of the United States.

"I want to find out who owns a building in Reno. Who should I talk to?" asked Sarah.

There was a long pause as the few active brain cells in the City Hall receptionist's head strung together in a chain long enough to come up with a response. "Tax office, maybe, or Central Registry."

"Can you connect me with Central Registry?" said Sarah.

"Just a second."

Sarah was put on hold for so long she was sure they'd been disconnected. Finally the line clicked and a man's voice came on.

"Central Registry, LeGrand."

"I'd like to find out who owns a particular building in Reno, if that's possible."

"No problem," said the man cheerfully. "Just give me the address."

"Thirty East Second Avenue."

"Okay. It'll take a minute. You want to hang on or do you want to call back?"

"I'll wait," said Sarah.

"Right," said the man. "Back in a flash."

Something in the easy voice made her think of Philip and she felt a pang of worry, but she forced herself not to think about it. LeGrand came on again.

"Thirty East Second?"

"Right," said Sarah.

"According to our records the building is owned by something called 21st Century Communications Ltd. That what you wanted?"

"Yes," said Sarah, her voice quavering with excitement. "Thank you very much." She hung up the phone and looked down at the papers spread out on the desk.

Like the fingers of a closing fist it was all coming together into a single, seamless unit. Twenty-first Century, Billy Carstairs' umbrella company, the Crusade, Eagle One, and NSS, Nevada Survival Skills. She opened the Reno phone book again and began flipping the pages, knowing in advance what she was going to find. She saw the listing she wanted and closed the book with a bang. The Gospel Way Evangelical Foundation had its Reno offices on the eleventh floor of 30 East Second.

"All the rotten eggs in one basket," said Sarah to herself. Five minutes later she was standing in front of the hotel, looking for a taxi. If Philip called, he would leave a message. If he showed up in Reno she would meet him later in his hotel room.

*　*　*

Riding across town, Sarah told herself that attack was often the best defense; stepping into the offices of Nevada Survival Skills, she wasn't quite so sure. The outer reception area was so offensively masculine it set the young woman's teeth on edge. The walls of the large, perfectly square room were covered in what looked like black leather, while the floor was fitted with a low-pile dark gray carpeting. The large couches and three armchairs were a match for the walls and the male receptionist sat behind a deeply varnished partner's desk that could have taken a dinner setting for twelve. There were no paintings on the walls and no magazines on the rectangular coffee table that sat between the two couches. There weren't any ashtrays either.

The receptionist, in shirtsleeves, was a dark-haired man in his early twenties. He looked up as Sarah entered the office, then got back to his typing. When she came up to the huge desk and waited, looking down at him, he glanced up again.

"Yes?" he said.

"I'd like to find out more about Nevada Survival Skills," said Sarah.

"We don't have a brochure," said the man. His voice was toneless and his expression was cool and bland. The man was acting more like a security guard than a receptionist.

"I don't want a brochure," replied Sarah. "I'd like to talk to someone in person, if you don't mind."

"NSS offers a comprehensive course in weapons training, anti-terrorist techniques, counter insurgency, survival tactics, and corporate security. Our clientele comes from the military, various police organizations and large corporations. Does that answer your questions?"

"It might," said Sarah. "I think I'd like a few more details, if you don't mind."

The man looked at her, silent, for a few seconds, then reached down and took a hidden telephone receiver off the hook, his eyes still on her.

"There's someone here who'd like information about NSS," said the man. He listened for a moment, then frowned. "Blue," he said finally. Sarah wondered why the person on the other end of the line wanted to know what color her eyes were, and then she realized that the mention of the color was probably some kind of code. The man hung up the phone. "Go through that door," he said, jerking a thumb toward an entrance behind the desk. "Mr. Freeman will see you. Second door on the left."

"Thank you," replied Sarah. The man went back to his typing again, and Sarah went around the desk to the door. She opened it and found herself in a wide hallway, doors placed on both sides, but widely separated.

She paused at the second door on the left and knocked. There was no name plate or anything else to show who Freeman was, or what his function was at NSS.

"Come," said a voice.

Sarah opened the door and went into the office. She'd expected a smaller version of the outer lobby, and she was surprised when she saw that the room was warm, friendly, and inviting. There was a wall of bookshelves to the right, filled to overflowing, facing a long credenza along the opposite wall, its surface cluttered with small pieces of sculpture, most of them Art Deco or Art Nouveau. Above the credenza was what appeared to be an N.C. Wyeth painting that was somehow familiar.

"It's an original," said the man standing beside the small, plain desk directly in front of her. Behind the desk was a floor-to-ceiling window wall that looked out over Reno.

The man was in his late thirties, tall, at least six-three, and very handsome. His skin was darkly tanned, the color intensified by the dark shadow of his heavy beard. The face was lean, the eyes deeply set, a shock of salt and pepper hair curling down over his forehead, ears, and neck. He looked like he'd just stepped out of an ad for Camel cigarettes, right down to the tight-fitting white jeans and the open-necked, pearl gray silk shirt.

"It's one of the illustrations from Treasure Island," he went on. "As a child I used to pore over those illustrations and imagine that I was Jim Hawkins. When the painting came up for auction I couldn't resist the temptation."

"It's quite lovely," muttered Sarah uncomfortably. She'd come into the office expecting some kind of John Wayne villain and here she was talking about art with a *Vogue* model. The tightly knit scenario she'd envisioned was beginning to fray.

"You look a little perturbed," said the man, smiling, his teeth glistening perfectly out of his tan. "I suppose you expected to find me wearing a beret, chewing a cigar, and cleaning my Dirty Harry."

"Something like that," admitted Sarah.

"Have a seat," he said, motioning toward a comfortable-looking red leather armchair. Sarah sat feeling more and more self-conscious with each passing second. The man went behind the desk and sat down himself. He leaned back, his face thrown into silhouette by the glare from the window at his back.

"My name is David Freeman."

"Sarah. Sarah Kirkland," she improvised.

Freeman smiled. "Reporter?" he asked.

"Why couldn't I be a client?" replied Sarah.

"You could be a client," said Freeman easily, "but you don't act like one. Our female students are usually with the military, the police, or they're executives. You're definitely not the military type, you're not tall enough to be a policewoman, and you don't dress like an executive. Simple deduction. And I'm right, I'll bet."

If only you knew, thought Sarah, but she nodded. "Yes," she said. "I'm writing a book."

"On survivalism?"

Sarah nodded, taking the cue he'd offered. "Yes, and anti-terrorism. From a woman's viewpoint."

"Interesting," said Freeman, nodding. "So what can I do for you?"

"I'm not sure yet," said Sarah, stumbling. More than anything she had simply wanted to see a Crusade operation at close hand. She certainly wasn't going to get any useful information from Freeman. "NSS is my first real contact with an ongoing business involved in survivalism. I guess you could say I'm trying to get a feel for it." The explanation sounded lame but it was the best she could do.

Freeman sat forward in his chair, his hands clasped together on the bare desk in front of him. "Well," he began slowly, "I think you have to have an understanding about what survivalism really is before you can appreciate the need for places like NSS. A lot of people think that survivalism is a fad, like bomb shelters in the fifties, or Davy Crockett coonskin caps. In some ways I suppose it is, but it's more a trend than a fad."

"What's the distinction?" said Sarah.

"Trends have long-lasting results," explained Freeman. "There's a boom in survivalism right now, and that will certainly pass, but hopefully the *idea* of survivalism is here to stay. Not that it's really ever been gone, but we're trying to bring it back into the American culture. Instead of a feeling of dependence on others, groups, organizations, governments, we're trying to foster self-reliance, you might even call it the old pioneer spirit. You don't need to think that World War Three is just around the corner, but if you're aware that you *might* find yourself in a situation requiring survivalist skills, then you'll take steps to educate yourself."

"Give me an example," said Sarah. She wished she'd had a steno pad or a tape recorder to give herself a little bit of journalistic credibility, but Freeman didn't seem to care.

"Take your pick," shrugged Freeman. "Trapped in your car in a blizzard, floods, lost on a camping trip, even something as simple as living in a big urban area where there is the chance of rape, mugging, break and enter. Survivalism teaches you how to cope."

"Generally or specifically?" asked Sarah, almost forgetting why she was there. Freeman sounded utterly lucid and logical.

"Either, or both," he answered. "We've got specific courses in everything from backwoods survival to special weapons training and anti-terrorist driving for diplomatic chauffeurs. You tell us your needs, and we'll set you up with the right courses. Everything is tailor-made for the individual or the group."

"What about political affiliations?" asked Sarah, risking the question. "From what I've found out already, there seems to be a tie-in."

Freeman shrugged. "Some groups have direct political connections I suppose, but not us. And most are fairly apolitical. Magnus Training Center in Pennsylvania is a group pretty much like ours, and the most political they get is a bit of a push for clients to join the National Rifle Association. Not the stuff of which scandalous stories are made. The people we and most of the other groups hire are almost all Viet Nam vets, Special Forces types, FBI, Texas Rangers, we've even got a few French Foreign Legion members on staff. They're practical guys—they don't give a hoot in hell for politics. They just don't want to see people dying or getting hurt for no reason."

"Which one of those categories do you fall into?" asked Sarah.

"Army Rangers," said Freeman. "Nam, Cambodia, and then The Fort Benning Ranger School. In some ways NSS is patterned after Fort Benning."

"Why did you leave the army?" asked Sarah.

"Money, frankly. An instructor doesn't make enough to ever get ahead. I went freelance."

"You were a mercenary?" asked Sarah.

Freeman laughed. "You keep on trying to put me into the cigar-chomping set," he said. "No, I wasn't a merc. The concept of mercenary soldiering repulses me, as a matter of fact. A soldier who fights without idealism as his best weapon is no soldier at all in my book."

"Then how does a soldier freelance without becoming a mercenary?" queried Sarah. "You said you quit for money."

"I became a consultant. Special weapons and tactics. Special Air Services in England, Groupement D'Intervention de la Gendarmerie Nationale in France, Special Unit 269 in Israel, GSG-9 in Germany. All anti-terrorist squads."

Sarah looked at the man seated a few feet away, trying to imagine him as an anti-terrorist commando. She shook her head.

"You certainly don't look the part," she said finally. Freeman chuckled. It was an odd sound, almost feminine, and somehow it didn't ring true. In fact none of it did. His looks, words, and movements were all too predictable, too theatrical to be real. It was as though she was watching a play unfolding, a play staged for her benefit.

"The toughest man on Kelly Hill at Fort Benning looked like he was sent directly from the angels. He shaved about once a month and he had moves like a dancer. One of the students called him a fag during an exercise and Terry had the guy's arm broken in two places and his jaw dislocated before he knew what hit him."

"The lesson being that looks can be deceiving?" said Sarah.

"Exactly." The plain, black telephone on his desk gave a muted, purring signal and he picked it up, his eyes still on Sarah. As he listened his hand went to a chain around his neck, and for the first time Sarah noticed that there was a small gold cross on it, the cross cut through the center by a red, enameled X. Fashion jewelry for the Tenth Crusade? Or a badge of rank and discreet recognition like a Masonic handshake?

After a moment, Freeman hung up the telephone without speaking again. He pushed his chair back from the desk and stood up. His expression had changed. The smile was still there, but it had become cold and distant. The interview, or whatever it had been, was obviously over. "You'll have to excuse me," he said, extending his hand across the desk. "Duty calls."

Sarah took the hand, wondering if the warm, dry grip had ever killed. She looked into his eyes and knew it had.

"You've been a big help," said Sarah. "Now at least I've got something to go on."

"Good," said Freeman, coming around the desk.

He escorted Sarah to the door and out into the hallway and the reception room, smoothly making small talk about the weather. As he took her to the main doors of the NSS offices Sarah felt a cold chill course through her body, followed by a faint, nameless anxiety.

Freeman waited with her at the elevator, and as the bell rang, announcing the elevator's arrival, and the sliding doors opened, the feeling of unease took form in her mind; she wasn't leaving NSS, Freeman was letting her go. She stepped into the elevator, absurdly glancing down at the floor, almost afraid that it was going to open beneath her feet. She turned, and as the doors slid shut she caught a last glimpse of Freeman. He stood stiffly, watching her, eyes unblinking, his body a weapon camouflaged in silk.

Her knees didn't stop shaking until she found herself outside again in the wilting heat.

In the twenty minutes it took her to get from the NSS offices to the Holiday Hotel her clothes were damp with perspiration and she felt emotionally exhausted. After her father's death her doctor had put her on tranquilizers and she'd spent a week living in a strange half-world of clouded thoughts and dusk light that dulled memory and kept reality at bay. She felt that way now, as though she'd been part of someone else's dream. What seemed real, the suite of offices, the handsome man in his silk shirt, the gold cross shot with red — they were all false, a mask to disguise something far more deadly.

She felt relieved as she stepped into her room. A long bath and a short nap would cure her, she was sure.

They took her from both sides, quickly, silently, and with a minimum of fuss. The two men, dressed in MEDIC-1 ambulance drivers' jackets pinned her expertly, one holding her firmly against the wall while the second quickly closed the door. The man holding Sarah kept one hand over her mouth and the other under her armpit and around her neck in a half-nelson. He was turned sideways, his left thigh and leg keeping Sarah's knees bent, preventing her from struggling. The man holding her stepped aside as his companion approached, allowing him to press the CO_2-powered syringe against Sarah's shoulder, close to the neck. He pressed the trigger of the gun-shaped syringe and the mixed dose of thioridazine and alcohol was injected. The combination, basically a mixture of a major tranquilizer and booze, brought on immediate results. Within a few seconds Sarah ceased to struggle and went limp in the first man's grip. By the time they had her laid out on the collapsible gurney they'd brought up to her room, the young woman's blood pressure had dropped, her pulse had increased and her pupils had dilated. To the casual observer she had the look of someone in fairly severe shock, and blood tests at a hospital would show a high level of alcohol as well as the tranquilizer. Another young person who mixed drugs and liquor, something the hospitals in Reno treated as often as they did sore throats.

The two "ambulance drivers" bundled a blanket around the comatose woman, wheeled the gurney out into the hall, and headed for the service elevator at the rear of the hotel. Five minutes later the two men loaded Sarah into the rear of a large Econoline window van. The van had been equipped to look like an ambulance and painted bright yellow, the name MEDIC-1 on both sides in electric blue.

Beyond the stares of a few onlookers in the parking lot no one paid any attention at all until the van roared out onto the street, siren moaning, and bright lights flashing. And no one noticed that while there were hospitals to the north, south, and west of the hotel, the ambulance was headed east, toward Route 80 and the desert beyond.

Chapter Thirteen

Philip Kirkland had driven through the Rocky Mountain night, exhausted, but running hard on the adrenalin produced by his escape. As he drove he tried to sort through the maze of conflicting thoughts and emotions that threatened to turn his brain into the same kind of porridge as Jackson's.

Finding Heather was still uppermost in his mind, but something else now seemed almost as important; the vague unease he'd felt before heading into the Ragged Mountain complex now had some real definition; Heather had been kidnapped by more than just a cult group, and her abduction *had* to be more than just the Crusade's desire not to lose a recruit.

He'd been hearing about cults since the late sixties, but this was the first time he'd heard of one that kept a secret arsenal and used sophisticated telecommunications to cross-index information on everything from finance to possible blackmail leverage. The fact that Sarah's father, a senator, had died in questionable circumstances relating to the Crusade was even more damning. This wasn't a straightforward Elmer Gantry-type group bent on shafting little old ladies out of their pensions, this was politics, power on a huge and obviously violent scale. He knew now that even if he found Heather tomorrow it wouldn't end there – the Tenth Crusade had something far more important than just a general's misguided daughter to hide, and one way or the other he was in too deep for them to simply let him walk away from it all.

It was then that he decided that whether he found Heather

or not he'd help Sarah uncover any evidence he could to pillory the Tenth Crusade.

Ironically, as he had driven towards Reno, the only station strong enough to cut through the radio shadows of the mountains had been WTGW, "Walk the Gospel Way"—Billy Carstairs' station. Rather than drive along in the black silence of the twisting mountain highway Philip had left it on, fascinated by the endless stream of cloying sentiment and holy terror being broadcast into the empty airwaves by Billy and the others at the station.

"I remember it, oh dear Lord I remember it, as clearly as if it was only yesterday. I met a friend who was working on something beneath his car, and I had the spirit in me that morning, so I said, 'Dave, you get out from under that car and let's talk about the Lord Jesus,' and he said, 'No, I can't, Billy, because I'm working on my car, and I have to get it finished.' So I didn't bother him anymore, I continued walking, and no more than a block or two away I heard this terrible sound, and I turned and ran back, and the jack had slipped on that car, and my friend Dave was crushed underneath it. He didn't know it, friends, but when he was talking to me, he was only a SPLIT SECOND FROM ETERNITY!

"A split second from eternity. Yes. Now think about that, friends, because I sure did. I grieved for Dave, and I had a burden for him. I told myself, Billy Carstairs, you're no Christian, you could have saved him if only you'd been a little tougher. If only you'd said, 'Now, Dave, GET OUT FROM UNDER THAT CAR BECAUSE I'VE GOT A LIFE AND DEATH MESSAGE FOR YOU!' If I'd said that, then he would be alive right now, and better than that, he'd be BORN AGAIN IN THE LORD!

"But he's dead. Dead because he didn't listen. Gone to Hell, because he didn't listen, lost forever because he wouldn't listen, because he wouldn't listen, because I DIDN'T MAKE HIM LISTEN! He was lost and never knew Christ before he died.

"And that's my sin, friends. MY SIN! I didn't talk loud enough for my friend Dave to hear. Just like millions of born-again Christians in this country. They're not talking loud enough, or long enough, or hard enough, and friends, this country is ON THE ROAD TO HELL!

"But that's the thing about Jesus, he's always teaching. I learned from my mistake, friends, my sin. I learned. And I'm TALKING PRETTY LOUD JUST NOW! I'm paying off my sin to the Lord just the way he wants me to. I'm telling you all out there, all of you people who've fallen asleep at the switch, I'm saying, WAKE UP AMERICA! Wake up and take a look around you. See what's happening to this country we love. I'M TALKING ABOUT COMMUNISTS IN CONGRESS! I'M TALKING ABOUT HOMOSEX-UALS IN OUR HIGH SCHOOLS! I'M TALKING CORRUPTION IN THE UNIONS, DEPRAVITY AND IMMORALITY IN GOVERNMENT!

"But we can change it, friends. We can bring America back! This country has been in the hands of the abortionists and women's libbers and the socialist liberals for long enough.

"And it's our fault! It's our responsibility. WE let America slip through our fingers. WE put America into the hands of the baby killers and the perverts. WE PUT AMERICA INTO THEIR HANDS!

"So we have to get it back. We have to fight for America, just like we fought for it two hundred and more years ago.

"RIGHT NOW! Right now, I'm fighting for America. Mostly I'm fighting for it in Washington these days, using our biggest weapon. THE WORD OF THE LORD! THE HOLY SCRIPTURES OF GOD! THE WORD AND THE LAW, FRIENDS! The law of God. The only law, and the only court you have to really worry about being judged by. The America Awake Foundation believes in that law, friends. We live by it day by day, and we're winning, praise God!

"But we need your help and your prayers. We can't do it alone. There's a lot of evil out there, friends, and, believe me, most of it's in Washington. So if you can help, we'd appreciate it, and you'd be doing something for your country, for your God, and FOR YOURSELF.

"So if you think America is worth fighting for, if you think America is worth saving, then send in your offering. You can send it to the America Awake Foundation, Box 8700, Wash-ington, D.C. Do it soon. Do it now!

"Don't be like my friend Dave. Don't leave it too long. Be-cause remember friends ... YOU'RE A SPLIT SECOND FROM ETERNITY!"

The longer Philip had listened the more difficult he'd found it to believe that Billy Carstairs was behind the Tenth Crusade. Carstairs was an old-fashioned tent evangelist and shyster, breathing fire and brimstone and milking his listeners for every penny he could. He might have the money to back something like the Crusade, but he didn't have the brains or the imagination. The sophistication Philip had witnessed was beyond anything Billy Carstairs had ever dreamed.

On the other hand, the Reagan Administration had been put into power by people just like Billy. You don't need brains to hand out brochures or staple up posters—you just need bodies. During the Nixon years no one had noticed Jesse Helms, the Republican senator from Carolina, and if they did pay any attention, it was to laugh. He was a Joe McCarthy clone, a buffoon. But by 1981, *Time* magazine was doing serious profiles on him, dubbing him a leader and power-monger among the neo-conservative elite. The same was true of Jerry Falwell, the honky-tonk preacher from Lynchburg, Virginia, who once referred to himself as a "big-mouth Baptist." In 1975, Falwell was a relative nobody as far as big league evangelism was concerned. Oral Roberts, Rex Humbard, even neophytes like Jim Bakker and his "Praise The Lord" Christian talk show, were talking to more people and making more money than Falwell. Yet by 1979, only four years later, Falwell was the man on top of the heap, a high-profile superchristian with a T.V. congregation of 18,000,000 and high rollers like George Gilder, the conservative economist, behind him, as well as Richard Viguerie and John Dolan, the man they called the "most feared consultant in Washington." Falwell's Moral Majority lobby became a catchword, and *Penthouse* magazine even interviewed him.

But maybe it made sense, thought Philip. John Dolan might be the most feared consultant in Washington, and Viguerie might be a political fund-raising wizard, but they were hardly what you could call charismatic. And that was the key. Falwell, Robison, Schuller, and his Crystal Cathedral, all had one thing in common: they could talk, and they could make the average, impressionable American *believe*. Falwell, whether he knew it or not, was a patsy. He was the king, but the others, the

Vigueries, the Dolans, and the Gilders were the whispering ghostly figures behind the throne. What Falwell's simple mind saw as power they recognized as merely pomp and circumstance. The world was ruled by the king makers, not the kings.

And did it come full circle? According to Sarah Logan, more than one international evangelical association with missionaries abroad had been tied into the CIA. It was, thought Philip, a paranoid's fantasy come true.

Dawn had seen Philip well into the crumpled hills and valleys of central Utah. He ate a quick breakfast at a truck stop just outside of Green River and then continued on, three Styrofoam cups of coffee on the dashboard to help him stay awake. Thankfully, Billy Carstairs faded with the climbing sun, and by the time Philip had reached the Fishlake National Forest, Falwell was gone, replaced by a drawling newsman reading a report about the latest exploits of America's own terrorist cadre, the Devil's Brigade.

The Brigade's first appearance had been flamboyant, an orgy of industrial bombings from one end of the United States to the other, followed by a sophisticated network of tape drops to radio stations, announcing their arrival on the urban terrorist stage. Their second appearance had apparently been far less dramatic, but its implications more terrifying; instead of attacking rail lines, hydro facilities, and communications towers, the Brigade had shifted to people—innocents with no relation to any possible political group or activity.

Once again the operation had been a combined effort, four different groups working in widely separated parts of the country. The targets were all family units in small urban areas: Hannibal, Illinois; Ironwood, Wisconsin; Sunbury, Pennsylvania; and Browning, Idaho. The procedures had been identical in each case, leaving no doubt that the four incidents were part of a central scenario. The families were attacked in their homes, bound and blindfolded, then taken to remote areas. In each case the father and husband had his Achilles' tendons severed, rendering him immobile, after which the wife and mother was raped and sodomized, then murdered. Then the children were dealt with, girls raped and sodomized like their mothers, the boys castrated, then murdered. Throughout the horrors, the husbands were forced to watch. Afterwards they were returned to their homes, blindfolded again. Each man was left with a simple message typed on plain paper: "NO ONE IS SAFE FROM THE DEVIL'S BRIGADE."

Of the four survivors, two men had been capable of giving descriptions. The attackers were male, dressed in black trousers, black shirts, and black nylon windbreakers with a small, bright red death's head symbol on the left breast. The men wore black wool ski masks to cover their faces.

According to the news reports, the FBI had taken over the investigation as soon as it became clear that there were interstate tie-ins, but the bureau had been unable to come up with anything concrete concerning the Brigade or the people in it.

As Philip continued across Utah and into Nevada on U.S. 50, bypassing Salt Lake City, the Devil's Brigade story took precedence over everything else. The grotesque killings seemed to have captured the imagination of the national press, and as Philip spun the dial on the car radio, he tuned in on talk shows in Utah, Nevada, and California, and the enraged voices of people filled the baking interior of the station-wagon. Everyone seemed to want some kind of action to be taken to stop the Brigade cold and more than one person brought up the Symbionese Liberation Army, the group responsible for the Patty Hearst kidnapping. Those men had been utterly destroyed by overwhelming police action and the general feeling was that the Brigade should be dealt with in the same way. But, as the hot-line D.J.s were quick to point out, you had to find them first, and that seemed to be the problem.

Philip had seen the results of terrorism in his work for years. He'd seen car bombs go off in Ireland, photographed hijackings in Lebanon, and he'd been sitting in the pizzeria around the corner from La Pagode in Saigon when a ten-year-old kid leaned a bicycle packed with gelignite up against the front window, killing eleven civilians and six American soldiers. Still, he was shocked by the Brigade atrocities, simply because they were happening in the States, not ten thousand miles away from home in somebody else's backyard.

He could see how effective the Brigade's tactics were. Philosophically the value of terrorism was to bring about political and social change through fear. It was a tactic used equally well by Ghengis Khan, Adolf Hitler, and a thousand others before and after. Even Harry Truman's use of the atomic bomb on Hiroshima and Nagasaki was definably a terrorist act, although at the time most people, with the exception of classical militarists, saw it as justified under the circumstances. The Devil's Brigade, like Baader-Meinhof and the Italian Red Brigades before them, used the most terrible of all the threats a terrorist could bring to bear—randomness. The FBI, running around searching for motive, or a connection between the attacks, would inevitably fail because the Brigade atrocities had no pattern, and thus could not be defended against. When they left their messages warning that no one was safe, they were simply stating a fact. They chose their victims at random, made no demands, and showed no mercy. The worst of it, Philip guessed, was that the kidnap-rape-murders were not an end in themselves, but only a prelude, an overture to a symphony of violence that was sure to follow.

The endlessly repeated stories on the deaths became even more irritating than Billy Carstairs' invective, and Philip had eventually turned the radio off, driving the last three hours through the arid, corduroy hills and valleys of central Nevada in silence, the killing heat, the glare, and the numerous cups of coffee he'd had churning his stomach and joining to give him a furious headache.

Now he was beginning to reach the outskirts of Reno. It was dusk, the sun had turned to a squat, orange oval shimmering down behind the Sierra Nevada in the west, the galaxy of neon and flashing bulbs slowly taking over, lighting up the night in yellow, red, and green.

Tired as he was, Philip remembered to take precautions. The car he was driving was stolen, and the chances were better than good that the Crusade people at Ragged Mountain had reported it. He drove down Virginia from Interstate 80, careful to keep his speed down, then crossed the Truckee River. He stopped to ask directions twice and finally found the Holiday Hotel on Mill Street. He doubled back onto Virginia, driving past the county courthouse, and slid the station-wagon into an empty slot in front of the Pioneer Hotel and Casino. The bright interior was open to the street, the rows of slots running back in aisles the length of a football field. There were hundreds of people, dressed in everything from evening clothes to shorts and halter tops, working at the long chrome arms, pulling and watching, pulling and watching, the incessant rumble and clash filling the air like the sound of galley slaves in chains.

Philip walked back down Virginia to Mill Street and the hotel, his feet dragging with exhaustion. Booking in at the reservations desk he got a couple of odd looks from the clerk, but as soon as he presented his American Express card, which he had dug out of his boot to pay for gas at a service station somewhere in Utah, the clerk perked up and things went smoothly. As the bellhop took him up to his room Philip sent up a silent prayer of thanks to the ad man who'd come up with the series of television commercials for Amex showing grizzled men in lumberjack shirts checking in at the Ritz.

With the bellhop gone, Philip dropped down on the bed, picked up the phone, and dialed the desk. He asked for Sarah's room and a few seconds later he was connected. He let the phone ring a dozen times and then hung up. They could have their reunion later.

Groaning with effort, muscles tensed in cords and bunches by almost twenty straight hours of driving, he managed to strip off his clothes and stumble into the shower. He stood under the rushing water, half asleep, and let the spray wash the last of his ordeal away. Still wet, he went back to the bedroom, turning off the lights as he went. He pushed back the bedspread and dropped down onto the cool sheets. He couldn't even remember when his head hit the pillow.

* * *

Philip woke, sitting bolt upright in the bed, covered in a sheen of tepid sweat. His hair was stuck to the back of his neck and his mouth was dry as dust. Blinking, he dropped back down onto the bed and turned toward the glowing dial of the digital clock radio. It was 3:00 in the morning. He rolled over,

156

dropped his arm over the bed, and groped around in his clothes for cigarettes. He found them and lit up, dragging in the smoke and cracking a huge yawn. He lay quietly for a few moments, blowing barely seen tendrils of smoke up at the ceiling, and tried to figure out what had brought him out of sleep. He could faintly remember a dream about being on a beach where the sand was black, covered with sunburned people, and with a blood-red sea pounding up on the shore. He let his mind run loose, fishing around for a meaning, but nothing came. He put the dream out of his mind; after two days at Ragged Mountain he wouldn't have been surprised if he'd dreamed about Eric parting Lake Erie with a machine-gun instead of a shepherd's crook.

But something told him that it wasn't the dream that had awakened him. On impulse he turned in the bed, found the phone, and, squinting in the darkness, he called down to the desk and asked to be connected with Sarah's room. It rang a dozen times, and he let it ring a dozen more, worry growing like an itch he couldn't scratch. He kept the phone to his ear, listening to the ring, and checked the clock again. What in hell could she be doing out at 3:00 in the morning? She wasn't the type to be wooed by quarter-slots and blackjack.

He hung up and lit another cigarette, stubbing the butt of the first one into the glass ashtray beside the phone. Something was wrong. If she'd found something there would have been a message for him.

He rolled up into a sitting position, and let the faint dizziness he felt pass away. He'd had almost six hours' sleep, and the burning edge of his fatigue was gone.

Sarah had room 514, the same floor as his. He rubbed his jaw, feeling the hard rasp of stubble. What if she wasn't there? He stood up and began dressing, aware of how stale the clothes were. One more day and they'd be standing up on their own. He put out his cigarette and went to the door, cracking it open. The hallway was an orgy of sunset red carpet and bright fluorescents. He squinted in the harsh light and stepped out, feeling like an intruder in the perfect, antiseptic vacancy of the corridor. He went down the hall, checking room numbers, until he found Sarah's. There was a Please Do

Not Disturb card dangling from the doorknob. He knocked, looking up and down the hall. Still empty. There was no response, so he knocked again, a little louder, and waited. Nothing. He tried the knob, and surprisingly it turned in his hand. He checked the hall a second time, turned the doorknob fully, and slipped into the room. It was dark, the only light coming from the large window at the far end of the room. Outside he could see the blinking lights on the casinos across the Truckee. The air conditioner hummed softly, keeping the air chilled.

He flicked on the overhead light and the Reno night scene disappeared, the window throwing back his own reflection. The room was empty. Double bed, desk, armchair, writing desk, and straight chair, chest of drawers. Standard and anonymous. The bed either hadn't been slept in or it had been made up by the housekeeper.

He spotted the litter of papers and the open telephone book on the writing table and crossed the room, seating himself on the straight chair. He riffled through the pages of photocopies curiously, quickly seeing what Sarah had been up to. The photocopies all related to companies in Reno that had the initials NSS. Bleary, his mind still fogged with sleep, he went through the copies, looking for some clue to which one, if any, Sarah had homed in on. There was nothing. He turned to the phone book and saw it immediately. A number had been underlined in the white pages for Nevada Survival Skills. The ball point had been pushed so hard it had cut through the page. The address was on East Second Avenue.

Philip sat back in the chair and thought. Nevada Survival Skills had been underlined in the book, making it likely that Sarah had found out something about it that made her think it was the NSS they'd discovered in the Barrington branch's garbage. Why wasn't she in her room at this late hour? The conclusion was obvious—she'd gone off and done something stupid like try to take on Nevada Survival Skills on her own. She was a great one for giving out advice about being careful, but his worst fears told him she hadn't practised what she'd preached.

"Shit," he muttered under his breath. He went back to the photocopies. He found the sheaf of information about Nevada

Survival and looked it over carefully, trying to see in it what had set Sarah off.

There wasn't much to go on. A couple of sheets with the company's corporate structure and two brief news stories about the opening of a new business in the Reno area. According to the stories, NSS was a survivalist-security company specializing in the training of individuals and groups, teaching combat, weapons, orienteering, and special driving skills. The instructors were ex-military and police types.

Philip put down the photocopies and lit a cigarette. It made sense. From what he'd seen at Ragged Mountain, the Tenth Crusade was heavily involved in weapons stockpiling, and NSS would be an ideal cover for a paramilitary training base. He tried not to think about *why* the Crusade would want a training base; there was no time for that now. He went through all the papers a second time, trying to find some reference to the actual location of the NSS camp, but there was nothing except the Reno address. He dug into his memory, came up with the number he needed, and picked up the phone.

Once upon a time Simon Adler had been the assistant bureau chief in Saigon for American Press. Unlike a lot of his colleagues Simon had made a point of going to where the action was rather than staying behind a desk. Admittedly, the fact that the action was often no further away than Tu-Do Street in Saigon made it easy for him, but still, he spent a lot of time with his correspondents. He and Philip had struck up a friendship quickly, and it had continued after the war was finally over. Simon's voice, coming across the wires from the AP New York night desk was like a touch of sanity after what seemed like an eternity of madness.

"What the hell are you doing in Reno?" asked Simon. After almost thirty years in the business the older man had a voice like cracked shoe leather, the result of a serious addiction to Muriel Cigars, Smith Brothers cherry cough drops, and Beefeater gin.

"Taking pictures of the tourists," said Philip.

"Sure," said Simon. Philip could almost see the yellow-toothed grin. "And you do weddings too." He paused, the sound of his cough like the death rattle of a monster from a fifties horror film. In Saigon there'd been a hundred bets laid on whether the Viet Cong or lung cancer would get Adler first. "Give me the goods, Philip. If you're in Reno that means it's four in the morning. What do you want that would make you miss your beauty sleep?"

"Do you remember that series you did on the whole survivalism trend a few months back?" asked Philip.

"Sure," answered Simon. "I remember a company called Mountain House — 'We'll Supply You Till Doomsday' was their motto, as I recall."

"That's it."

"So?" prodded Adler.

"Did you ever pick up any information on a group called Nevada Survival Skills?"

There was a long silence. "No, not that I can recall offhand," said Adler finally. "But that doesn't mean anything. Hang on while I ring it through the computer." There was the sound of a match being struck and an obscenely wet sucking sound as Simon worked up a Muriel. The line buzzed and clicked in Philip's ear, counterpoint to the air conditioner behind him in the room.

"Anything?" asked Philip after a long five minutes.

"Sec," grunted Simon, talking around the cigar. There was another wait, then the journalist coughed again, and spoke. "Yeah, here we go. File from our guy out in L.A. Nothing much to go on really. We never used the material in the story. Funny little squib on it, though."

"Like what?" asked Philip.

"A photographer. Freelancer working on a thing for *National Geographic*. Disappeared about two months ago. Same locale as this NSS place."

"Give me the locale," said Philip.

"All it says here is Tonopah," answered Simon. "Maybe an old abandoned Air Force base, according to this. Mean anything to you?"

"Not much. Is that all?"

"Just about. The Nevada Survival Skills camp is somewhere in the Yucca Wells-Tonopah area. The photographer was found in the desert about twenty miles out from Yucca Wells; that's where they took him for the coroner's inquest too."

"What killed him?" asked Philip.

"Snake bite. Rattler. Three times on the arm, according to this. Must have fallen into a pit of them or something."

"Your guy doesn't make any connection between Nevada Survival Skills and the dead photographer, does he?" asked Philip.

"No," answered Simon. "The squib on the photographer showed up because his files are cross-indexed by geographical area." There was a pause. "Why do you ask? Do *you* have a connection?"

"No," answered Philip.

"What are you on to out there? If you come up with any good survivalist stuff I could probably use it."

"If I get anything, I'll let you know," said Philip. He thanked Simon and hung up.

He stood, yawning. "Where the hell is Yucca Wells?" he said, looking around the empty room. He grunted. He wasn't even going to think about Yucca Wells until he'd had some breakfast. He left Sarah's room the way he'd found it, dark, the air conditioner humming its low-key dirge into the silence.

Chapter Fourteen

Heather Foxcroft sat in the corner of the cold gray room, trying to keep her memories at bay, concentrating on the slow movement of a small brown insect that was crossing the relative infinity of the concrete floor. She forced herself to remain immobile, but the welling panic was beginning to consume her, and the roach's progress was slowly ceasing to hold her concentration. Finally, her present bounded by the featureless room and her future too frightening to think about, she escaped to the only thing she was sure of: her past....

She sat, cross legged, on a wide flat stone, high on a hill above the gleaming lodestone of the great stupa at Bodhnath. Beyond the huge, white domed building the deep green fields formed a monochrome pathwork of alternating furrows that reached all the way to the walls of Katmandu, a mile away. Above it all, the temple, the city, even the hill, were the mountains; great white fists of snow-covered rock, the lofty abode of unimaginable gods.

Somewhere, perhaps within the walls of the stupa, there was the sound of a ritual drum, and then a gong, echoing forever across the deep basin of land to the Himalayas. She listened, and to the dull beat of the drum she spoke her own litany, her last link with sanity.

"I am Heather Foxcroft. General Foxcroft is my father and I am his daughter. I am twenty years old and this is Katmandu, the end of my journey."

And, as always, the ritual failed. She was still afraid. She tried to empty her mind, the way the guru in the Freak Street ashram had told her to. Empty yourself, let the sky and the mountains and the earth at your feet come in and *be* you. Let them take your body and *become* your body. Forget yourself.

But the mountains remained mountains and the sky remained sky. Instead of emptiness and peace she felt a soft warmth spreading out from her thighs and the aching hollowness she always felt when she thought about Philip. He was half a world away and yet the remembrance of him could take her, rape her more effectively than the frozen white giants of the Himalayas only forty miles away.

She could have Philip if she wanted to, have him inside her. She could have Philip's hard reality instead of the distant metaphysics of the mountains but it would mean denying everything she'd come to believe. It would mean all the time and all the tens of thousands of miles she'd traveled had been for nothing. And if she admitted that, admitted that it had all been a waste of time, an escape rather than a seeking journey for the truth? Madness.

She was crying, tears trickling down into the corners of her mouth. Her whole life, the world she had been raised in, had been so selfish, and now she was being selfish again. She wanted to love Philip and forget about everything else, but how could she do that when the world was so big and so unhappy?

She'd seen so much of it. The beggars, shivering on the Métro air vents in Paris, the blind children squatting in the dust of the Marrakesh medina, a bent-backed old man staggering under his immense load, a *hamal*, crossing the Galeta bridge in Istanbul, an opium eater, his robes in shreds, drowned in his own vomit on the road into Peshawar. It was too much.

The mountains gave her no answer, and she wanted to die, or to go home, wherever that was ....

* * *

Sarah watched the girl across from her, who sat cross legged on the concrete floor of the high-walled and windowless room they shared. The girl was staring up into the bright glare of the single tube of fluorescent lighting in the ceiling. Sarah watched her, hypnotized by the look on her face. She'd been like that for hours, motionless and wide eyed and by Sarah's estimation she was either in some kind of schizophrenic fugue or she'd been drugged into oblivion. Whichever it was, the woman obviously had no idea where she was, and for that Sarah envied her.

From Philip's description Sarah knew that the catatonic woman was Heather Foxcroft, which made her curiosity even more acute. Even as she was, slack faced and staring, Heather was beautiful in a strange haunting way that defied real analysis. She was wearing the blue and white Crusade uniform, but even the severe lines of the skirt and blouse couldn't hide the lithe, muscular body underneath. Philip had said that she'd been a dancer years before.

Sarah found herself thinking about Philip and Heather together and she felt a twinge of jealousy. She frowned, irritated at her thoughts; here she was in what amounted to a prison cell, miles from anywhere and she was thinking bitchy thoughts about another woman.

"You just complicate things," she said, her eyes on Heather. "Not only do I have to get myself out of here, I have to play hero and drag you along with me. It's not fair."

There was no response from the glassy-eyed woman huddled in the corner.

Sarah stood up and crossed the floor to the only door. It was wide and solid, covered with a roughly fabricated skin of galvanized sheet metal. Once there had been a doorknob, but it had been patched over with a small square of the same metal, attached rudely with more than a dozen wide-headed nails. Sarah felt her throat constrict. Locked-room mysteries might be fun to read, but the reality of being inside one was something else again.

She went back to her place on the far side of the room from Heather and slumped down again, her back against the rough concrete wall. She began putting all the facts together in her mind, assembling the data the way she would for any research project.

From the time she had been drugged in her room at the

Holiday Hotel she could remember almost nothing, except being transferred from one vehicle to another. She had also come out of her haze long enough to realize that they had gone from a paved road to an unpaved one at some point. By the time they'd reached their destination she was aware enough to recognize that she was at some sort of military base. She had vague recollections of a series of large hangar-like buildings, rows of paint-peeling barracks, and some old-fashioned, curve-roofed Quonset huts. The building she'd been taken to was much clearer in her mind, and she assumed that by then the drug had really begun to wear off. Her "prison" was surrounded by a high chain-link fence topped by a triple row of barbed wire angled inward. The building itself was a single-storey factory-like structure made from cinder block, and shaped like a truncated L. The door she had been led through was old and scarred, the small window to one side of it broken in several places. The interior gave off the same aura of age and abuse. The walls were bare concrete as was the floor, and there was a dank musty odor everywhere.

So what did it all add up to? Her best guess was that she was at an out of use air base—the hangars and Quonset huts pointed to that quite clearly. The condition of the buildings seemed to indicate that it had been abandoned by the military a long time ago, so either NSS had rented or leased the property from the government or they were using it without permission. It didn't matter which, really, but if it *was* an old U.S. Air Force base it did tell her a few other things. For instance it meant that although it was off in the boonies somewhere, it was accessible without too much trouble, and was probably located fairly close to a town of some kind. On the other hand, an air base, even an old one, would still have some of its security systems in place, including a perimeter wire and sentry posts.

She let out a long sigh and looked across at Heather Foxcroft; she still hadn't moved. Sighing, Sarah crossed her arms on her upraised knees and dropped her head down, blocking the light.

"Now I lay me down to sleep, I pray the Lord my soul to keep. And if I die before I wake, I pray the Lord my soul to take." Her father had taught that to her when she was a little girl and, remembering it, she had to bite her lip hard to keep back the welling tears. As she sat, head cradled in her arms, she heard the memory of her father's voice and felt more alone than she had ever felt in her life. Finally she slept, and the voice dissolved into her dreams, while across the room the motionless woman stared blindly into the overhead light, her thoughts years and thousands of miles away.

*　*　*

...Sister Angela, who had once been a young American woman from Boston named Heather Foxcroft, a name she had now almost forgotten, walked slowly along the filth-encrusted length of Chitpore Road in the heart of Calcutta, the hem of her white and blue habit brushing the earth, the small pouch at her waist bouncing on her hip. As usual, her back was aching, the old dancing injury made worse through years of the back-breaking labor she endured as a novice in Mother Teresa's Sisters of Charity. She had come to learn that the pain was a good reminder of her mortality and would bring her closer to those she aided deep within the teeming slums of the ancient city.

She was unfit, unfit to serve. Almost every night, in the few hours between the last mass at midnight and the rising prayer at 4:00 A.M., she dreamed, and her dreams were never of Christ or God or the holy state she so desperately craved; they were always of the world, and of the past.

But why did she question everything, why couldn't she just accept, and take Christ's joy in one delicious draught? Why did she sometimes, even awake, crave the touch of a hand on her breast, Philip's hand, or his lips on her lips? Was she that filled with lust? Was she that consumed by sin?

It had been six years since she'd felt a man's body, seven since Philip had last been with her. There had been a dozen men between Philip and her joining the Sisterhood, but it was always Philip she thought of.

Just then, she spotted the sleeping figure of a small boy, curled up in an impossibly small space between two tiny

166

shops. She stopped. The large, thick-jowled man on the left was squatting in his stall, selling tea by the cup and deep fried sweets. To the right another man was selling spiced betel nuts wrapped in leaves. Above them both, a counter had been laid and a third merchant was hawking pills for potency.

She bent low and reached in between the wooden posts and touched the small child's naked back. Lice crawled on his scalp, and as her eyes adjusted to the dim light Heather saw a large iridescent fly creep into the boy's partially opened mouth. She realized that the skin was cold to the touch. The boy was dead. She stood and informed the three merchants.

"We know, little Sister," said the man selling betel nuts. "He was dead when we came early this morning."

"Then why have you not moved him, or called for someone to take him away."

"He is not ours, little Sister," said the heavyset man selling tea. He had poked his head out from beneath his counter stall and eyed her mildly. "He is no trouble to us dead after all. If he were alive he would have only tried to steal from us."

"As it is he is very quiet," smiled the pill vendor. "Unlike the street." He waved a hand at the teeming throngs of men, women, children, and animals choking the narrow thorough-fare. "His discretion is a lesson to us all." The pill vendor noticed the pouch on Heather's hip and he frowned, backing away to the rear of the splintered wood counter that was his stall. "You are one of the slit-bellies," he said softly.

Heather nodded, resisting the urge to press a hand to the small of her back. "Yes," she said. It was one of her main functions for the Mother House. The pouch carried a number of basic surgical tools—clamps, scissors, and a scalpel. Each afternoon she would make her way from the Mother House and her work in the hospital there, heading down Chitpore to the banks of the Hooghly River. She would travel along the bank north towards the immense span of the Horah Bridge, looking for bodies in the muddy, silt-filled water. It was a favorite place to suicide, and many of the people who tried to take their own lives were pregnant women. If she could catch them early enough it was her job to quickly perform a Cae-sarian on the spot in an attempt to save the unborn child. In five years she had done the operation more than 300 times and she had managed to bring a total of eleven children into the world. As she stood on the filthy street, a hundred odors—foul, spiced, and sweet—fighting for attention, it occurred to her that the child dead between the stalls could easily have been one of those eleven.

"What's the point?" she whispered, staring at the child's corpse. "What's the use?"

From the Mother House in Calcutta, to the lepers of Shantinagar, and beyond to the *Ciudad Perdidas*, the lost cities of the poor, in Mexico City. Hindi, Malayalam, Bengali, English, and Spanish mixing in her mind until any individuality she'd once had was lost.

And then, after eight years, the fear. Afraid because her time in the novitiate was over, and she was to go to Rome to take her final vows. She had been instructed to return to her family one last time to say goodbye. She would have two months to visit, two months in a world that had forgotten her and which had changed too much for her to understand. And so she found herself in a long-distance telephone office on the Avenida Juarez, her own voice sounding in her ears as though it were a million miles away, the English she spoke sounding stilted and foreign to her. With tears running down her face, she said: "Janet? It's Heather. I'm coming back. I'm going to Boston...."

* * *

The door of the cell swung open, slamming back against the wall, and revealing a blank-faced man wearing unmarked desert camouflage fatigues, paratroopers' jump boots, and a black beret. He had a Colt .45 Commander holstered on his webbing belt, and a converted Ruger Mini-14 strapped across his back on a quick release harness. To Sarah he looked no more than twenty.

"Up!" he said.

Sarah did as she was told, casting a quick glance at the woman in the corner. Heather Foxcroft was no longer staring at the light; while Sarah had dozed she'd fallen asleep as well.

The figure in the doorway stepped aside. "Out!" he said.

Sarah crossed the room and went out the door, edging past the uniformed man. She found herself in a narrow hallway that dead-ended a few feet from the door on the left. To the right there was a fifty-foot corridor lit by a row of old-fashioned casement windows. Criss-cross bars had been roughly plastered from the inside. The light pouring in was almost painfully bright; mid-morning sun by the looks of it.

"Move!" said the guard behind her.

Sarah moved, sneaking glimpses out the windows as she passed. The sun was just visible over the mountains and from its position she judged she was looking almost due east. There was a narrow packed gravel compound, more of the chain-link fence she'd seen when she was brought here, and beyond that there was nothing but desert for a mile or more. A ridge of hills ran as far as she could see in either direction where the flatlands ended.

As she went down the corridor she noticed several doors on her left, and from the heavy locks and hasps she assumed they were cells like the one she and Heather Foxcroft had shared.

The corridor turned onto the short arm of the L-shaped building—now she was headed west. There were no windows along the section of hall, only doors on the right, equipped with ordinary doorknobs. Offices, she thought to herself. As she came abreast of the third door the guard spoke again.

"Stop!" he said. Sarah did so. The guard came forward, tapped lightly on the door, then reached forward and opened it. His eyes never left Sarah. She stepped into the room beyond and the guard closed the door behind her.

"Good morning." It was David Freeman, from the Reno Nevada Survival Skills office.

Freeman was dressed in the same uniform as the guard, with the exception of his hat. Instead of a fatigue cap he was wearing a long-billed baseball cap with a small insignia patch on the front; a silver sword on a black background. The office was far different from the one in Reno. Instead of antiques and original oils there was nothing but a plain gray metal desk, a wooden swivel chair, in which he sat, a wooden straight chair for visitors, and a row of battered-looking dark-green filing cabinets. There was a schematic map on the wall. From where she stood she could make out the outlines of a few buildings and a heavily inked runway pattern. A plan of the complex? Over his shoulder she could see out the window. The blank rear wall of a corrugated metal building filled up the entire view. One of the hangars she'd seen. She crossed to the straight chair and sat down without being asked.

"This suits you better," she said after a moment.

"What does?" he said.

"The office. This is the real Mr. Freeman."

"*Colonel* Freeman," he corrected.

"In whose army?" asked Sarah.

"U.S. Marine Corps," he said, smiling.

"That's no Marine Corps uniform," she answered.

He shrugged. "I'm not in the Marines any more."

"So what are you in?" asked Sarah, unable to keep the sneer out of her voice.

Freeman frowned. "Miss Logan, I don't think you appreciate the situation you're in right now. You're hardly in a position to ask *me* questions."

"Why did you call me Logan?" asked Sarah, shocked. "I told you my name was Kirkland."

"You lied," said Freeman, leaning back in his chair. "Your name is Sarah Juliette Logan, daughter of the late Senator Andrew Duggan Logan. We have clear evidence that you and your accomplice, a Mr. Philip Kirkland, were involved in a break-in at the Barrington, New York headquarters of the Tenth Crusade Christian Mobilization Association. The evidence includes videotapes showing you inside the headquarters as well as fingerprints and audio recordings of your conversations while you were ransacking one of the offices there. In addition, there is an outstanding warrant in Canada, issued by the Toronto Metropolitan Police for Mr. Kirkland, as a suspect in the murder of a woman named Janet Margolis. Once again, there is a considerable weight of evidence. There is also a warrant out for Mr. Kirkland in New York City, where he's wanted for questioning in the disappearance and possible murder of Miss Heather Foxcroft. Apparently Mr. Kirkland called the New York City Police and tried to tell them that Miss Foxcroft had been taken from his loft by force, but in consideration of the charge against Mr. Kirkland in Canada, the New York police feel that Mr. Kirkland may be responsible for her disappearance. Since you have been with Mr. Kirkland for some time, all of it after Miss Foxcroft's disappearance and after the murder of Miss Margolis, you are classifiably his accomplice. To be blunt, Miss Logan, you are in very deep shit."

"This is unbelievable!" said Sarah, stunned. "You know as well as I do that Heather Foxcroft is in a cell in this building right now."

Freeman smiled, and shook his head. "The woman who shares the cell with you travels under a Mexican passport. The name on it is Sister Angela Delicata and the address is the Convent of the Sisters of Charity, Mexico City. She was found wandering around on the streets of Denver, Colorado, and she was taken in by a member of the Tenth Crusade Christian Mobilization Association in that city and she was sent here to rest and recuperate."

"You're crazy!" whispered Sarah.

"No, just careful," replied Freeman. "We don't make very many mistakes and when we do we rectify them." Sarah opened her mouth to speak but Freeman held up one hand, stopping her. "Please, Miss Logan. I don't want to get involved in a long conversation with you at this point. I don't have the time to waste. I want some answers to a few specific questions. If you give me any trouble answering those questions you will be dealt with very harshly. Understand?"

"Yes," said Sarah. She was damned if she was going to let him know how frightened she was. And she wasn't going to be stupid enough to lie.

"Good," he replied, nodding. He sat forward in the chair, opened a drawer in his desk, and brought out a small cassette recorder. He placed it on the desk and turned it on. "First question. Where is Philip Kirkland?"

"I have no idea," replied Sarah. "The last I knew he was going to try and get into the Tenth Crusade compound at Ragged Mountain, Colorado."

"You haven't seen him since that time?"

"No."

"Did you make any provisions for meeting with him again?"

"Yes," said Sarah. "He said he'd meet or call me at the Holiday Hotel in Reno."

"Why Reno?" asked Freeman.

"I was going there to continue my investigation."

"Investigation of what?"

"The murder of my father by the Tenth Crusade."

"Your father committed suicide," replied Freeman. "He blew his brains out with a shotgun, if I remember correctly."

"He was driven to it by your people."

"Anyone who commits suicide is driven to it by something, Miss Logan. In your father's case I assure you it wasn't the Tenth Crusade. It's far more likely that he killed himself out of remorse."

"For what?" asked Sarah hotly.

"He had been carrying on a homosexual liaison with a much younger man for some years, Miss Logan."

"That's insane!" blurted Sarah. She stood up, the chair slamming onto the floor.

"Sit down," instructed Freeman. He waited until Sarah picked up the chair and seated herself before he went on. "I know it may come as a shock to you, Miss Logan, but your father was quite definitely a homosexual. We have evidence."

"Lies!" said Sarah, her voice catching.

"I'm afraid not, Miss Logan. The young man's name was Terence Coopersmith."

"Terry was one of my father's assistants!"

"Sure," said Freeman. "He was also your father's lover until he went back to law school. Paid for by your father, I might add."

"You blackmailed him!" said Sarah.

Freeman shook his head. "No, we asked for his support. He refused."

"What kind of support?" asked Sarah. "What kind of sick law did you want him to vote for?"

"You're hardly in a position to call any law we might want to see enacted *sick*, Miss Logan." He let out a sighing breath. "As a matter of fact we wanted his support in our fight for the repeal of certain elements in the federal abortion statutes. As I said, he refused."

"Bastards!"

"Please. We've veered from the track. You said you wanted to carry on your investigation in Reno. Once again, why Reno?"

"Because of NSS."

"Where did you see the name?" he asked.

"Barrington. Philip and I stole their garbage. There were some old Telex tear sheets."

"Marvelous," said Freeman, frowning. He leaned forward and checked the tape in the cassette machine. "And what did you find out about NSS?"

"Nothing," said Sarah. "Except you, the Billy Carstairs people, and Eagle One share space in the same building."

"What do you know about Eagle One?" asked Freeman, suddenly interested.

Sarah shrugged. "Just that it fits into the whole pattern. Sam Keller is a big-time Conservative. When the religious roundtable was set up before Reagan was elected he was in like Flynn. He gave money to anyone who looked hot."

"You seem to have done a great deal of investigating," said Freeman. "Too bad you weren't on our side. You've got skills we might have used."

"I still don't know what side you're on," said Sarah.

"God's," answered Freeman, and there wasn't the slightest hint of humor in his voice.

Chapter Fifteen

In Reno just about everything except the public library is open twenty-four hours a day, and by 8:30 in the morning Philip Kirkland was already twenty miles outside the city in a rented car. He followed Interstate 80 east to Fernley, then turned off the turnpike onto Alternate 95, hopscotching south down Lyon County, then turning east again into Mineral, reaching the County Seat in Hawthorne just before 11:00. By then the day was already broiling hot, but the tourists were out in full force with their funny hats, buying souvenirs at the general store and asking directions to the old Luck Boy mine where the occasional nugget could still be found. Philip headed for the relative sanctuary of the Hawthorne municipal offices. He spent an hour in the dusty stacks of the County Seat Registry, and eventually found what he was looking for in the 1947 Survey Ledger.

The ledger was nothing more than a collection of maps, covering the county in square-mile sections. Using the information he'd been given by Simon Adler, Philip went through the maps, concentrating on the sections within the boundaries of Tonopah, just across the line in Nye County and Yucca Wells, which was located on Route 23, roughly halfway between the towns of Luning and Gabbs. A triangular section of Esmerelda County jutted up into the area he was searching, but according to the State map he was using for reference, that area was part of the Monte Cristo range of mountains and was unlikely to have been used for an air base.

The base, when he finally found it, was located eight miles

east of Highway 23 on a secondary road that wasn't even shown on the State map. From the looks of it, the secondary road had once connected the Gabbs-Luning road with Tonopah, but had been replaced by another road slightly to the north at some later date. There was a third road, this one marked only on the survey for the base itself that ran two miles to the south, cutting through a series of drumlins, eventually opening up into a clear plateau area about half a mile square – the base. On the chart it was merely indicated as USAF B55D/USWD XMV-9, but in now faded ink someone had added in another designation: Pilot Peak air base, undoubtedly named for the mountain located twenty miles or so to the south on the State map. Since the base didn't show on the survey for the following year it probably meant that the place hadn't been in existence long enough for it to have received anything more than the letter-number designation, adding to its anonymity.

The scale of the survey was large enough to show buildings and runways and, using a piece of paper borrowed from a dozing clerk, Philip roughed out a quick sketch of the place. Whoever had designed it had liked the number three, because it seemed that the buildings had been erected in trios. There were three large hangars, three Quonset-style barracks buildings, and three peaked-roof warehouses clustered around the northern end of the single runway. There was also a large square building behind the hangars that had most likely been used as a maintainence shed, a control tower, and an L-shaped structure that was either a mess hall or the base office.

The half-mile square was delineated by a perimeter wire with guard towers every two hundred yards as well as a sentry post at the main gates. According to the small-scale map on the next page in the ledger the actual area of the reservation went out well beyond the perimeter wire, extending to the beginning of the access road. The small-scale map also showed contour lines indicating that except for the plateau area the base itself was on, the surrounding terrain was a series of rippling hills. Like Ragged Mountain, the Crusade installation at Pilot Peak was the quintessence of privacy – which was going to make it a very difficult place to get into. Philip sat in the dim cool room and tapped his pencil against his teeth, looking down at the charts in the Survey Ledger and at his own sketch. He was vaguely aware of the hollow echoes of voices and laughter from elsewhere in the building, but his mind had taken him back in memory to his days as a photographer in Viet Nam.

In many ways the situation he was faced with was like the problem of rescuing downed helicopter pilots in the jungle. On three or four occasions Philip had gone out with the rescue crews and he'd seen the difficulties of taking people out of hostile territory at close hand. Using Sikorsky "Jolly Green Giant" helicopters, and aided by Rockwell Bronco Forward Air Controllers, the rescue crews would swoop into the "down" zone and pick up any survivors of the crash while an escorting group of propeller-driven A-1 Skyraiders gave covering fire. The rescuers were further aided by high-altitude radar picket planes which monitored ground offensives by the enemy, usually anti-aircraft fire and guideline-launched SA-2 surface-to-air missiles. Even with such massive support the missions were extremely dangerous, and more than once the rescue crews themselves were shot down and had to be rescued. Sometimes the efforts made to rescue downed aircrew went too far. Philip had once done a photo story on a rescued navigator who'd been in the jungle for twelve days. In that time three helicopters were shot down by anti-aircraft fire and a Rockwell Bronco FAC plane was shot down by a surface-to-air missile. In all, seven men were killed trying to rescue the single navigator, and one of the people shot down in a rescue helicopter had to be rescued himself. Philip had costed the mission out at roughly $3,000,000, and that didn't take into consideration the absurdly wasteful loss of human life.

In its simplest sense, the tactics used by the Air Force rescue teams relied on diversion, and high speed, and from the information he'd gathered about Pilot Peak, the same would apply there. But while the Air Force could call up long-range artillery fire, as well as using the Skyraider fighter planes and sometimes even offshore support fire, he was going to be going in alone against an enemy he knew nothing about, over unfamiliar terrain. If it had been Viet Nam any officer in charge of such a mission would have refused to go; Philip couldn't. Not only did he feel morally obliged to make the attempt, he knew that there was no one else.

That was assuming Sarah was even there, of course. As far as he knew the Crusade or NSS could have spirited her halfway around the world by now. He had a brief impulse to simply walk away from the whole thing and go back to New York, but he shrugged it off, the thought leaving him with a faintly queasy feeling in his stomach. He was far from being a hero but he knew that he'd never be able to rationalize quitting now by putting it down to common sense. Sarah's and Heather's lives were at stake, and leaving them now was tantamount to murder.

He closed the ledger thoughtfully, leaving it on the table in the high-ceilinged room for the clerk to deal with. He picked up his sketch, folded it, and slipped it into his breast pocket. It was already past noon and he still had some things to do in Hawthorne before he set out for Pilot Peak.

Philip found a sporting goods store and put his credit card to work. According to the map he was going to have at least a two-mile walk over some rough terrain to reach the perimeter fence of the base, and it wasn't going to be a Sunday stroll. He picked out a sand-colored packsack and began filling it with the basics: canteen, hiking boots, an idiotic-looking facsimile of an Australian bush hat with a turned up brim, a lightweight nylon hunter's coverall in desert camouflage, a Canadian made Grohmann hunting knife, with a five-inch blade, binoculars, a waterproof watch, and a firestart kit with a magnesium rod and a striker.

He moved across the store to the glass cases and racks of firearms and weighed the pros and cons of taking a gun with him. He'd learned how to shoot reasonably well in Viet Nam, but spraying the countryside with an M16 on full auto with your eyes squeezed shut didn't make you a sniper. Not to mention that firearms were noisy and heavy as well. He decided that a gun would be more trouble than its potential worth.

He took his pile of equipment to the cash register, and five minutes later he was driving out of Hawthorne, heading east.

He stopped twice before reaching the town limits, once at a grocery store where he bought a quarter-pound of hard cheese and a box of raisins, and then again at a gas station where he filled the gas tank and his canteen. As he drove away from the wind-scarred Union 76 pumps he checked his watch. It was 2:00. Another hour would see him in Yucca Wells. That should leave him plenty of time to reach the base by nightfall, which was when he wanted to arrive.

The land between Hawthorne and the Luning turnoff was arid and dusty, pumice and sienna in a dozen shades, relieved here and there by irrigated fields that were almost lurid green by comparison. On either side of the low tongue of flatland were the stunted hills of the Gills Range and the Excelsior. It was the hottest part of the day and the blacktop shimmered with heat ripples as Philip squinted at the road ahead. Within twenty minutes his eyes were sore and he kicked himself mentally for not buying a pair of sunglasses in Hawthorne.

He reached the Yucca Wells turnoff and swung to the north, the well maintained highway changing abruptly to the pitted and cracked tar-macadam of the side road. He began climbing almost immediately, the road swinging back and forth in wide, unbanked curves around the bases of the low hills.

The land was desolate except for clumps of sagebrush, and stunted, intermittent patches of desert grass. As Philip took the car higher the hills began to blend down into a huge, gently undulating plateau, unfenced, untended, and barren. This was no man's land, unfit for almost any growth, inhabited only by spiders, snakes, scorpions, and nomadic carnivores.

At last the town of Yucca Wells appeared out of the heat shimmer like the ghost of an oasis. It was almost as desolate as the land surrounding it, and if there ever had been yucca trees nearby they had long since disappeared. The battered, weather-worn buildings, all false-fronted like a Hollywood ghost town, were dribbled along both sides of the narrow road like an idea gone wrong. Of the town's twenty buildings, more than half were tumbledown, no more than skeletons and piles of gray splintered wood, shattered windows staring blindly at their equally depressing neighbors across the way. Philip slowed the car to a crawl, looking out both sides and wondering for what reason the town had been originally built. Presumably, at least by its name, it had been a watering spot, perhaps a stagecoach stop on the way to Gabbs, or Austin farther north.

The only sign of life was a gas station at the far edge of the almost dead community. There was no brand name sign, just a sandwich board propped up in the packed earth which announced "Harky's Cheap Gas." There was a single pump in front of a low stuccoed garage, an old-fashioned round-top Coke machine and an immensely fat man in an undershirt sitting at a rudely constructed picnic table set off to one side. The man was drinking out of a Styrofoam cup and smoking. Philip pulled in to the station and came to a halt a few yards away from the picnic table. He saw that the man had some kind of gray rag tied bandanna fashion over his head to protect him from the heat. The man paid no attention to Philip's arrival.

Philip got out of the car and was struck instantly by a stupendous blast of heat. He walked over to the picnic table and sat down across from the fat man. Philip saw that the man was tanned the color of mahogany except where the undershirt covered him. The flesh beyond that line was fish-belly pale. He wondered if the man always wore the same undershirt, or if it was one of a matched set. The fat man was sweating hard, the moisture running in streams down the deep-cut lines of his bulldog face, and sparkling in the gray-white bristles scattered across his descending chins. Huge mirrored sunglasses obscured the man's eyes entirely. He lifted his cup and Philip noticed a plain gold wedding band embedded in the flesh of his third finger. He tried to imagine what the man's wife could possibly be like and then gave up. At another time or place he would have asked permission to take the man's photograph, but he had far more important things to do now.

"You like some coffee?" asked the man. His voice was as deep as his huge, flabby chest. "It's hot."

"No thanks," answered Philip. He wiped sweat off his forehead with the back of his arm. He glanced over at the Coke machine and pointed. "Any Cokes in that?"

"Not since fifty-two," answered the man, smiling. "Had a fight with the guy who drove the truck for them. Called me 'Fatty.'"

"Oh?" said Philip.

The man nodded. "I hit him. Once. In the mouth. Broke his jaw, I think. Left half his teeth in the dirt too. Never came back. Neither did anybody else for that matter. That car's a rental." It was a statement, not a question.

"That's right," said Philip.

"Got one of those rental plate holders. Saw it right off. Tourist?"

"You might say that," answered Philip, wondering how much to say. He decided to take a chance. "It's more like a nostalgia trip, I guess. I'm looking for the Pilot Peak air base."

"Why?" asked the man. "You're too young. Base closed down just after the war. The Second War."

"I know. My dad flew out of there. I was in Reno on business, so I thought I'd take a look. My father told me some good stories about it."

"I was a mechanic there," said the man. "Learned my trade at Pilot Peak."

Philip groaned inwardly. If the man asked him about any of his father's experiences at the base he'd be in trouble.

"What did you work on?" asked Philip, hedging.

The man grimaced. "T.B.F.s, Dauntless, Wildcats. Whatever was on the ferry roster to San Diego. Your old man one of the ferry pilots?"

"That's right," said Philip, relieved. What he knew about World War Two airplanes wouldn't have filled a matchbook cover.

"What was his name?" asked the man. "Maybe I knew him or something."

"Smith," said Philip quickly. "Bob Smith."

"Knew a bunch of Smiths. Didn't spend much time with the officers though; just the other greaseboys."

"Is the base close?" asked Philip, reeling the fat man in from his reminiscences.

"Close enough," said the man. He lit a cigarette from the

butt of the other, then took a sip of his coffee. He put the cup carefully down on the table and licked his lips. "Go maybe seven, eight miles north, you'll see a highway to the right. Old 221. Eight miles along that and you'll see a line of hills and dips. Road right through the middle of them about three miles, maybe less. Then the base. Not that there's any point."

"What do you mean?"

The man ran his palm down his chin and neck, then flicked off the sweat. "Been bought out. Some kind of training camp for businessmen. Shooting, driving, that kind of thing. I don't think they'd take kindly to visitors."

"Maybe I'll pass on it, then," said Philip. "It's probably all been changed anyway."

"Not much," said the man. "I was out there when they started up. Helping them with the electrical and plumbing. They were putting in some kind of race track, but else it was pretty much like it was back in my time. Dogs though. Big ones. Dobermans. They train them, I think. Scared the piss out of me. Chained in pairs."

"I think I'll definitely pass on the base, now that you mention it," said Philip with a weak smile. "I'd like to make Salt Lake City in one piece." He stood, preparing to go. "By the way, you don't know where I could get some sunglasses do you?"

"Nope," said the man. "Just these here I got on. Nice, don't you think?"

"They're just the kind I was looking for," replied Philip, reading the tone in the man's voice.

"Cost me ten bucks," said the man.

"I'd pay fifteen for glasses like that."

"I'd take it."

Philip pulled out some bills, counted off the fifteen and laid them on the picnic table. The man slid the glasses down his nose and put them beside the money. The man's eyes were totally out of keeping with the bulldog face. They were large and clear, the irises a deep, almost iridescent green. A woman's eyes. The beautiful eyes in the seamed, sluggish face were an obscenity.

Philip picked up the glasses and slipped them into his pocket with the folded sketch of the Pilot Peak base. "Thanks," he said.

The fat man bent his head in acknowledgment. "Nice doing business with you," he smiled, the eyes searching Philip's face. "When you came in I was afraid I wasn't going to be able to sell you nothing at all. Name's Harky, in case you're back this way."

"Bob," said Philip.

"Bob," said the man thoughtfully. "Just like your dad. Now that's nice."

Philip smiled, waved, and turned away. He walked back to the car and drove off, feeling those slick green eyes on his back for miles.

He found the side road without difficulty and turned down it, slowing immediately on the neglected surface. Grasses were growing up through cracks in the worn pavement, and the shoulders had actually begun to crumble. There was nothing on either side but the monochrome flatlands and Philip felt a twinge of fear, wondering how long he would last without a car. A few miles further on he spotted the corrugated rise of the hills Harky had mentioned and he slowed even more. He reached into his pocket and pulled out the sunglasses, wiping them on his sleeve before he put them on. As soon as he did his nostrils filled with the sour-milk odor of the fat man, and it was almost enough to make him sick.

He tried his best to ignore the smell and scanned the country on the left. There was no sign of humanity anywhere. He reached the road leading north to the base and stopped, looking down it. The road cut through the hummock hills, veering slightly to the right. It looked as though it led nowhere. He waited for a few moments, taking in the empty landscape, then backed and filled until he had the car facing the direction from which he'd come. He'd noticed a small cut in the land half a mile back—hopefully large enough to hide the car. Driving west he reached the cut and pulled off the road, the tires barely creasing the rock hard surface of the desert; there would be no telltale tire marks to be seen if someone drove by. He angled the car behind the bulk of the jutting outcrop and got out. He walked back to the highway and checked the eastern and western approaches. There was no sign of the car. Snapping off a branch from one of the sagebrush clumps that lined the side of the road he went back along his route and brushed out the faint indentations made by the passage of the car. Then, satisfied that he was hidden from anything except an intensive search, he began unloading the car. Ten minutes later he was on his way, pack on his back and the canteen bouncing on his hip.

In the Hawthorne municipal offices Philip had estimated the distance from the road to the base at three miles; in the end it turned out to be more like ten. Some of the hills were so steep that Philip had to skirt them entirely, making long detours as he attempted to find another route north, adding hours to his journey.

By the late afternoon Philip was exhausted. He stopped briefly in the lee of a large striated outcropping of rock and made a rough meal of his raisins and cheese, taking care not to drink too much water. He had been traveling for three hours and in that time he estimated that he had covered no more than half the distance to Pilot Peak. The only thing in his favor was the steadily lowering sun which was now behind him and to his right. As it fell behind the hills the temperature dropped off quickly and walking became more comfortable, although he could feel blisters rising on his heels and on the sides of his feet. He knew that he was on a one-way trip—one way or the other he was going to have to find some other way out of the base. Even walking alone the trip would be impossible; his water was almost gone and even if he traveled at night he knew he'd never make it. If he succeeded in finding Sarah or Heather, trying to walk out of the semi-desert would be suicide.

He cursed himself for being a hundred different kinds of fool, but he kept on, his feet digging down into the crumbling sand, their weight like pigs of lead strapped to his ankles. The pack on his back chafed at his shoulders and armpits, and the sweat in his armpits trickled down his sides in long sticky trails that dragged at the sodden fabric of his shirt. Every exposed portion of his body had been sunburned terribly within a few hours, including the tender tissues of his nostrils and his lips. The sunglasses he'd purchased from the obese man at the gas station proved to be almost useless; they cut the glare well enough, but they were cheap and unpolarized so his eyes had swollen three-quarters shut before he'd traveled a mile. Continuing his course after his brief meal, he found himself wondering if he was going to make it at all.

By late evening he was little more than an automaton, pushing himself forward by will alone, his feet rising and falling heavily, the muscles in his calves and thighs long seized and cramped to the point where the pain was almost like a familiar friend. He lost all sense of time, place, and purpose; he only knew that he had to keep walking or he would die. He forced himself to think about what it would be like to die alone in the terrible wasteland of stone and sand, his body slowly desiccating, pulled apart by turkey vultures, the marrow of his bones cleaned to ivory by hordes of crawling insects. Eventually even those horrible visions stopped working and every agonizing step became a battle between his body and his mind.

Then, suddenly, it was over. He dragged himself to the summit of yet another of the infinity of undulating hills, his bare hand grabbing at the thick horny stock of a mesquite bush for leverage. And there it was, laid out like some complex child's toy in the flat-bottomed valley below. He stood there dumbly, mouth hanging open for a moment, then dropped down to his knees and slithered backwards down the slope. The last of the sun was directly behind him and if there were any lookouts posted he would have presented a clear silhouette on the skyline.

He squeezed his eyes shut and waited for the pounding of his heart to subside, wondering how close he'd come to having his brains blown out. He had a brief, hideous flash of the photo he'd taken of the Viet Cong agent and the aftermath—the crumpling, loose-jointed fall, the spraying flecks of gray and scarlet, the seeping blood that puddled around the corpse, highlights sparkling brilliantly in the sunlight. Then it passed.

He pulled himself back up the slope and took a second look, only the top of his head and his eyes above the line of the hill.

He took off the sunglasses, jammed them into the flaking sand, and wiped the thin film of dust and sweat from his face.

The camp was at least a mile away and from where he lay he could see the high, barb topped perimeter fence. The base was much the way he'd seen it laid out on the chart, with a few additions. The single, dead straight line of the runway, the clusters of hangars, warehouse, and barracks were the same, but another building had been added close to the entrance gate, and there was a winding asphalt track laid out between the runway and the northern line of the fence. The track was a looping figure eight that wound around two large rock outcroppings. Scattered across the base, clumps of mesquite and creosote bush had taken over, their heavy roots gripping the hard-packed soil, but other than that there was no vegetation. Shadows fell like slabs of solid black from the buildings, making it difficult to pick out detail. Philip dropped back down the slope again and shrugged the pack off his back. He opened it up, found the binoculars and went back up the rise.

Seen through the lenses, the shadows fell back, instantly revealing that the Pilot Peak air base was far from deserted. At the end of the runway, beside one of the immense old corrugated metal hangars was a paved lot filled with vehicles of all kinds from half-tracks, jeeps, and eight-tons to a scattering of what looked like old Sherman tanks. There was another grouping of trucks and jeeps within the high-fenced confines of the L-shaped administration building between the hangars and the driving track, as well as several automobiles. Except for the cars all the vehicles were painted the same color—a dusky green-beige that blended in perfectly with the surrounding countryside. A mile, even with binoculars, was too far to make out minute details, but Philip was almost positive that the tanks, half-tracks, trucks, and jeeps all carried the U.S. Army star. He lowered the glasses, and stared out across the cooling valley.

Behind him the sun had dropped even further and the ground was rapidly being swallowed up in a creeping veil of purplish shadow. In an hour the entire base would be shrouded in darkness. Philip frowned, confused. The mark-

ings on the military vehicles didn't make any sense unless....
He picked up the glasses again and squinted through the eye-
pieces, trying for a last look before the sun was gone. If those
were U.S. Army vehicles that meant that the government, or
at least the Pentagon, was involved with NSS and the rest of
the tangled skein of events he'd been thrown into. It didn't
seem possible, but the Tenth Crusade itself had been laugh-
able to him only a few days before.

There was no doubt about it—they *were* U.S. Army insignia.
He moved the binoculars, sweeping down across the base to
the wire. As the darkness rolled in he could pick out lights in
the barracks and around the hangars. He checked the area directly outside the perimeter fence. If he was dealing with the
army he'd have to expect more sophisticated security. The
chances were good they'd have remote sensors outside the
wire, or even movement monitors like the high resolution
night sights and ground radar that had been used at fire bases
in Viet Nam. It was too late though—the shadows were ob-
scuring everything and the flat, mottled terrain was almost
completely invisible. He was going to have to go in blind.

He waited for over an hour, letting the night completely
blanket the valley below, and while he waited he tried to come
up with a plan that allowed him some chance of survival. As
far as his approach was concerned there was little choice; one
way or the other he was going to have to come down the hillside into the valley with almost no cover at all beyond the occasional patches of mesquite randomly scattered on the
downside slope. In Hawthorne he'd assumed that he could get
through the fence anywhere along its length, but the bolt
cutters he'd purchased wouldn't do him any good if the fence
was wired to sensors that led to a security office within the
camp. If the fence *was* hooked into a security network his only
other chance would be to go in through the main gate, and
that was almost certainly going to be guarded.

Eventually he decided to go for the southwest corner of the
fence. The area on the other side was solidly overgrown with
mesquite and creosote which would hide him reasonably well,
and if, on examination, he found that the fence was linked to
a security system he could follow the fence east to the road

and the main gate. Before the shadows had obscured every-thing he'd seen that there was a shallow gully that ran parallel to the fence, probably resulting from subsidence caused by the building of the perimeter. It wouldn't give him much cover, but it was better than nothing.

If he found that he could get in through the fence he would make his way north along the fence line to the cluster of hangars at the end of the runway, then cut behind them across the motor pool lot and from there get to the adminis-tration building. Which was where his plan ended. The ad-ministration building was totally exposed, visible from the main gate, the barracks, and the hangars. Hopefully the base remained unlit at night, but even if it was dark, getting through the second line of fence that surrounded the small building was going to be hairy. But again, he had no choice; it was the only building that seemed likely as a place to keep prisoners.

With the coming of night the air cooled dramatically and as he stripped off his clothes and changed into the camouflage coveralls Philip found himself shivering. He finished off the last of his water and prepared his equipment. He stowed the firestart kit in one of the zippered leg pockets of the coveralls, strapped the sheathed hunting knife to his waist, and slipped the bolt cutters into one of the coveralls' thigh pockets, and then went over the top of the hill in a rolling crouch, keeping as much of his body as possible from silhouetting against the sky. It was still too early for the moon, but even so he felt horribly exposed as he slithered down the hillside, heels dig-ging into the sand to keep him from moving too quickly. He made the best use he could of the limited cover, pausing be-hind each bush to check the base as he went down. Except for a few lights the place was dark and silent. No sirens, no sud-den alarms, and no detectable movement. He thought about the dogs the fat man had mentioned and swallowed hard. Guard Dobermans were trained to attack silently and he knew he'd have almost no warning if they came after him. The thought of being savaged by half a dozen of the silent creatures brought bile to his throat but he kept on, concen-trating on the terrain immediately ahead.

The fence loomed up in front of him. He checked the dimly illuminated dial of his watch and blinked; somehow time had compressed so that the five minutes he was sure had passed was in fact almost half an hour. He wondered if the long trek across the sand had taken too much out of him, distorting his perceptions dangerously. To get in and out of Pilot Peak he was going to need all his wits about him.

He dropped down into the shallow gully that ran beside the fence and came out of it on his belly, as he crossed the last few yards to the chain-link and barbed-wire barricade. Beyond it he could make out the dark, tangled mass of undergrowth that ran for at least two hundred yards along the north-south line of the fence. If he could get in there safely he'd be all right for a while.

He brought his face to within a few inches of the fence and peered at it carefully. As far as he could tell it was ordinary chain link, no different from the fencing they used to cordon off school yards. There were no trip wires laced through the links that might be linked to sensors and none of the insulators that would indicate the fence was electrified in any way. He fished the small bolt cutters out of his coveralls. He turned again, moving up on his elbows and brought the cutters to the wire. Then he paused, thinking hard.

On the way down the hillside he'd seen no evidence of distant warning devices and now, here at the fence, there were no security measures either. If this really was some kind of clandestine military base, linked however bizarrely to the Tenth Crusade, then it had been put together very sloppily— too sloppily. Then he saw the obvious answer and, with it, the diabolical implications. What if NSS and the Tenth Crusade had faked the insignia on the vehicles, making them look like official army materiel? Dressed in army uniforms and driving what looked like army vehicles, NSS and the Crusade would have *carte blanche* in the area. The only thing they'd have to worry about would be a check made by a legitimate army unit, and as far as he knew there were no army bases close to Pilot Peak. And what if it wasn't just Pilot Peak? What if they had places like this all over the country?

"Paranoia strikes," he muttered. NSS and the Crusade were

clearly rich, powerful, and dangerous – he'd had proof enough of that, but it was hardly *Seven Days in May* material. Knebel's book had been fiction, this was real life.

On the other hand, why not? He thought to himself. What was to stop a bunch of loonies like the Crusade from thinking they could take over the United States and make it safe for the godly. They might not succeed, but they could make one hell of a mess failing. The times were certainly ripe for it, the increasingly frequent attacks by the Devil's Brigade had the country up in arms and, according to Sarah, the huge upsurge in pseudo-Christian groups in the past few years would give a fascist bunch of zealots like the Crusade a firm base of support. He cut off the train of thought; there was no time for philosophy, he had a fence to get through. He took a deep breath, held it, and squeezed the bolt cutters down hard.

Silence, except for the timpani beat of his heart, loud as thunder in his ears. Second cut, his ears so tuned that he heard clearly the snicking of the thick blades and the parting of the metal. Still nothing. He waited, listening, the muscles of his legs cramped and tensed, ready to run at the first sign of trouble. Except there was nowhere to run to. If the alarm was raised now they'd bring him to ground in minutes. He blinked the sweat out of his eyes and cut again, opening the rent in the fence enough to squeeze through. He lay on his back, putting the bolt cutters back into the pocket of his coveralls. Above him the stars glistened like ice, cold and distant witnesses to his break in. Hopefully they were the *only* witnesses.

He pushed the fence back roughly, closing the opening, then bellied forward until he was completely hidden in the mesquite. He sat up in a crouch, his head barely showing above the dense bush, and looked around. From the looks of it he'd made it into the base undetected. Directly north he could make out the line of the fence and the dense shadow of the buildings two hundred yards away. To his right he could make out the peaked roofs of the barracks buildings, but the only light showing there were the single harsh bulbs over the doors; the barracks themselves were dark and shuttered, blind to his intrusion. He wrinkled his nose, fighting back a choking sneeze. The creosote bushes, coming to life in the coolness of the night were emitting the acrid odor that gave them their name. If he got out of Pilot Peak alive he was going to smell like a paint store, but that would be a small price to pay.

Breathing through his mouth, he moved forward through the bush in a crab walk, picking his way carefully, his eyes darting from side to side. After ten minutes he reached the edge of the undergrowth beside the service road that led in behind the hangars. This, he knew, was going to be the most dangerous part. The only way to get to the administration building was by cutting across the taxi area at the end of the runway, then through the motor pool. If there was a guard posted with even average night vision he'd be a goner. Keeping low he went down the service road at a run, expecting a shouted order to halt at any second, the muscles of his back tensing for the single cracking shot. It never came. He reached the rear of the nearest hangar and huddled in the deep shadow, his breath coming in long ragged gasps. When his breathing slowed he crept along the wall to the corner and looked around it, wincing as his boots crunched on the pebble-strewn ground.

From his vantage point he could see across the pitted asphalt of the taxi-way to the motor pool, his line of sight partly obscured by the bat shape of a small plane tethered to the tarmac in front of the far hangar. Unlike the other transport he'd seen the plane had no marking except the normal registration sequences on the tail. He let his eyes roam back and forth.

Nothing, nobody. Like everywhere else, this part of the base seemed deserted. Warning bells started to ring dully in his mind. How could the whole base be unguarded? If they were worried enough to use Dobermans, then why no human security? It didn't make any sense. He ignored his instincts and stepped out from under the protective shadow of the hangar.

He sprinted across the open space. The motor pool to the left of the hangar was unfenced and seconds later Philip was threading his way through the high shapes of the parked vehicles; they were old; vintage surplus. The jeeps were all the low bed type used during and just after World War Two and the trucks were Dodges and Chevrolets from the forties and fifties. It was like the parking lot for a John Wayne war movie.

The administration building, if that's what it was, sat alone, equidistant from the hangar and the driving track. Philip estimated that he'd have about a hundred-yard run across open ground before he reached the fence. He could see small floodlights at the fence corners, pointing inward, but they were dark. If he could make it unseen to the rear of the building he'd have the structure between himself and the rest of the camp. From the hill he'd been able to see that there were no other structures between the building and the perimeter wire some five or six hundred feet to the north.

He studied the building carefully, looking for some way in. The fence around it was about ten feet high and, like the perimeter, it was topped with a triple strand of inward-facing barbed wire. There was only one entrance that he could see – a gate facing the road and even from a hundred yards away he could make out the large padlock and hasp sealing it off. Inside the fence were the cars he'd seen from the hillside, parked at the side door. Above the door a single light burned, casting a puddle of yellow light in a small circle over the three-tiered concrete steps leading up to the simple, roughly painted wooden door. Hundreds of bugs swarmed around the light in a frantic swirl of movement, but they were the only sign of life.

The building itself was as plain as the door, a one-storey structure of brick, shaped in an L and cut with ordinary casement windows every few feet. From where he stood he could see small peaked protuberances in the roof. Skylights? More than anything it looked like a small factory or warehouse from the thirties. Like the rest of the installation it seemed to have been given a minimum of maintainence. Grime had washed down from the tar and asphalt roof in long smudges, the window frames were dried and peeling and the concrete line of crenelations along the roof was broken and cracked. He also noticed an area of cleaner, and obviously newer brick and mortar on the long side of the L. The rectangle of new masonry was about twenty feet from the nearest window and parallel to it. In the not too distant past a window had been bricked in and if the building was being used as a stockade it made sense that the window had been bricked in to provide a security area – a cell.

Philip checked his watch. It was almost 10:00; he'd been inside the Pilot Peak base for a little more than half an hour, and he was pressing his luck. He gathered up the last shreds of his courage and energy, then sprinted the hundred yards across the road and the intervening ground between it and the fenced building.

"Horseshoes up my ass," he murmured to himself, dropping to the ground at the rear of the fence. Behind him there was nothing but pitch-black night. He unzipped his pocket, took out the bolt cutters and he snipped the fence, checking again for wires before he began. Three minutes later he was through and running for the back of the building.

He came around the corner in a crouch and stopped. Ten feet away was a loading platform and a large, battered service door. Parked by the loading bay was one of the most decrepit trucks he'd ever seen. It was a right-hand drive 30 hundred-weight Chevrolet, built in Canada during the forties for the British Army Long Range Desert Group. Basically it was little more than a huge open cab pick-up truck, raised on massive leaf springs and equipped with fat desert-use tires. The side was cut out to provide space for a radio transmitter and there were no doors or windshield. There was a giant I-beam front bumper in front of the old-fashioned hump-back hood, extra batteries and jerry cans on the short running boards and pierced metal sand skids racked on mounts along the sides. There was also a fifty-caliber machine-gun on a pintle mount at the rear of the truck bed, and a pair of carbines clipped to mounts beside the driver. The sand-colored metal of the truck was pitted and filthy, and eaten through with rust. The entire vehicle was coated in a gritty layer of sand that had built up on all the greased parts of the truck like old some kind of grotesque, crumbling mold.

Using the massive bumper as a step Philip quietly climbed up onto the loading platform and crossed it. The wooden door was partially slid back, and a sliver of light cut out into the night. He peered in through the crack. Inside he could see a large storage area, half filled with long wooden crates. Philip had seen crates like that before, at military staging bases around the world. They were as identifiable as the heavy kraft paper bags used by liquor stores—weapons boxes. He was looking into an arsenal. A deserted one.

He listened for a moment and when he was sure there was no one close by he pushed the sliding door back another foot and let himself in, returning the door to its original position once he was inside. He made his way around the stacks of boxes until he reached an interior door. This one too had been left ajar. Whatever else they were NSS was hardly security conscious; undefended perimeters, unarmed guards, and arsenals with open doors.

Philip eased open the door and found himself at the apex of two dimly lit corridors. One led straight ahead to the front door of the building, while the other veered off to the left. The left-hand corridor would take him down to the place where the window had been bricked up. He started down it, muscles tensed and ears tuned to the slightest sound. He'd managed to walk ten feet before his luck ran out.

A door opened at the far end of the corridor and a man appeared, his back to Philip. He seemed to be carrying a tray of some kind. Philip stopped dead in his tracks and the man turned, shutting the door with one hand and balancing the tray with the other. Philip had a single glimpse of the uniformed figure's startled expression before all hell broke loose.

There was no time to think. As the guard dropped the tray and fumbled at the holster strapped to his belt Philip jumped forward, tackling the man and throwing him backwards. He managed to get his elbow across the guard's throat, and with his other hand he jerked his knife out of its sheath on his leg. The guard was still trying for the gun at his waist when Philip brought the knife around, driving it hard into the man's side, feeling the long blade slice below the ribs, cutting into the kidneys and lungs. The man beneath him twitched and the air was filled with the smell of excrement as the corpse voided itself.

Philip sat up, panting from exertion, still straddling the body. For a moment he thought he was going to be sick, but the feeling passed, replaced by a hard, cold anger. Kill or be killed; the old law had reasserted itself, and Philip was flooded with the adrenalin surge of victory. He was still alive, and that was all that mattered. He stood up slowly, leaving the knife in the man's side. Taking a deep breath he stepped over the corpse and went to the door at the end of the wall. He opened it and stepped into the harshly lit room.

Chapter Sixteen

"Philip!" It was Sarah. Behind her Philip could see the huddled form of Heather Foxcroft. Strangely, he felt no surprise at seeing her there. It was as though the three of them were intimately tied into some game that none of them understood. He studied the woman who had once been his lover without emotion. She was still wearing the same clothes as when he'd last seen her, soiled and crumpled after so many days. He moved past Sarah, motioning her to be silent, and bent over Heather. She was droning some kind of chant and there was no light of recognition in her eyes. She was Heather, but whatever mind she'd had was gone. She was a shell. He touched her lightly on the shoulder, then stood up. He crossed the room to Sarah.

"Come on," he whispered urgently. "We've got to get out of here. Now!"

"What about her?" asked Sarah, turning to look over her shoulder at Heather.

"Bring her. I'll carry her."

"What happened out there?" asked Sarah.

Philip stared at her coldly.

"I killed somebody," he said, the words taut with emotion. "I killed somebody." He pushed past her and went to Heather. He reached down, took her under the armpits and dragged her to her feet. The woman's eyes stayed shut and the chant went on. He twisted around, getting one arm around her shoulders and under her arm, and began to drag her toward the doorway, her feet half walking and half stumbling.

"End of the corridor and then right," he grunted, instructing Sarah. "There's a loading platform and a truck. Move it!"

She nodded once and headed out the door, Philip close behind with Heather. He went out into the corridor in time to see Sarah pause as she saw the body, then step over it, her shoulders tensing. He went after her, ignoring the corpse. Heather's feet trailed through the pool of blood, leaving two weaving lines of scarlet along the floor.

He turned at the end of the hallway, kicking the door open wide with one foot and hauling Heather through. Ahead of him, Sarah was waiting at the large wooden door. He paused long enough to hit the light switch on the wall, plunging the large storeroom into darkness.

"Open the door," his voice grated, Heather's weight dragging on his arm. "Slowly!"

Sarah nodded again and did as she was told, moving the sliding door back on its oiled track without a sound. Philip took a deep, grateful breath of the cool night air and pushed his chin forward, urging Sarah outside.

"Now what?" she asked, as he joined her on the open platform. Philip closed his eyes wearily and thought. There were only two choices—try and go back the way he'd come, or bully their way out in the ancient truck parked a few feet away. Then it was out of his hands. A deep, slowly growing moan filled the air like some kind of mechanical baying hound. A siren.

They'd found the hole in the fence.

"Get into the truck," said Philip.

"That?" asked Sarah, staring at the sand-crusted behemoth.

"For christsake!" snapped Philip. "Just do it!" He pushed Sarah toward the truck. She dropped onto the ground, then clambered up into the driver's seat. Seeing that she was behind the wheel she shifted over and waited. Philip let Heather down onto the edge of the platform, dropped to the ground himself, then eased her over the side. She was as limp as a doll now, completely lost in whatever world she'd conjured up in her mind. He hauled her to the rear of the truck, pulled out the pins on the tailgate, and hoisted her up, dropping her like a sack of flour beside the pintle mount of the machine-gun.

In the distance the sound of the siren kept on climbing, joined now by the sound of whistles and the roaring of some kind of engine. Philip banged the tailgate shut, threw in the cotter pins and then raced around to the side of the truck, jumping up into the driver's seat. He found the ignition, a large key ready and waiting, and twisted. The engine was silent.

"Shit!" he groaned. "What the hell is wrong?" He peered at the dashboard, checking the gauges in the darkness.

"There!" exclaimed Sarah. "A starter—on the floor by your foot!"

He looked where she was pointing and saw a large dull metal button on the floor beside the long, bent-handled shift lever. He rammed his foot down and the engine fired heavily, shaking the whole vehicle. He grabbed the shift lever, pushed down on the clutch, and smashed the metal rod around in a screeching, grating search for reverse. He found it, popped the clutch and they roared off backwards, the force of the motion throwing Sarah forward, cracking her raised arm into the dash. He twisted the huge wheel to the left, manhandling the unfamiliar shift into a forward gear, then stood on the accelerator, sending the large machine forward in a roostertail spray of sand. Before he'd even seen it in the darkness they'd reached the fence, the I-beam snagging the chain link and cutting through it like so much cheesecloth. Both he and Sarah ducked instinctively as the fence shattered around them and then they were through, racing across the hard-packed earth toward the runway. Out of the corner of his eye Philip could see headlights flashing on in the motor pool area. He dropped into another gear just as they reached the edge of the tarmac, the truck leaping into the air as they bellied into the low gully at its edge. They dropped down onto the asphalt with a jaw-smashing thump, the sudden change in surface almost tearing the wheel out of Philip's hands. He hung on as the truck skidded across the runway in a long drunken yaw, and then he was back in control, aiming the truck at the dark shadow of the gatehouse five hundred yards ahead and, ignoring the road, he took the most direct route.

The truck dropped off the far side of the runway, skidding on the loose ground, the huge tires biting hard. A hunching shadow reared up out of the night and before Philip could react the truck was cutting a swath through the thick area of brush between the runway and the gatehouse. The air was full of branches and twigs as the old Chevrolet bulldozed forward, and then they were through and onto the smooth pavement of the approach road, less than a hundred yards from the gatehouse. For the first time since the beginning of their helter skelter ride Philip risked a glance behind. In the split-second-look he saw headlights in the distance, coming up from the motor pool area. He turned his attention forward again, figuring the odds as he manhandled the truck toward the gate. The vehicles he'd seen in the motor pool were almost as cumbersome as the one he was piloting and, with the exception of the few jeeps, just as slow. They had a small chance if they could keep the distance between them constant and if they could reach his rental car without incident. There wasn't much leeway though; the vehicles behind were no more than half a mile back, and that left him with not much more than a thirty-second headstart. Half a minute between freedom and sudden death.

They reached the gatehouse, the heavy bumper catching the inside corner of the small building and demolishing it as they hammered into the chain-link fence. Philip ducked as a piece of timber whirled over his head and then the air was filled with the sound of the gate rupturing. The truck swerved again and Philip could hear the screeching howl of metal as a piece of the chain link caught in the left side wheel well. He dropped down another gear and jerked the wheel around, knowing that if they lost a tire now they were finished. The fencing finally let go, spinning out under the truck and almost tearing out the exhaust as it went. Then it was gone and there was nothing but the deep roar of the engine and the thunder of the tires.

"They're getting closer!" yelled Sarah in his ear. She was

turned around in the high-backed seat looking down the road behind.

"Can you drive this thing?" yelled Philip, peering ahead, his eyes closed to slits against the sand-filled wind. The road in front looked arrow straight, cutting between lines of low scrub covered hills on either side.

"I think so!" answered Sarah, her eyes still on their pursuers.

"All right! I'm going out on the running board! Put your foot down on the gas when I move and then take the wheel! The road ends about two miles along. Swing right when you get to the intersection and keep on going no matter what!"

He lifted his foot off the gas and the engine faltered slightly, picking up again as Sarah brought her weight to bear on the pedal. Philip waited until her hands were on the wheel and then slid off the seat, hanging onto the raised edge of the dashboard, feeling with his feet in the darkness for the running board. He stepped down, giving Sarah full control and turned half out over the road until he was sure she was all right. The truck seat was high and she had to almost stand to be able to reach the pedals but she seemed to have it. He inched back along the running board until his feet hit the metal flange holding the spare batteries and then climbed onto them, grabbing the lurching seat and hoisting himself back onto the wooden box enclosing the radio transmitter. He dropped down into the bed of the truck, almost stumbling on Heather. She was curled into a tight ball on the floor of the truck, moaning loudly. He stepped over her, swaying with the movement of the truck and grabbed onto the thick cast iron tube of the pintle mount for support.

The Long Range Desert Group trucks used by the British Army in World War Two had been equipped with two basic weapons that could be mounted on the pintle. A long-barreled Boys anti-tank gun and the classic Lewis machine-gun with drum magazine that had proved itself in the First World War. Both types of armament had become obsolete years before and NSS had replaced the lighter weapons with a Browning M2 50-caliber machine-gun from the Springfield arsenal. The heavy machine-gun was loaded using hundred-round link belts joined together and fed up from a box bolted to the floor beside the mount.

Philip had fired some light weaponry in Viet Nam, but never anything as heavy or complex as the Browning, and never under the high stress conditions of combat. He grabbed onto the handles of the heavy gun and almost lost his balance as the weapon swung wildly on the well-greased mount. He righted himself, saw the ammunition box at his feet, and, holding onto the gun with one hand, he reached down, flipped open the lid and grabbed. He pulled up one free end of the belt and peered at the slot breech, panicking as the lights from the approaching vehicles hit him in the face. He ducked instinctively, jamming the free end of the belt into the slot, hoping like hell that he'd done it right. He dragged the gun around to bear on the road behind and on the swinging beams of light, then pulled down on the twin triggers. Nothing happened. There was a wasp-buzz of sound to his left and then the solid *thunk* of a bullet striking metal, followed by a whining ricochet that almost deafened him. The truck lurched as they hit a pothole and he almost lost his footing a second time. What had he done wrong? He bent over the gun, checking the belt, and then he noticed the large rod-like lever sticking out of the body of the gun. One of the commanders he'd worked with in Viet Nam had kept an old-fashioned Thompson M1A1, the famous "Tommy Gun," and it had a smaller version of the same thing. The word "slide" came into his mind and without thinking he pulled back on the rod and felt the belt move up a notch. He stood over the gun again, lined up the yard-long barrel, and then downed the triggers.

It felt as though his arms were being torn out of their sockets. The gun jerked and bucked sending out a spitting stream of bullets, every sixth a tracer that left a wavering line of blinding white behind it. He bore down hard on the twin handles of the machine-gun, trying to keep the barrel pointing down the road, but it was almost impossible. Within thirty seconds he had sprayed 350 rounds down the road and the tip of the barrel was glowing a bright, cherry red. He tore his fingers off the triggers, the monstrous sound of the firing still ringing in his ears. He stared back along the road, looking for the lights. One pair of headlights was tilted up into the sky, which meant he'd probably done some damage, but there were still more, strung out in a line, at least six vehicles, by his count. NSS wasn't about to give up easily.

The truck lurched and swerved a third time and Philip lost his balance completely as Sarah, who had never driven anything much larger than her TR7 took the turnoff onto the old highway at full speed and in fourth gear. The Chevrolet pitched over sharply, almost lifting onto two wheels, coming out of the turn in a drunken fishtail that left Philip on the metal floor of the truck, his head smacking hard into the sharp edge of the wheel-well cover. He screamed as the metal tore into his scalp, and he rolled away, bouncing off Heather, then climbed into a crouch as Sarah regained control of the truck. He got to his feet and grasped the handles of the Browning again. With blood from his head streaming down over his face he looked back and saw that the people chasing them had lost at least another few hundred yards. Their margin was increasing.

Too late he realized that Sarah had no idea of what he was planning. He dropped his hands from the gun and turned toward the front of the truck, hauling himself forward using the protruding side panel struts to hang onto. He put one knee up onto the radio box just as the hummock where he'd hidden the car streamed past, no more than a deeper shadow in the darkness.

"Shit!" he said, slamming his fist down onto the rear of the seat.

Sarah turned, startled. "What's the matter?" she called out, her words torn away by the wind.

"Nothing!" he yelled back. "Just keep your foot on the gas." He stumbled back to the gun and pulled it around to the rear again, determined to keep the hounds on their heels at bay as long as he possibly could.

The lights were gone. He peered into the night, wondering if his eyes were giving out, and swept a hand across his brow, pushing back the trickles of blood. Still nothing. Either they'd doused their headlights or they were no longer chasing them.

He reached out, grabbed the side panel closest to him, and made his way back to the tailgate. He looked again. No lights, no dark shapes on the road close behind. No bullets. They were alone on the highway. There was no doubt. They'd given up the chase. He sank down onto the floor of the truck and let his head rest against the bouncing edge of the tailgate, exhausted.

He gave himself five minutes, then checked the road again. Empty. He dragged himself forward to the back of the seat.

"There's a crossroad in a couple of miles," he yelled, leaning over Sarah's shoulder. "Hang a left."

"You sure you don't want to drive?" asked Sarah.

Philip shook his head. "I'm going to stay back here for a while yet. It looks like we're okay, but you never know."

"That's putting it mildly," she grunted.

They continued on to the turnoff and headed south on 361. Philip vaguely remembered a telephone booth beside Harky's Cheap Gas. It was time to call in reinforcements; he'd had enough of playing Zorro to last him a lifetime. He was fairly sure that the people at Pilot Peak had decided that discretion was the order of the day and that shooting up trucks on the highway was no way to keep a low profile. The area was virtually uninhabited, but there was always a chance of another car being on the road. He also had a pretty good idea that NSS wasn't about to give up that easily either. The faster he called the cops the better.

By the time they'd come within a couple of miles of Yucca Wells the moon had come up over the horizon, coating the demi-ghost town in a pale silver sheen. Philip breathed a deep sigh of relief and started for the front of the truck again. The U.S. Cavalry was only a phone call away.

As he reached the seat the road ahead suddenly burst into brilliant light, blinding him and making Sarah involuntarily jerk the wheel around. She lifted her foot off the gas and the deep throb of the old flathead six-engine dropped. Another sound superseded it, a yammering stutter followed by the same insect buzzes that had signified fire from the NSS chase vehicles. They were being fired on. Sarah stood on the brakes and the truck swerved into a spinning drift, throwing Philip back onto the floor of the truck. He clawed his way up the pintle mount, grabbed the handles of the Browning, and turned it toward the light, his fingers jerking down on the triggers. The heavy gun whipped out of his grasp as Sarah rammed the truck back into gear and floored it again, jerking the truck off the road and onto the soft shoulder. Philip found the handles again and turned the gun until it was pointing over the silhouette of Sarah's head, black against the burning light ahead. He had a brief strobed image of a huge, fat man carrying some kind of weapon, no more than a hundred feet ahead, and then he hit the triggers again, concentrating on taking out the light. There was a splintering explosion and then the spotlight Harky had mounted on his pick-up truck disintegrated and Philip swung the gun around as they roared past, half on the shoulder and half on the road. He walked the Browning around in a sweeping arc, watching as the tracers bit into the cab of the pick-up and then found Harky himself, the huge chunks of lead ripping into the man's belly, chest, and head, pieces of flesh flying in all directions, the already dead remains of the fat man spinning and jerking in a dance more horrifying than Edgar Allan Poe could have conceived in his most tortured nightmares. Then Yucca Wells was gone and they were alone in the desert once again.

Chapter Seventeen

They reached the outskirts of Reno at 4:00 in the morning, just as the truck was running out of gas. Philip had managed to remove the Browning from the pintle mount en route, and they'd thrown it, the hunting knife, and the seat-mounted carbines into a ditch halfway along Walker Lake. Even without the weaponry the truck was conspicuous, so they parked it beside a wrecking yard on McCarran Boulevard while Sarah went to a telephone booth and phoned a cab. While she went into Reno to rent a car Philip slept in the truck, wondering how long it would be before a curious cop pulled over to check out the bizarre vehicle.

Sarah returned at dawn, driving a huge, jet-black Lincoln – the first car she'd found for rent. They managed to get Heather into the spacious back seat and then they drove to the Holiday Hotel. Leaving Heather asleep in the Lincoln, Sarah and Philip went to their rooms, showered and changed, then checked out. Reno being the kind of town it is, no one paid any attention to the fact that Philip was dressed in a filthy camouflage coverall and Sarah looked as though she'd slept in her clothes for a week. An hour after arriving Philip was behind the wheel driving them out of Reno toward Interstate 80 and San Francisco, Heather comatose in the back seat, and Sarah dozing beside him.

San Francisco seemed like the only logical place to hide out while they made plans. Sarah had told him about her conversation with Freeman and the implications were clear: NSS and the Tenth Crusade were setting him up to take the fall for the kidnapping of Heather and the murder of Janet Margolis in Toronto. Both were capital crimes which meant he'd have the FBI after him as well as the Royal Canadian Mounted Police in Canada. And that wasn't even taking into account little things like derelict rental cars, stolen station-wagons, breaking and entering, and killing two people the night before. If he'd ever had a chance of convincing the authorities that something was terribly wrong at the Tenth Crusade and NSS it was long gone now. He'd moved into the Charlie Manson class of criminal now, and he was scared. Like any animal being hunted his thought processes had shrunk to the immediate future. All he could think of was getting away from Reno as quickly as possible and finding a place to go to ground, and San Francisco was the nearest big city.

It took Philip slightly more than six hours to cover the 226 miles between Reno and San Francisco; he kept well within the speed limits and drove carefully, not wanting to attract any attention. Sarah slept fitfully for the entire journey, rousing herself finally as Philip guided the living-room sized car into the noon-hour traffic crossing the Oakland Bay Bridge.

He'd spent enough time in the city over the years to know roughly where he was going and after three quarters of an hour twisting and turning through the maze of one-way streets, steep hills, and main drags, he found the Civic Center on Van Ness. While he stayed with Heather in the car, Sarah went to look for some kind of accommodation. She came back half an hour later with a bag of sandwiches, a quart of milk, and an address. According to her the tourist office was swamped since it was high season, and there were almost no hotel rooms available, but they'd managed to come up with the name and address of a woman who rented out bungalows to tourist families by the week. Sarah had jumped on it, making a quick judgment that a private house would be better than a room or a suite in a hotel. She'd phoned the woman from the tourist bureau and reserved the bungalow sight unseen. They ate the sandwiches and drank the milk on the drive across town, reaching the address just after 2:00 in the afternoon.

The bungalow was located on Greenwich Street on the eastern flank of Telegraph Hill in an area that looked like a transplanted Cape Cod resort. Because the hill was so steep the locals had installed wooden step-sidewalks down the slope, the boardwalk effect matching the pastel wood houses and the picket-fenced gardens. The woman was waiting at the rental bungalow when they arrived and rather than try to explain Heather's strange condition Philip dropped Sarah off telling her to tell the landlady that he had some errands to run. He gave Sarah twenty minutes and then went back. When he returned he found Sarah busily airing out the small two-bedroom cottage and making tea. They managed to get Heather into the house without attracting any attention, and put her in the rear bedroom.

"You finish making the tea," said Philip. "I'll get her into bed."

Sarah looked at him curiously, gave a little nod, then left the room. Philip began stripping Heather's filthy clothes off. Underneath the soiled skirt and blouse she was wearing a plain white cotton bra and matching underpants, and though he'd seen her naked a thousand times he felt strangely shy about taking them off. He could hear the kettle boiling in the kitchen and he found himself thinking about Sarah, oddly embarrassed that he was in the bedroom with Heather while she was nearby.

But, too tired and confused to make any sense of what he was feeling, Philip left the underclothing on and gently drew the sheet up over Heather. Then he went back to the kitchen and joined Sarah. The kitchen was small, no more than an ante-room to the larger dining area. A small window looked out across the city over the rooftops of the houses down the hill, the bright sun glinting off their brightly colored exteriors. He sat down at the formica-topped dinette table and Sarah put a cup of tea in front of him. He added milk from the unfinished quart Sarah had bought and sipped the hot drink gratefully. His body felt like lead and he had to fight to keep his eyes open. He stared at her blearily over the rim of his cup, struck by how attractive she looked and even in his exhausted state he felt a twinge of arousal.

The hard traveling and harder time she'd spent at Pilot Peak had worn the primness off her. Her mouth, instead of being set so firmly and tightly, had loosened into a wide, sensuous curve, and the dark shadows of fatigue around her eyes had softened enough so that they set off the pale blue of her eyes. Her posture had changed as well; instead of sitting like a very proper lady she sat on the chair opposite, one leg tucked up under her thigh, her elbows resting on the shining brown surface of the table as she worked at the tea. If she'd change the dumpy style of her clothes and her hairdo she'd have the potential of being quite pretty. He resisted an urge to reach across and pull the pins now barely holding up her long auburn hair, and took another swallow of tea instead.

"You're looking pretty good considering everything you've been through over the past few days," he said.

She flushed slightly and stared down into her cup intently, as though she was trying to read their future in the dregs. "Thanks," she mumbled finally. Philip watched as her small fingers played with the fluted edge of the saucer. She had delicate hands, almost as small as a child's, the nails short and without color. The movements she was making were gentle and sensitive and Philip found himself wondering what her touching him would feel like. He blinked, confused by his train of thought. He'd gone through hell finding and rescuing Heather and here he was getting turned on by someone who was almost a total stranger. In the bedroom, undressing Heather he'd looked at her body and what had he felt? Certainly not lust ... love? Or was the sad ache he felt looking down at her simply the lonely realization that the clock couldn't be turned back and that the woman on the bed was no longer the Heather he'd loved and made love with in Paris. Inadvertently he groaned aloud.

"What's the matter?" asked Sarah, concerned.

He shook his head. "Nothing. It's all catching up to me, I guess. I'm not used to being a fugitive from justice."

"Why don't you sleep then," said Sarah. "The beds are all made up, or you could sleep on the couch or you could ... you could sleep anywhere you wanted to." The words came out in a rush and she flushed again.

"I think maybe the couch," he said, standing. He swayed, holding onto the back of the chrome and plastic chair for support. "Thanks for the tea, Sarah," he said, and smiled.

"You're welcome, Philip," she answered, her voice quiet. His smile turned into a grin and she looked at him angrily.

"What's so funny?" she asked.

"Nothing," he said soothingly. "It's just that you've only called me Philip once since we met. We're making progress."

"Go to hell," she said, but she was smiling through the blush on her cheeks. Philip gave her a little wave and then headed for the couch in the living room at the front of the bungalow.

*   *   *

The vertigo of her thoughts had ceased, replaced by splinters of real time interspersed among the ragged trails of memory. Heather was sure that she had been in a car, with Philip, but of course that was impossible. She was an instrument of the Lord now, and Philip was anathema to His will. Her body, feeling the comfort of cool sheets, relaxed, but her mind continued on, searching through the labyrinth of questions, searching endlessly for an answer....

She sat back with her back against the trunk of a heavy-boughed oak in the small Boston cemetery, her eyes closed, oblivious to the incessant mutter of the city around her. When she breathed she could smell grass and rich earth, and if she kept her eyes shut she could imagine that she was somewhere else, somewhere she wanted to be.

It was as though she'd traveled in a huge circle through a dozen years and, sitting there, her mind wandering, she wondered perhaps if growing old meant taking a very long and complicated route home again.

Heather Foxcroft opened her eyes and looked at the worn headstones scattered around her, trying to imagine herself among them, peaceful and silent. Death was so close to her in the graveyard she could almost feel herself sinking into the ground, seeking it, wanting it.

A movement caught her eye and she turned. A young man

had stepped out through the French doors of his office onto the tarred roof of a lower section of the building with its rear facing the cemetery. He stood, looking into the graveyard, looking at her, smoking a cigarette and enjoying the early summer breeze. He was dressed in a three-piece suit that might have been tweed. Back Bay born and raised and every inch a Harvard man.

She might have married a man like that once. If her father had had anything to say about it. Or maybe she would have tried to please him even more and married an Annapolis boy, living the life of a Navy wife. It could have been that way. Maybe it *should* have been that way.

The man on his informal balcony returned to his office, turning his back on her and the spell of what might have been was broken. She stood up, the pain in her lower back swelling to a burning lance that seemed to tear up through her spine. She adjusted the folds of her habit and walked down the sloping path that wound through the headstones to the street. She stopped for a moment at the sign on the low wrought-iron fence: THE GRANARY BURIAL GROUND. Then she turned and walked up the gentle grade to Park Street and Boston Common.

She crossed the park and went into the Common, her sandals smacking the asphalt paving in a slow rhythm. Frisbees and dogs, old men on benches, a kite flying high over the pale green grass, the glint of the gold dome on the State House across the way on Beacon Street. Hundreds of people enjoying the early afternoon. All of it so familiar it almost didn't register. But it did, just, and hurt deeply, because it didn't belong to her any more, and the memories were safer than the reality. She wanted pain and work and the mindless joy of Mother Teresa's God. Not reminders of her past which led in turn to Philip and all the rest.

As Heather went past one of the benches close to the path a young woman with a small bag on her lap stood up quickly, as though startled, and the bag fell to the ground. Dozens of rolls of coins spun out onto the asphalt and Heather automatically stopped, knelt down, and helped the woman gather them again.

"Thanks," said the woman. "There was a bee or something. I thought I was going to get stung. Are you a nun?"

The question was straightforward and innocent. Heather nodded. "Yes I'm with the Sisters of Charity."

"Mother Teresa," said the woman, bobbing her head. "I've heard of their good work. You must be very happy to be doing the Lord's work under her guidance."

"Yes," said Heather, slightly taken aback. The woman she was talking to looked to be in her late twenties, with brown hair cut short and wearing a blue pleated skirt and a white blouse. Heather knew that some orders had very loose dress codes and wondered if the girl was a nun herself. She asked and the woman laughed.

"No," she answered. "Not a nun. But I work for Christ too. I'm with the Tenth Crusade here in Boston."

The approach had been smooth, controlled, and accurate.

"The Tenth Crusade?" asked Heather. And that was how it began.

She was willing to do almost anything to get out of Boston, which she had thought would feel to her like home, and the prospect of spending time with her father in Washington was horrifying. She agreed immediately to the woman's offer of a weekend in the country at the Crusade's farm in Lexington, Massachusetts.

She spent the next few days after her return to Boston in a half-trance state, her mind whirling with the implications of the weekend. Here was a group that worked for God, and yet did so using the best of their talents, rather than like dray horses, yet at the same time loved and worshipped Christ with the same zeal she felt herself. The years she'd spent with Mother Teresa began increasingly to fade and she found her thoughts returning to the Tenth Crusade. When she went to visit Janet Margolis, she had the address of the Toronto Crusade headquarters. She was quietly sure that she had reached a turning point in her life....

*   *   *

Philip slept until the early evening. He awoke quickly, sitting up and listening, muscles tense. Then he realized where he was and relaxed. He stood up and walked to the small picture window that looked down Telegraph Hill. The setting sun was at his back but there was enough light left to splash down on the stepped houses below him, turning them into a glowing patchwork of colored light. Beyond them the city was sinking into evening, dark shadows sweeping down from Coit Tower across Pioneer Park. Between the park and the foot of Telegraph Hill he could look down into North Beach and he could almost taste the fresh cannolis and the panettone, a round sweet bread filled with raisins and candied fruit that he'd fallen in love with while doing a story on the Italian-Mexican-Basque neighborhood. Memories of other days, he thought, before all this went down.

He turned away from the window, frowning. He could hear voices, speaking softly. He went back through the living room and dining room, pausing at the small kitchen alcove. Sarah wasn't there, but there were several large shopping bags on the counter. Obviously she'd been out.

The voices were coming from the back bedroom. He made his way down the dim hall to the rear of the house and paused, listening at the door to Heather's room. He could hear Sarah, her voice low and soothing. He cracked open the door and peeked inside. The lights were off in the room, the only light coming from the curtained window on the right. Sarah was sitting by the bed and he could see the blink of the battery light on a cassette tape recorder. Sarah looked up as he poked his head into the room. She raised a finger to her lips, motioning for silence, and stood up carefully, like a mother rising from a sleeping child. She tiptoed toward the door and Philip stood back as she left the room. She closed the door tightly and went back down the hall, Philip following. She went into the kitchen and sat down on one of the chairs, letting out a deep sigh. She hit the stop button on the recorder and placed the small black-cased machine on the table in front of her.

"What were you doing in there, and where'd that machine come from?" whispered Philip.

"She started to come out of it about an hour after you fell asleep," answered Sarah, speaking quietly. "That coma or whatever it was. I went in to check on her, and I could tell her breathing had changed; it was more like ordinary sleep. Then she started talking."

"She was doing that before," said Philip.

"Not like this. She was making sense, or at least she wasn't doing that weird chanting. I started picking up words, names. Important ones. So I went out, bought a tape machine at an audio place I saw on the corner, and picked up some food for later."

Philip shifted uneasily in his chair and frowned; there was something almost obscene about recording Heather talking in her sleep.

"I don't know if you should have done that," he said. "I don't think it's ... I don't know, right. And what did you hope to gain?"

"We don't have any choice," answered Sarah. "We've run out of leads to follow and somehow I think we're running out of time as well. Whatever she has in her head that can help us, we need."

Philip shook his head. "I don't buy that," he said. "Heather is an innocent victim of all this. Someone who was mentally vulnerable in the first place. They recruited her and I think something must have just snapped in her head."

"And I don't buy *that*," answered Sarah. "She's more than just another person blissed out by a cult group. In the first place I've never heard of a cult group forcibly taking someone back into the fold the way they took Heather from your place in New York and, second, why was she being held at the NSS place? No, Philip, your lady friend is someone special to the Crusade. And important. I didn't tell you this before, but Freeman as much as admitted that the Crusade had been blackmailing my father. He said my father was ... was .... " She stopped, her voice breaking.

Philip reached out across the table and touched her hand. "You don't have to tell me," he said softly.

Sarah shook her head, fighting back tears. "No, it's okay," she managed. She took a deep breath and went on. "Freeman said my father was a homosexual. Gay. I don't think I believe him, but he had *something* on dad. Maybe it's the same with

Heather. You said her father was a General."

"Joint Chiefs," said Philip, nodding. "Chairman of the Defense Appropriations Committee."

"And my father was a senator, on half a dozen different committees, including a Senate investigating committee looking into the possibility of taxing parachurch businesses. Maybe the Crusade is, or was, using Heather as leverage against her father."

"It's insane, magnificently insane," muttered Philip. He patted his shirt, wanting a cigarette badly.

"I bought you some," said Sarah. She stood and went to the bags on the counter and pulled out a package of cigarettes and a packet of matches. She slid them across the table to Philip and sat down again. They were Chesterfields. He lit one and dragged deeply and sent out a long plume of smoke. Sarah grimaced.

"You're marvelous," said Philip, dragging again.

"I'm a masochist," grunted Sarah. "Anyway, you were saying?"

"It means the Crusade is blackmailing on a gigantic scale. And doing it systematically."

"Lobbying taken to its ultimate conclusion. These people think they're working under some kind of divine law that supersedes any others, so blackmailing would be nothing more than a means to an end."

"The logistics must be incredible!" said Philip. "Most of the information they gathered would be useless unless they could correlate it to something else. You'd have to have a cross-index system."

"They've got the facilities for that, if you tie in Charles Todd."

"The fundraiser you told me about? The one who works for Billy Carstairs and the America Awake people?"

"That's him," said Sarah grimly. "I read a news story that said he had more than three hundred thousand names on his mailing lists. That's a pretty good data base for cross-comparison. Not to mention the fact that Carstairs and the Crusade both work on local and State levels as well. They've probably got information dossiers on everybody in public office from mayors and assemblymen right up to State senators. Do your homework well enough and spend enough money and you could come up with enough leverage to sway the entire country if you wanted to."

"And money would be no object, not with Keller Pharmaceuticals and Eagle One behind you. Christ! It's diabolical!"

"It's old-fashioned pork barrel politics," said Sarah, her face barely visible in the rapidly fading light. "It's what most of these people are used to. Billy Carstairs was born and raised on it. So were most of the other New Right types: Jesse Helms, Phyllis Schlafly, Joe Coors, Falwell. To them it's as American as apple pie. The up and comers like Dolan and Viguerie are just refining the old techniques, upgrading them. And now it looks like Todd and Carstairs and all the rest have taken it that one step further."

"And what about the guns?" said Philip. "What about that arsenal I found at Ragged Mountain, and the NSS set-up at Pilot Peak? What the hell does that mean?"

"I don't even want to *think* about that," said Sarah. "The Crusade and NSS are about as extreme right as you can get. That puts them out in crazyland with the white supremacy groups—the Klan, Minutemen, Rockwell's Nazis. Give a fringe group enough money and power and they aren't a fringe group anymore. Hitler was nothing until he got I.G. Farben and the others behind him. And those big businesses never thought twice about the law either. Boeing was making airliners in Seattle for Lufthansa that could be turned into Condor bombers by sealing up the windows, and I.T. and T. was doing military work for Germany long after Pearl Harbor."

"Money and power," said Philip.

"That's it."

There was a long silence. The light in the small room was almost completely gone. For a moment Philip felt as though he was a helpless spectator watching the world end. When the sun set it would be for the last time. The Dark Ages, Tenth Crusade style.

"Hitler all over again," he said. "Surely it can't happen."

"Yes it can," said Sarah. "Listen to the tape." She rewound

the tape and then pressed the start button. There was a hollow hissing sound and then Heather's words tumbled into the air, jumbled and sometimes meaningless, but with enough sense in them to send a chill down Philip's spine as he listened in the deep-shadowed room on Telegraph Hill.

"Whoever refuses to confess that Jesus Christ is come in the flesh is antichrist and blessed ... is the nation whose God is the Lord.... No, I can't, no.... It's all in Todd's book. Jericho. It will be Jericho.... Blessed are the dead who die in the Lord from henceforth...their works do follow them and no greater sacrifice can be made. I want...Philip, I want.... Jericho *will* come! The promise was made and the Lord's instrument will be purged of sin and yes, yes, all power on earth is given unto me. I will be Jericho! Todd's book says it.... Daddy why did you, why did you, did you do what they said you did ...they told me about you, Philip, they told me that the sin, the sin had to be purged. Die! We are nothing unless we can die, all of us, die for Christ! Fight for Christ! The scripture gives us the way and Todd's book. Todd's book. Why did they do this to me, why did they make me, make me? No! I can't do that. Don't! Don't do that! Philip! Deep. So deep. I want it to be deep. PHILIP!"

It went on that way, for both sides of the tape, ninety minutes in all. When the tape was over they sat in the darkness together without speaking, the silence and the shadows making the terrible litany seem unreal. When he spoke at last Philip had to swallow hard, and even then there was no way he could keep the tremor out of his voice.

"So ... what do you get from all that?" He lit a cigarette, the match flaring and then dying, bringing back the night.

"She mentions Todd, or Todd's book, dozens of times. She used the name of Billy, too. Presumably she means Billy Carstairs. I think, uh, I don't know how to say it, but it sounded to me as if she'd been raped or tortured. When she mentions you it's almost as though she's calling out for you to save her or something. I'm sorry, but–"

"Forget it," said Philip. He took a deep shuddering breath. "Christ! What did they do to her?"

"You could call it a lot of things," said Sarah, an ice-cold thread of anger in her voice. "Technically I think it's called 'behavior modification.' And a long way from a Skinner Box or rats in a maze. While I was taping what she was saying I ... checked her over a bit. She's got puncture bruises on the inside of her elbows and behind her knees, which probably means drugs. She'd ... she'd also urinated while I was out, so I kind of rolled her over and changed her underwear. I, um—"

"What?" said Philip.

"I noticed she was pretty torn up ... down there. Vagina and rectum both. I—"

"Aww, Jesus!" moaned Philip. He pushed himself away from the table, the chrome chair falling backwards. He went to the window and stared out at the firefly lights of the city. He began to cry, hot tears rolling down his cheeks. He swayed and reached out to hang onto the window frame, leaning his forehead against the glass. His whole body shook violently as a stunning, overwhelming rush of fury tore through him.

Through the anger he felt a soft touch and turned away from the window. Sarah stood beside him, one hand making small circles on his back. He groaned, still crying, and put his arms around her, pulling her close, feeling her body pressed against his, her cheek on his chest.

"We'll get the bastards, Philip. They'll pay," she whispered.

Chapter Eighteen

Philip and Sarah went through the tape of Heather's ramb-lings again and again that night, trying to establish some kind of pattern or overall meaning. By midnight they'd come to the same conclusion: the trail which had begun with the stolen garbage in Barrington, New York, now pointed toward Wash-ington, D.C. and Charles Todd. By Sarah's count Todd's name appeared on the tape a total of seventeen times, almost invari-ably in the phrase "Todd's book." Carstairs' name came a close second at fourteen occurrences. The name "Jericho" cropped up more than either of them—a total of twenty-four times. From what the two could piece together, Todd and his book and Carstairs were tied to Jericho, possibly a code name of some kind.

"Joshua fit the battle of Jericho," said Sarah, listening to the tape again.

"And the walls came tumbling down," finished Philip. "I don't know, Sarah, maybe it's all just babbling. Maybe none of this means anything at all."

"I said it before, it's all we've got. Heather has been savaged by these people, and they didn't do that to her without some reason."

"It's all so pat," said Philip. "Right from the start it's all been too easy. Like a trail of breadcrumbs. One thing leading to another. Take out the melodrama, the window dressing, and it's a pretty easy trail to follow. Now this. It's as though they let us have Heather, knowing that she'd come out of it. We hit a dead end and, presto! we get a new lead, something to take us a bit further on. Goddamn it, we're being led around like a donkey with a carrot in front of its nose!"

"What difference does it make?" asked Sarah. "We can't go back, so we have to go forward, even if it's along some kind of prearranged path. Face it, Philip, we don't have any choice."

"I suppose you're right."

"So what do we do next?"

"We find out just what Todd's book is," said Philip. "Which means we go to Washington."

"We can't go together," said Sarah, rubbing the back of her neck and yawning. "The authorities and the Crusade will be looking for you and Heather together."

"I've already thought of that," answered Philip. He lit a cigarette and went to the kitchen window. He felt a surge of emotion come over him in a wave but he held it in check, telling himself that it was Heather who had suffered, not him. He turned and looked at Sarah, her face pale in the weak light from the overhead fixture.

"Didn't you mention something about your grandmother having some kind of summer place close to D.C.?" he asked. "We were on the plane to Denver."

"The Fredericksburg camp," said Sarah, nodding. "It's not really in Fredericksburg, but that's the closest town. It's on the Potomac. It was granddad's hunting lodge."

"Could you get into it, if you wanted?" asked Philip.

Sarah shrugged. "I suppose so. They always left the key with Dan Hocker in Fredericksburg. Hocker Realty. He took care of maintenance and things like that."

"I want you to go there. Take Heather there and stay with her. I think the Crusade people would do just about anything to get her back, and you as well."

"What about you?" asked Sarah, frowning. "You've got the FBI to worry about as well."

"I'll go after Todd. Like you said, he's all we have to go on now. Either I come up trumps with him or I might as well cut my own throat. We've got to get some hard evidence against the Crusade, or any of them, before we can go to the authorities or even the press."

"Why don't we just lie low here," said Sarah. "If you try to get at Todd it would be like going from the frying pan into the fire."

"We can't risk the time," answered Philip. He came back to the table and sat down, butting his cigarette into the saucer. "Carstairs is riding high on this Devil's Brigade thing. I was listening to the radio while we were driving down from Reno. He's called for a big rally in Washington on Monday. I've got a sneaking suspicion things might get violent. Those guns I saw at Ragged Mountain and at Pilot Peak weren't for looks. If we can get something concrete on Carstairs and the others before then maybe we can nail them to the wall and get out from under all this. And I want to get Heather some professional help, quickly. We can't give it to her here."

"Okay," said Sarah grudgingly. "I babysit Heather while you go into Washington. Then what?"

"If and when I get something, I'll get in touch with you at the Fredericksburg place and you'll bring Heather into D.C."

"Why don't we reverse it?" asked Sarah. "You stay with Heather at Fredericksburg and I'll do the investigating. It's my hometown after all. I've got better contacts there than you do."

"Sure," said Philip. "That's just the point. The Crusade knows it's your turf too. They'll be looking for you. It's the obvious place for you to go to ground. Not to mention that having me and Heather at your grandmother's place might attract too much attention. If we were going to do it that way at all you'd have to go to Fredericksburg, explain things to this real estate man, and then go back to D.C. Frankly we can't afford the time."

"All right," said Sarah. "You've made your case. When do we leave?"

"Tomorrow. Separate flights. I'll give a false name and wear dark glasses or something. You can take Heather with you in a wheelchair. Tell them she's your sick sister. It's dangerous to use my Amex card at this point so you'll have to use yours to get me some cash—for a ticket, and expenses—before we split up. And the phone number of your grandmother's place. There is a phone, I hope."

"There's a phone," said Sarah. "It's on 'quiet service.' Pay as you go, but it works, and I want you to use it."

"What do you mean?"

"I'm not going to sit out in the bush waiting for you to 'come up trumps,' as you put it. I want you to check in with a call every four hours. Miss a call and I go to the police and tell them the whole story. To hell with the consequences."

Philip thought for a moment and then nodded. She was right; there had to be some kind of fail-safe, a back up in case things went wrong. Even if the police didn't believe her, he stood a slightly better chance against the FBI than he did against the Crusade.

"Okay," he said finally. "If we get morning flights that will put me into D.C. some time around the middle of the afternoon, Washington time. You'll need a couple of hours at least to get to Fredericksburg. Let's say I make my first call at midnight."

"Fine," said Sarah. "I'll get us some seats."

* * *

Philip's flight landed at Washington National Airport at 4:50 in the afternoon. It was high summer, and, this being Sunday, central Washington was deserted except for roving bands of tourists intent on taking in one more monument before checking out the roller skating waiters at La Niçoise on Wisconsin Avenue.

The flight had been uneventful except for a few nauseatingly anxious moments at San Francisco International. Sarah and Heather had taken the Lincoln and Philip had gone in a taxi and when he arrived he found the place swarming with security guards toting M16s and at least three SWAT teams complete with sniffer dogs. His first urge was to run like hell, but after a few moments he realized that neither he nor Sarah and Heather were the objects of the high-profile security measures.

According to the man at the smoke shop where he'd ducked in for a new pair of sunglasses—the extent of his disguise—the police had been out in force for almost a week, checking out a continuous stream of threats from the Devil's Brigade. The scuttlebutt from pilots who came in and out of his store was that the same kind of thing was going on all over the country, so Philip wasn't surprised when he found that Washington International was on an alert basis as well. Even so, he didn't relax until his cab was across the Francis Scott Key Bridge and heading into Georgetown.

Having checked in a phone book at the airport he came up with two addresses for Charles Todd: Charles Todd Consultants on South Capitol, and his home address on P Street. Somehow he was sure that Todd wouldn't keep anything relevant to the Crusade at his office, so he decided that his best chance would be to get into Todd's Georgetown residence.

The taxi dropped him at the Georgetown Inn on Wisconsin. After checking in he went up to his room, where he took a long and relaxing bath. He dressed, left the hotel and headed down M Street, Georgetown's main shopping drag. He eventually found an open restaurant and went in for the first good meal he'd had in a week. By the time he was finished it was almost 8:00. He went back to his room, and lay down on the large, comfortable bed to think things through while he waited for the night.

As he lay naked, the cool breeze from the air conditioner fanning over him, he realized that for a hardened criminal he was pretty naive about how to break into somebody's house. Except for the fiasco at Barrington, the closest he'd ever come to break and entry work was a photo story for *People* magazine about a famous jewel thief who'd written his autobiography and had a bit part in the movie based on it. That and old "Naked City" reruns were his only sources of inspiration.

The jewel thief, whose name inevitably was Doc something or other, had said that of all the attributes a good thief should have to succeed, cowardice was the most useful. The whole idea was to minimize the risk right from the beginning. If you couldn't get the risk factor below an acceptable level, then dump out the whole idea. If you did proceed, the crime should be committed with care that approached paranoia. Doc never did a job unless he was sure the occupants would be gone for a minimum of thirty days, the burglar alarm was ten years out of date, and that there wasn't the slightest possibility of a dog being on the premises. Dogs, he said, were the worst, and he'd dropped his pants on the spot, showing off a puncture scar on his left buttock that had come from a miniature poodle with fangs like a piranha. *People* had declined to use the shot of the thief's rear end, but the story had stuck in Philip's mind.

He decided that he wasn't in a position to ask for too low a risk factor. If Todd didn't answer his telephone after twenty rings Philip would assume that he was out for the evening. Other than that he would have to fly blind. He had no idea if Todd had a burglar alarm, but he'd have to risk it. If Todd kept a dog he'd defend himself with the only weapon in his possession—the ornamental letter opener he'd found in the hotel room desk.

"Real forward thinker you are," he said to himself as he lay smoking in the darkened room.

Presumably anything useful at Todd's place would be on a computer tape somewhere, and if Todd was the computer whiz he'd been made out, it stood to reason that the man would have a terminal in his home, linked to the ones in his Capitol Hill offices. That in turn meant codes, bypasses, entry keys, and all the rest of it. Philip knew enough about computers to play Alien Blitz on a VIC-20 and to operate a VDT unit in a magazine or newspaper office, but that was it.

The whole idea of breaking into Todd's was beginning to seem more and more ridiculous, not to mention risky. Doc's second cardinal rule was time. In and out with the minimum expenditure of that precious commodity. In forty years of rifling the boudoir bureaus of his "benefactors," Doc said he'd never dallied longer than fifteen minutes. That was his break point, even if he *knew* beyond a shadow of a doubt that the owners were five thousand miles away.

Philip sighed, butted his cigarette, and lit a fresh one. He stood and walked naked to the window. He smoked, watching the trickle of evening traffic moving down Wisconsin Avenue from the suburbs of Burleith and Glover Park.

The whole idea was insane. Breaking into Todd's house was grasping at straws. Even if he didn't get caught the chances of actually finding anything were minimal. The break-in would simply compound the crimes he'd already committed.

But he had to do *something*. In the beginning his involvement had been totally personal; all he wanted to do was find Heather and make sure she was all right. The psychiatry of *why* he felt so obligated was irrelevant. But it had gone beyond that, first because of his involvement with Sarah and the death of her father, and now because he sensed that the Crusade was involved in a plan of monstrous proportions. Sarah was right, he was sure of that now.

The Crusade was a bunch of roving, redneck zealots who used Christ as a banner to carry through their multiple frustrations. Have-nots who wanted to have, xenophobes who wanted to strike out blindly and viciously at anything or anyone who saw the world in any other way than themselves. Germany after Versailles, the Depression, and massive unemployment, the United States after Viet Nam, Watergate, and the Iran hostages. The fury of impotence.

"Bullshit," said Philip aloud. And he knew it was. He didn't give a good goddamn about the psychology of it all. They'd hurt someone he cared for, they were trying to hurt him, and he wanted revenge. Pure and simple, and the most dangerous of all motivations. Sarah had said it the night before: "Get the bastards."

He looked at his watch. It was 10:30.

He called Todd's number, listening to the echoing jingle and not sure if he wanted it to end or not. He let the phone ring twenty times and then he hung up. Ten minutes later he was on Wisconsin Avenue heading north toward P Street.

*　*　*

Sarah guided the rental compact down the twisting roads that led from Fredericksburg to the Potomac Tidewater shore, every passing farm and stand of trees bringing back memories of her childhood and summers spent with her grandmother. The house itself was located on a thumb-shaped inlet a few miles upriver from Fairview Beach and for Sarah it had been a place of slow dreaming and expectation. Each summer from the age of six to her adolescence she'd wanted to be something different, from ballet dancer to botanist, and the sixty-five acres of the estate had given her the world to make her fantasies come true, at least for a few bright weeks. She'd worn a makeshift tu-tu and gone spinning through the cool mosses of the birch dells on the property, played Huck Finn with her cousins along the bullrush shore, examined flowers, caterpillars and dew worms with a microscope her father had given her for Christmas, and read *Anne of Green Gables* in her small lofted room on the third floor of the house, wishing that she had red hair and freckles too. When she tried to make a pattern of her childhood, Fox Run, her grandmother's name for the place, provided the connecting thread of memory.

Beside her on the seat, Heather stirred, mumbling something unintelligible in her uneasy sleep. Sarah reached out and gently pushed back a few strands of hair that had fallen across the woman's face.

Even after all she'd been through, Heather was clearly still a very beautiful woman and Sarah felt a brief twinge of resentment. She looked away and concentrated on her driving. Around her, the rolling hills and woodlots were lowering as they came closer to the Potomac shore. Another ten miles and they'd be home free. Sarah glanced at Heather again and smiled sadly, wondering what it would be like to have memories like hers, to remember the strange places and stranger people, seen not as a tourist from the window of a train, but as a traveler, with the heat on her face and the dust of miles on her feet.

Beside her, Heather made waking sounds again and Sarah frowned, biting at her lip as she drove. Ever since they'd landed at Dulles, Heather had been showing signs of coming out of it. Thankfully she'd been virtually comatose for the whole flight; having a person who'd been as traumatized as Heather wake up in the rear seat of a Jumbo halfway across the country could have been dangerous and embarrassing. Even having her come back to life at Fox Run could be a problem. She was hardly equipped to deal with someone in Heather's condition, and it was a long way to the nearest hospital. Sarah began to wonder if bringing her out into the country was such a good idea after all.

Heather was still sleeping when she made the turn off to Fox Run. She took the car carefully down the mile-long dirt road that led to the property, the sides of the car brushing the overhanging branches of the closely planted ash and alder. The sound was familiar and comforting and Sarah began to relax. The property was isolated from its nearest neighbor by half a mile, its only link to civilization being the telephone. If she was going to be able to put the events of the past few days beind her, Fox Run was the place to do it.

The road widened suddenly and Sarah found herself on the circular drive that led around to the front of the high, two-storey white house, a scaled down version of Tara. The grass on the half-acre lawn was long and yellowed and the once carefully tended beds of hydrangeas and wild roses had been allowed to spread in a tangled riot. The fee paid to Hocker Realty by her father's estate for maintenance obviously didn't include landscaping. She drove around to the front of the house and parked.

Four tall, fluted pillars supported a deep portico shading the nine casement windows and double-doored entry, while above the gently sloping slate roof gleamed dully in the late afternoon sun. Except for the grass growing up between the bricks of the walk and the untrimmed lilacs planted around the porch it was exactly as Sarah remembered it.

She got out of the car, went around to Heather's side, and managed to get the woman out and on her feet. They walked slowly up the walk to the steps and when they reached the door Sarah supported Heather with one arm around her waist while she fitted the key into the lock. She pushed open the door and brought Heather inside.

The air was heavy and musky, the furniture in the dark, marble floor foyer was covered with ghostly dust clothes. A lump rose in Sarah's throat. As far as she knew no one beyond the caretaker had been inside the house since the summer, two years ago, when her grandmother had died.

Rather than deal with the winding spiral staircase Sarah managed to get Heather into the family room just beyond her grandfather's "summer office." The family room had once been what Grandmother called an orangerie, for some reason, but two generations of children had first transformed it into a large playroom, and when they were grown it had become a guest room, complete with a hide-a-bed and an ensuite bathroom.

She eased Heather onto the old battered couch, then covered her, using a light blanket she found in the room's large walk-in closet. When she was sure Heather was comfortable she left her and began going through all the rooms in the house, pulling off the dust covers and opening the windows.

There were seven rooms on the main floor, all clustered around the oval hub of the entry and the spiral staircase. At the front of the house, with windows looking down onto the sloping lawn, the screening trees, and the wide reaches of the river beyond were the "summer office," in reality an old-fashioned library, complete with dark wood paneling and floor-to-ceiling bookcases, and the large living room, filled with the heavy eighteenth-century British and American furniture her grandparents loved so well. The dining room led off the living room, separated from it by sliding doors that Sarah could never remember seeing closed. The furniture was much the same as that in the living room, and a full dozen upholstered chairs still stood around the massive cherry table. At the rear of the house, facing the entrance road and the dense screen of trees at the edge of the lawn were the kitchen, breakfast room, and laundry.

For some reason, Sarah had always thought of the second floor as being much younger than the first. The furniture in the large master bedroom-sitting room her grandparents had used was light, mostly wicker and bamboo, and the three other bedrooms were equally bright and airy. Finally, going up the last flight of the narrowing spiral staircase she reached the room that had once been hers, a small, slope-roofed area with two old-fashioned skylights set into the ceiling and a pulley-operated ladder that could be pulled down to give access to the captain's walk on the roof. On hot summer nights her father had sometimes allowed her to take a blanket and a pillow up into slightly cooler air outside, and she would lie there, staring up at the endless shoals of hard, bright stars in the black sky, waiting for the shining face of the moon, or if she was lucky the hair-thin trail of a comet. She allowed herself a brief moment in the room, letting the memories flood, and then, holding back the gentle wave of sadness she felt, she went back down to check in on Heather.

The sleeping woman had tossed off the blanket, and from all appearances it looked as though she would soon be waking. Her eyelids were fluttering, her lips were moving, and she was making small movements with her hands, the long, beautiful fingers jerking weakly like small, trapped birds. Sarah went back to the car, brought in the groceries she'd purchased in Fredericksburg and, after making herself a cup of tea, she went back to the family room and sat with Heather. And waited.

*　*　*

… She lay in the gray room, huddled on the small, filthy bed. The room was filled with the odor of sex, raw and thick like the perfume of a noxious plant. She could find no comfort in any thought or memory, because now there was no memory for her except the nightmare of the men who had taken her, again and again, filling her, tearing her, abusing her.

"Purification." That's what the voice had kept on saying. It was all to purify, for her sin was an endless one, a rustling fugitive in her soul that hid in dark corners and refused all but the severest exorcisms. Philip was the key, for he was the object of the sin, and her lust for him, her endless, clawing lust was the chancre that had to be removed.

Hence the purification. The removal of sin by the process of making the sin abhorrent. Sex again and again until her thighs ran with blood and she screamed for mercy.

And the voice kept its promise. A young, almost Christ-like face would swim into view. There would be an instant's pain so tiny in comparison with what had gone on before it was almost no pain at all. And then the rush of peace and sleep, and the soft voice that kept its promise, whispering quietly to her from out of a deep and comforting blackness.

"When lust hath conceived, it bringeth forth sin, and sin,

when it is finished, bringeth forth death. Do you know those words, Heather?"

"It ... it's from James."

"That's right, Heather. From James. From the scriptures. The Law, Heather, do you understand that?"

"Yes."

"And you want to obey the law, don't you, Heather?"

"Yes. But no more of pain please, oh God, please."

"The flesh lusteth against the spirit and the spirit against the flesh. Do you know that?"

"Yes."

"Do you believe that?"

"Yes."

"Would you rid yourself of lust, of sin?"

"Yes! Please, yes!"

"But you don't want the pain, is that right?"

"Yes! Stop the pain."

"Heather! Unto you it is given in the behalf of Christ not only to believe in him, but to suffer for his sake!"

"Yes!"

"Rejoice, Heather! Inasmuch as ye are partakers of Christ's sufferings that when his glory shall be revealed, ye may be glad with exceeding joy."

"Yes, please, yes!"

"Remember, Heather! Ye shall be hated of all men for my name's sake but he that endureth to the end *will* be saved! Do you believe that, Heather?"

"Yes!"

"Do you want that, Heather?"

"Yes!"

"Will you do anything for that, Heather?!"

"Yes! Yes! God, yes! I want—"

"Then listen to me, Heather, listen to my voice and what I have to say to you. Listen to me, Heather...."

*   *   *

"Heather? Are you awake now, Heather?"

"Umm." A groan that sounded far away. Someone in pain.

Her own voice. She opened her eyes and out of the dusk light she saw a face. Dark hair, large eyes, pretty eyes. A woman.

"Who ... who are you?"

"I'm a friend of Philip's. My name is Sarah Logan, and you're safe now. No one is going to hurt you."

Chapter Nineteen

The dark green leaves of the maples planted along the narrow sidewalks of P Street rustled softly in the night breeze; it was a dry sound: death rattles and whispering shrouds. He walked on, counting door numbers along the gently sloping ranks of brick townhouses, each with its own vest-pocket garden below a bay window, filled with summer flowers, their colors bright in the parlor lights.

He came to Todd's address and stopped. The house appeared completely dark. Unlike a lot of the tall, narrow buildings along the street, Todd's stood alone, luxuriating in a three-foot gap on either side, keeping the neighbors at arm's length. Since he wasn't about to stand on Todd's doorstep to rifle the door he slipped down the alleyway between the houses, bending low as he moved out of the pale yellow light from the reproduction gaslights on the street.

He was looking for a basement window. Doc's third rule: people tend to give the least security to the things they value least. Garages and basement windows were usually the most poorly defended. In New York you put chain locks on your closets and broken bottles along your basement window sills. In Georgetown it seemed that people weren't quite so paranoid; the basement window on the alley had no break-bar or any other form of security that Philip could see. He looked up the alley, checking the street, then fell to his hands and knees, looking more closely. The window was caked with grime, the panes flecked with cobwebs on the insides but there was no evidence of any kind of electronics. Philip reached out and pushed against the low edge of the window. He felt the slight give of dry rot and then the harder resistance of some kind of obstruction. Either the window was nailed shut or there was a hook on the inside. He pushed harder and from the feel he had located the problem. A simple catch on the upper edge. He sat down on the cool bricks of the alley and lifted one leg, tapping the upper right pane of glass in the window with the heel of his boot. There was a crunching sound and then the soft tinkle of falling glass. Philip glanced out at the small rectangle of light that marked the street. Still clear. He leaned forward and picked away the large shards of glass still stuck in the ancient putty, then reached cautiously into the newly opened gap, feeling for the catch. He found it and pushed hard. The catch held for a moment, then swung back. The window was open. He took the letter opener out of his jacket pocket, inserted the flat edge of the handle into the crack between the bottom of the window and the sill, then levered up. There was a small grating sound and then the window popped up. Without waiting Philip shimmied forward, keeping the window up with one hand, and fitted his body into the narrow space between the window and the sill. He squirmed around once his legs were inside, feeling for a foothold, while he squeezed the rest of his body into the hole. His feet touched something hard, and he ducked his head, pulling the window shut as he went into the basement backwards.

He stepped down onto the floor of the basement, feeling around blindly, groping with his hands. He touched whatever it was he'd been standing on and felt the rough texture of wood. A crate of some kind. Ignoring it, he moved across the basement, his arms outstretched, sweeping the air directly in front of him. He found a wall, followed it, and eventually came to a corner. Except for the pile of boxes by the window, the basement seemed remarkably tidy. The locker in the basement of his loft building was a death trap by comparison.

He licked his lips and swallowed. His mouth had gone to cotton balls and his heart was going at about twice its normal rate. He wondered if people like Doc tended to die young from stress. If he had to do this kind of thing for a living he would have died of fright years ago.

He turned the corner and kept going until his head smacked hard into a post that had come out of nowhere, sneaking between his blindly flailing arms. He stifled a grunt of pain and found the post with his hands. The support for a staircase? He ran his hands along it and a few seconds later felt a protruding lip of wood. A tread. He breathed deeply, trying to slow his pulse rate, and tiptoed forward, keeping his hand on the stair. A few seconds later he found the bottom step and began to climb. Keeping one hand on the two-by-four banister on his left, and the other held out before his blind eyes, he moved upward until his outstretched fingers touched the smooth surface of a door. He stopped at the head of the stairs and listened. There wasn't a sound except the whistle of air through his nostrils. He found the doorknob with his hand and, wincing, turned it. The door opened silently and he stepped out into Charles Todd's kitchen.

Cool light washed down from a recessed overhead fixture, bathing the stark, galley-sized room in a smooth white glow. Todd, it seemed, believed in efficiency; the room was Bauhaus and NASA mixed; dark brown formica counters, brushed aluminum drawer and cupboard pulls, a Cuisinart, a microwave oven inset into the wall, a Braun coffee grinder, and a gleaming ultra-modern espresso maker.

Philip closed the basement door gently and eased across the dark-blue tile floor to the kitchen entry. Beyond it was a narrow hallway leading to the front door. He went down the hall, peeking into the rooms that led off to the right. The dining room—a long, narrow room with a butcher-block table and a half-dozen chrome and leather armchairs, and what looked like a Persian Tabriz prayer rug hanging on the stark white wall. Beyond the dining room was a small boxy living room or parlor facing the street outside, furnished with more leather and chrome, and with an unmistakable Rosenquist slash of color hanging on the wall. Todd was a "less is better" advocate, by appearances, or more likely the place had been done by a decorator and didn't reflect Todd's taste at all.

Philip checked his watch at the bottom of the side hall stairs. He'd been in the house for eight minutes, more than half of Doc's allotted time. He went up the thickly carpeted stairs to the second floor, anxiously aware that if Todd came home now he'd have no escape route. He reached the top of the stairs and did a quick check of the four rooms that opened onto the landing. Two bedrooms, one clearly for guests, a bathroom, and a study. Ignoring the other rooms Philip went into the study, shut the door, and flipped on the lights. Pay-dirt.

The study was small and windowless, located at the rear of the house above the kitchen. Three walls were filled with floor-to-ceiling bookcases, all the lower shelves filled with identical plastic binders about three inches thick. The fourth wall, on either side of the door, was given over to banks of filing cabinets. In the center of the room was a large rectangular desk that held a squat gray computer terminal, a printer, and a tall stack of accordion-folded printouts. In front of the terminal was a comfortable-looking armchair. Everything in the room was spotlessly clean and Philip could hear the faint ticking sound of an air conditioner. Philip sat down in the chair and stared at the screen of the terminal display unit. The machine's cursor clicked on and off in the upper left-hand corner of the screen. Todd was no believer in economy; the terminal was permanently on line, ready to go any time the man wanted to use it, which in turn meant that it was probably connected to Todd's own computers at his office rather than to some kind of time-sharing arrangement.

"Now what?" said Philip to himself. The machine was an IBM, the same as the display writers he'd occasionally used in wire service and magazine offices around the world. He squeezed his eyes shut, trying to summon up the pitifully small fund of knowledge he had about them. Only a tiny trickle surfaced. He opened his eyes and stared at the keyboard. Tentatively he reached out and tapped the "run" key on the left-hand side of the keyboard. The cursor made a little clicking pop and began to move. "Name of document."

Philip typed out: "Tenth Crusade." Nothing happened. He hit "restore," the screen cleared and he went back to where he'd started, this time typing in: "Nevada Survival Skills." Nothing again. Sweat began forming on Philip's forehead and his hands were going clammy. He rubbed them on his thighs and wanted desperately a cigarette. He was running out of time. What the hell was he doing wrong? He had one more possibility. He entered the word "Jericho." Nothing.

"Shit!" he whispered angrily. He looked at his watch. Seventeen minutes. He'd broken Doc's cardinal rule. He had a vague recollection of a leggy woman in the New York AP office talking to him over coffee one afternoon about display writers and word processors. Philip had been more interested in the possibility of going out on a date with her than learning about the innards of the machines she used, but one small item stuck in his mind. She'd said that one of the most difficult things to keep on top of was that when you wanted to call back something from a file you had to enter your request in exactly the same way as it had been originally filed. If you entered your document with a capital letter the first time you couldn't retrieve it by typing in the name of the document with a lower case opening. If you forgot how you'd entered it, it was lost for good.

Philip cleared the screen and tried again, this time punching up "Jericho" without a capital letter. Nothing happened. So much for the tall word-processor lady.

"Damn!" he muttered. He leaned back in the chair and for the first time he noticed the small wall plaque hanging on one of the crosspieces of the bookcase beyond the desk. "bE ACCu-rAtE."

Philip frowned, then shrugged his shoulders. It was worth a try. He pushed "enter" again, then tried: "jERICho."

Almost as though by magic the screen cleared itself and gave him back:

A. Create Document
B. Revise/Update
C. Paginate
D. Special Instructions
E. Task Selection

"Hallelujah!" whispered Philip. He hit "run" and then the letter A to create the document. The "menu" of options disappeared and everything filed under the word Jericho began to come up on the small screen in front of him.

JERICHO
Address delivered to first general meeting of Christian
   America Political Action Committee/CAMPAC held at
   Eagle One Institute Summer Seminars, Aspen Colo-
   rado/8-12-82
Attended by:
J. Steenbaker/American Conservative Coalition for Truth
A. Kronen/America Awake Foundation
C. Todd/Charles Todd Consultants
J. Snow/U.S. Senate
S. Keller/Keller Pharmaceuticals/Eagle One*
D. Freeman/Nevada Survival Skills
*chairman
Speech delivered by the Chairman...........
   —Gentlemen: I must say it's a great pleasure to see you
all here today. We've come a long way in the past four years
and the formation of CAMPAC is the fruit of our labors.

I don't need to go over the history of why our various
groups and organizations came together, we all know the
reasons. The leadership of this country has become pro-
gressively more unstable over the past two decades, and
we've been led into a state of moral and financial decay. It
can't go on, and that's what we're all about. We've tried to
re-establish the values of American life which we all hold
sacred, and we've made great progress, but the time has
come for some strong, definite action. Words aren't enough,
gentlemen. And if we're going to get this country back on
top of the heap we're going to have to act hard, and fast.
Our efforts to put President Reagan into office were successful, but like most politicians, Mr. Reagan used his
friends and then tossed them away when he no longer
needed them. We've been slighted, my friends, and that
slight has to be redressed, or we're all going to do down
with the ship.

As of this moment we have all the logistical problems
under control. Thanks to the efforts of Mr. Kronen and Mr.
Freeman we've established Crusade offices from one end of

the country to the other, concentrating, as we agreed earlier, on the Midwest and the South Central States. We've got people in every major town, headquarters offices in most State capitals, and some kind of leverage at virtually every level of the political and administrative ladder. Mr. Todd's work has given us the inroads we didn't have before, which has given us access to key people both in Washington, labor, and the business sector. We've learned from long experience that you can bring a liberal to water, but making him drink requires a little bit of metaphorical arm twisting.

−pause−

And I mean that as more than a joke. Christianity has enjoyed a huge upswing in the past little while, due in a large degree to the advent of television. The Pro-lifers have been a big help too, but it's not enough. We've had Reverend Falwell and the Moral Majority, the religious roundtable, and maybe forty or so parachurch organizations in the country in addition to our own, but it's no more than a drop in the bucket. You all know the words to the hymn, "Onward Christian Soldiers"−well, that's what we have to be, soldiers for this country of ours, fighting a war that's as real as any other we've fought. Only this time the battlefield is inside our own borders. We can't go marching through the streets with banners like the hippies did and expect to get anywhere; the odds are against us. We've got Jew liberals running all the T.V. networks, gayboys as mayors of major cities, and commies in Congress. If we really are going to be soldiers for Christ then we've got to act like soldiers. We've got to be ready to fight tooth and nail to win, and *we will win*, gentlemen, because our cause is just.

But to win we need a catalyst, something to bring all those parachurch people together under our flag; we can't go on bickering between ourselves the way we have been. God is God, gentlemen, and the word of God is as plain as day. It's the liberals and the commies who use the divide and conquer technique, and we can't fall for it any longer.

Which brings us to Jericho. That's my name for it, anyway. Mr. Freeman has detailed it out under my direction, and most of you have heard something about it, but after

I'm finished maybe we can get down to brass tacks with this thing. If we do it right, we can force the President to go along with us, and frankly I don't give a damn if he follows our lead because he believes in what we're doing, whether it's because it's politically expedient, or whether it's because Mr. Todd here has a file on the man's time in Hollywood that makes Chappaquiddick look like a kid stealing candy from the five-and-dime.

Anyway, I've talked enough. I want you all to get together with Dave Freeman and go over the plan the way we've outlined it, and come back tomorrow so we can iron out the details.
                              —Message—
Enter————2021/2025/3225/7684/8556/9997
for additional ref.
                              end

Philip keyed in the additional documents and sat forward as the material came onto the screen.

After twenty minutes, his head was spinning. There was no single file that outlined Jericho in detail, or in fact even spelled out specifically what it was, but there were enough references to specifics to let Philip know that his feelings about the Tenth Crusade being involved in something violent were true. From what he could make out the Crusade was to form a sort of quasi-militia all across the United States once Jericho had been accomplished. There were arms dumps in Charlottesville, Virginia; Tampa, Florida; St. Louis, Missouri; Spokane, Washington; Ragged Mountain, Colorado; and Houston, Texas. If Jericho was successful, all the Tenth Crusade State headquarters would be notified by Telex, and the weapons would be distributed using transport and personnel provided by NSS.

But what was Jericho itself? The material on the computer was choppy, referring to other files and to information that was apparently common knowledge to those concerned. The constant use of acronyms and symbol words didn't make it any easier. He was able to decipher a few basic facts.

It was clear that Jericho was to take place in Washington.

The name appeared dozens of times in connection with Jericho, although, strangely, it was often referred to as *The* Washington, almost as though a phrase had been started and then left unfinished. The Washington what?

It was also obvious that Nevada Survival Skills was involved in Jericho, and not just to transport arms after the fact. There was a complex analysis of routes and times from the Charlottesville arms drop to D.C., and several estimates of required manpower and equipment. The phrase "target positioning" was also used several times, and at first Philip had thought that Jericho might be some wild plan to assassinate the President, but then he remembered that Keller had referred to forcing the President to go along with them. So, if the "target" wasn't the President, then who, or what, was it?

In the end, Philip decided that it didn't matter. Better men than he could spend time figuring out just what it all meant. The fact that he had a list of arms dumps, and descriptions of plans to distribute them was enough. On top of that, there were scattered references in the material to people who'd been co-opted by the Crusade, undoubtedly in the same way Sarah's father had been blackmailed.

He hit the "end" key on the console and the screen cleared, then returned to the original "menu" he'd been given. He typed in "D" for special instructions and that took him to a "print document" function. He turned on the printer beside the console, entered the document name and then hit "enter" again. There was a small popping sound from the computer and then the printer began working, the daisy wheel rippling back and forth with a tiny stuttering sound. The sheets began to roll out of the printer and as they came Philip let them fold into a neat stack in his hand. The whole process took less than five minutes and when it was done Philip put the stack down beside the printer, returned to the console, and tried to wipe out the last of his instructions. He couldn't afford to have Todd return to find the last tidbits of the Jericho file glowing on his video screen.

Eventually he gave up and simply turned the computer off, then on again. He'd done something wrong, because the cursor no longer showed in the upper-left corner, but he doubted that Todd would notice. It was then that he checked the time.

Two minutes to twelve. Christ! He'd been in Todd's study for more than an hour. Not only had he outstayed his welcome, he'd also almost missed his check-in call with Sarah. Two more minutes and she'd call the cops. There was no phone in Todd's computer room, but he'd seen one on a small table in the downstairs hall. He left the room at a run, then plunged down the stairs. He reached the telephone, found the scrap of paper with the Fredericksburg number on it in his jacket pocket, and dialed.

Sarah answered halfway through the first ring. "Philip?"

"Yes."

"Thank God! Where are you? What did you –"

"Look, I don't have the time. Right now I'm standing in Charles Todd's front hall putting a long-distance tab on his bill. I think I've found what we want. Todd, NSS, and all the others are involved in something big happening in Washington. I haven't figured it out yet, but they keep on referring to 'The Washington' something or other. Christ, who knows, maybe they're going to blow up the Washington Monument. Anyway, I'm all right and on my way out. I'm booked into the Georgetown Inn. Meet me there tomorrow at noon. Okay?"

"Yes, but...."

Philip heard the gentle snick of a key being inserted into the lock of the front door and at the same instant he realized that the phone was dead. The line had been cut, either at his end or hers. There was no time to think. He stood there in the dim hallway, the phone in his hand, and watched as the front door of Charles Todd's house opened. A short, balding man with glasses stepped into the hall. He was dressed in evening clothes. Behind him were two much larger men in ordinary suits. The short man smiled and walked toward Philip, his hand outstretched.

"Ah, Mr. Kirkland," said Charles Todd. "Nice to meet you at last."

*   *   *

"Philip?" There was no answer, not the slightest crackle or

hiss on the line. It was dead. Sarah pushed down the buttons in the phone cradle and listened again. No dial tone. The disconnect had been at her end.

"Damn," she said softly. That was all she needed. With the phone out she had no way of getting back to Philip, even if it was only to confirm that he'd got back to his hotel safely. She stood up, yawning, and checked the newly set mantel clock above the fireplace in her grandfather's library. Five past twelve. From the back of the house she could faintly hear the rattling of dishes. Heather was making tea for them.

The transformation in Heather Foxcroft had been just short of miraculous. She'd come out of her half-sleep, half-trance state in the late afternoon and by supper time she was utterly transformed. She'd borrowed some clothes from Sarah, bathed and brushed her hair and generally took on the characteristics of a normal human being. For the first little while she'd been nervous around Sarah, but as they talked and Heather began to really understand that she was safe, the tensions eased. The only problem was that she seemed to want to talk about nothing except Philip and her relationship with him. A couple of times Sarah gently brought up the subject of the Crusade, but Heather calmly told her that she didn't want to talk about her experiences yet.

Sarah walked slowly out of the library and went out into the foyer, wondering what Philip would think when he saw Heather. She bit her lip. There was no way around it, Heather was a beautiful woman and, by the looks of things, recovering from her ordeal nicely. She'd be lucky if she got a Christmas card from them every so often.

When she reached the kitchen she saw that Heather had laid out the tea things on the old, honey-yellow maple table, complete with a tray of sandwiches.

"Midnight snack," Heather smiled from the counter where she was tidying up.

"You didn't have to go to all that trouble," said Sarah, seating herself.

"It was no trouble, Sarah," answered Heather. "You've been awfully nice to me, it's the least I could do." Sarah smiled.

As she began filling the cups the kitchen phone rang, startling her and making her spill her tea all over the table. It wasn't a normal ring. It was a long, unbroken trill that seemed to go on forever. Then it stopped.

"What the hell was that?" Sarah said, frowning.

Heather turned from the counter and stepped toward the table. Sarah had a flashing image of bright light on steel as the other woman brought the bread knife down toward her. Sarah lurched away, screaming as the razor-sharp blade sliced through her clothing at the shoulder. Sarah dropped to the floor, one hand clutching her shoulder, then rolled away across the tiles as Heather came after her, the knife raised to strike again. Her eyes were glazed and there were flecks of saliva on her lips.

Sarah's foot found the rungs of a chair and she pushed hard, sending it skittering across the room to tangle in the approaching woman's legs. Heather slipped on the spattered trail of blood left by Sarah, and stumbled over the chair, falling to her knees. The knife flew out of her hands and Sarah struggled to her feet, one hand still clutching her shoulder.

"Heather! Stop!" she screamed, but the other woman showed no sign that she had heard. She pushed away the chair and crawled rapidly over the tiles, heading for the doorway leading to the rear entrance.

Groaning, Sarah staggered around the table. She lunged across the room, trying for the telephone on the wall, but as she reached it the red casing seemed to explode silently, sending a whirling shower of plastic in all directions. Two inches from her head a gaping hole appeared in the perfect white surface of the kitchen cupboard, followed by a splintering crash from somewhere. Glass tinkled and there was an ear-splitting metallic whine from the direction of the sink.

Ducking, the sheer panic making her feel faint, Sarah found the doorway. She lurched through the hall beyond as a chunk of wood the size of her hand was torn out of the frame, disintegrating, splinters hitting her cheek and upper arm. There was no time to think, she had to get away from the madness erupting around her like some demon poltergeist. She stumbled forward, looking back over her shoulder, but Heather was still on the floor of the kitchen, groveling at the base of the cupboards.

Ahead the air was filled with the sound of breaking glass and it seemed as though the furniture and the very walls themselves were exploding all around her. Even as she watched the top of the newel post on the stairs dissolved into matchwood and the large, ornate mirror on the opposite wall shattered into a million glittering shards that erupted forward like the blossoming of a terrible crystal flower. Sarah dropped down onto the floor, arms above her head, screaming as the entrance hall filled with flying glass. She felt a stinging pain in her leg and, looking down, saw a shallow, trough-like wound across her lower thigh.

"Stop it!"

But it went on, a hideous symphony of destruction that was slowly but surely tearing the house apart. There was a coughing sound from outside the house and then the front panel of glass in the main door shattered. A smoking canister the size of a soup can hit the marble of the foyer and rolled heavily toward her. She screamed, crabbing away from the small gray cylinder, coughing as the coils began to spread gas fumes.

It was only then that Sarah fully understood what was happening. Fox Run was under attack, men outside using silenced weapons to destroy the house and anyone within. Freeman. NSS, God! How had they tracked her here, a continent away? It didn't matter. They'd done it, and now they were trying to kill her. She dragged herself to her feet, gagging on the fumes, and hobbled across the hall to the library, her leg burning like she'd been branded, obliterating the pain of the slash in her shoulder. As she reached the doorway a second canister came through the shattered front door, this one striking the floor and then exploding with a roar into white hot flame, the shock wave smashing into Sarah's back like a huge fist, thrusting her into the room beyond.

Hammered into the desk her grandfather had used, she rebounded and fell to the floor beneath the window, now nothing more than a gaping hole, the glass and frame shot away. She sneezed and coughed simultaneously, almost vomiting, tears from the gas running down from her burning eyes. Outside in the hall the fire was taking hold, tall tongues of flame licking up the wallpaper with a deadly crackling sound. Panic surged up in her and without thinking she clawed her way up, using the ragged edge of the window sill for leverage. She stood, her back braced against the side of the window, and with a groan she swung one leg up and out through the hole. A third canister came through the riven door, this one a concussion grenade. Screaming, hands covering her ringing ears, Sarah literally fell out of the window, landing sprawled in the lilac beds below.

No one seemed to have noticed her somewhat unorthodox exit from the house and shielded by the blackness of the night she rolled out of the lilacs onto the lawn and began to run for the trees, less than two hundred feet away. She reached the safety of the alder grove without being hit again and fell to the ground, her face hard into the soft, sweet smelling earth. She crawled further into the protective screen of the trees and then turned, looking back at the house.

Smoke was pouring out of all the main floor windows and the doorway at the front of the house, a deep rose-colored glow flickering angrily through the gray-black billows. A reddish light was beginning to grow in the second-floor windows as the flames spread up the spiral staircase. Sarah knew that unless the fire was quickly dealt with the entire house would be consumed.

As she watched the house burn she saw the silhouettes of running figures; men carrying weapons, dressed in tight fitting black suits, their faces covered by some kind of cowl or hood. They seemed to be everywhere, scurrying forward toward the house like huge, foraging army ants. A squad of four reached the front doorway, half hidden by the dark bulk of Sarah's parked car. Two moved to either side of the door while the other pair barged in through the door, tearing what was left of it from its hinges. When the first two had entered the other two followed. Sarah didn't wait to see any more. It wouldn't take the men long to realize that she wasn't in the house, and when they found her gone they'd come after her.

She stood, gritting her teeth against ragged surges of pain that swept over her in sawtoothed waves, then moved off through the trees, her unsteady feet guided by a vague memory from her childhood.

When she was ten her father had given her a boxed set of the Narnia books by C.S. Lewis and she'd read them all, one after the other, enthralled by the strange, metaphorical kingdom the writer had created. That summer, Fox Run, with its woods, waters, and quiet places, became her Narnia, and once, while pretending that she was Jill from the Silver Chair, she came upon a small glade on the Fox Run property that could have been taken whole from Lewis's imagination. There was a small, spring-fed pond in the center of the clearing, the waters of the tiny pool spilling out in a winding freshet that disappeared among the trees. On a steep slope on the far side of the stream there was an immense, twisted oak, its roots so old the ground around had been thrust up in hunch-backed mounds. Half hidden by small shrubs and weeds Sarah had discovered a cave beneath the roots, large enough in her mind to be the entrance to the Narnian "Underland," the home of the Bism gnomes, and ruled over by the Lady of the Green Kirtle, Queen of the Shallow Lands. In reality it was little more than a cubbyhole between two ancient roots, but that summer it was enough. By the time she was twelve she had discovered, much to her dismay, that the Lewis books were written by a theologian and were really nothing more than children's parables, and she hadn't returned to the oak and its small cavern again. Now, seventeen years later, the clearing and the bolt hole might provide her with sanctuary once again.

Chapter Twenty

Philip sat in one of the living room's armchairs and smoked a cigarette while Todd sat on the patterned silk couch on his left. The two heavyset bodyguards had disappeared, but Philip knew they weren't far off. The front door of the house was only fifteen feet away at the end of the hall, but it might as well have been fifteen miles.

Todd was beaming happily, toying with a small, delicate liqueur glass one of the guards had brought him. The drink was a dark amber color and Todd sipped it as though it was some rare ambrosia. He looked extremely pleased with himself and Philip felt as though he was some kind of exotic butterfly that had just been pinned to a card by a lepidopterist. His mind was working furiously, trying to come up with some way out of his predicament but it was futile. Beyond his own problems he was also worried about Sarah and Heather: Why had the phone gone dead?

"You look worried, Mr. Kirkland," murmured Todd, gently placing his glass on the coffee table in front of the couch.

Philip tipped his ash into the ficus benjamina beside the chair and shrugged, trying to keep calm. "I'm waiting for you to phone the police," he answered. "You have caught me red-handed after all."

Todd laughed quietly. "You know perfectly well I'm not going to call the police, Mr. Kirkland," he said. "Not yet, at any rate. You'll do us no good."

"Us?" said Philip.

"Ah, yes," said Todd theatrically, his thin eyebrows rising.

"Us. Them. The paranoids' delight, the mysterious conspiracy bent on destroying civilization as we know it. Is that the 'us' you're questioning, Mr. Kirkland."

"If you say so," said Philip, not sure if the man was just pulling his leg or if Todd was certifiably insane.

"And now you think I'm mad, don't you?" said Todd, astutely reading Philip's expression. "Well," he continued, "I can assure you that I'm not mad. A touch of megalomania, perhaps, or maybe you can just call it a good healthy American desire for wealth, position, and power."

"That sounds sane enough," said Philip. "In fact it's about the sanest thing I've heard in quite a while."

"I understand," nodded Todd. "You've no doubt been listening to the ravings of that young woman you've been traveling with. Senator Logan's daughter. She's convinced that her father was driven to suicide by the people I'm connected with."

"Was he?" asked Philip bluntly.

"Almost certainly," answered Todd blandly. "He was a weak man, and to say that is being kind. He was a closet homosexual who was also a politician. In this day and age you can be one of the two, but being both simultaneously is dangerous. In his case fatally so. But it was the weakness that killed him, not us. Politics is a rough game."

"Blackmail isn't playing by the rules," said Philip.

"Don't be naive, Mr. Kirkland," said Todd. "It's a question of semantics. Eisenhower was blackmailed by the Russians, Kennedy was blackmailed by everyone from Hollywood starlets to U.S. Steel and Nixon had so many political favors to pay back after his election he wound up being blackmailed by the entire world. Blackmail is *the* rule in politics, Mr. Kirkland."

"And maybe you're rationalizing a criminal act," said Philip.

Todd lifted his shoulders in an eloquent gesture of disdain. "It doesn't matter, Mr. Kirkland. It's the one thing I've learned in dealing with people over the last thirty years or so. You may be able to change people on superficial levels, but the basic nature of an individual cannot be changed by *anything*. Conservatives in this country have bent over backwards to accommodate the democratic process, but a liberal is still a liberal, a communist is still a communist. It comes down, in the end, to numbers and power. If you have the numbers you have the power, if you have the power, the numbers will come out of hiding and support you."

"*Mein Kampf,*" said Philip dryly. He was getting tired of Todd's political science lecture, but he was a captive audience nevertheless.

"Ah, Miss Logan again. She's the one who thinks that conservatism in the United States is equivalent to Naziism in the thirties, yes?"

"Something like that," replied Philip.

Again the shrug from Todd. "Perhaps. She may not be too far off the mark. The question is, would that necessarily be bad?"

"Most people would think so," said Philip.

Todd shook his head. "I disagree, Mr. Kirkland. The Nazi ideology has received some very bad publicity over the years, I will admit, but its roots are based firmly in sound political and especially social principle. In essence Hitler wanted to rally a dying nation around a common cause, to give the people of Germany a united purpose. He saw the threat of communism long before anyone else, and he acted, using it to create that common front. He saw Germany being used by foreign powers, and he took steps to remove them. He recognized that his country was being ruled by an aging and reactionary group of people and he dealt with that as well. He gave Germany purpose, direction, and strength. Surely those are positive things."

"His methods were a little on the vicious side," said Philip.

"His methods suited the situation, just as ours do. We no longer have the time for due process in America. Another five years, and one more Hindenburg like Reagan, and this nation will be on its knees."

"So what are you going to do, start World War Three?"

"Dear me, no," said Todd. "Quite the contrary. We have enough problems of our own to overcome without trying to take on the entire world. No, the answer is to clean up our own dung heap, and a dung heap is what we've become."

"So the Tenth Crusade will become the nation's garbagemen?" said Philip. "From what I've seen they've got more potential as an American version of the Brownshirts."

"Militia," corrected Todd. "A moral police force."

"Whose morals?" asked Philip. "Yours, Billy Carstairs'?"

"For now, yes," said Todd. "Billy's morality, his adherence to biblical law is perhaps a trifle rigid, but rigidity is what we need now. The people of this country have forgotten a very basic principle, a principle on which this country was founded."

"Tell me," said Philip.

"Freedom is a right, Mr. Kirkland, but it is a right that must be earned to be appreciated. The people of the United States have taken their freedom for granted for too long, so they must be taught a lesson."

"With your people as the teachers, right?"

"Precisely. Every one of the basic freedoms in this country has been abused to the point where they mean nothing. Remove those freedoms for a time, and when they are returned they will be appreciated. You may think that the law according to Jerry Falwell, or Billy Carstairs is simplistic, but Mr. Kirkland, *it is a law.* Now we have anarchy."

"And anything is better than nothing as far as you're concerned."

"You're being obtuse, Mr. Kirkland. The Bible states that there are ten basic laws to life and that adherence to those laws will bring peace. I believe that. The Ten Commandments are good laws, Mr. Kirkland, and a fine place upon which to build a nation. We have a country that has gone to hell, fifth columned by a small group of humanists who took control simply because this country *was* democratic. Well, secular humanism has brought us inflation, unemployment, rampant immorality, and a decline in national pride that is unprecedented. Now it's our turn."

"I think you're full of shit," said Philip mildly. He butted his cigarette in the plant. "And I also think you're mad as the fucking March Hare."

"Of course you do," answered Todd benignly. "And, as it was so eloquently put by Clark Gable, 'Frankly, my dear, I don't give a damn.'"

"So let's get on with it," said Philip.

"Get on with what?" asked Todd. "You really do think I'm Dr. No or some such, don't you?"

"I think you're planning some kind of violent demonstration to coincide with Billy Carstairs' rally tomorrow. I also have a sneaking suspicion that the Tenth Crusade is intimately tied in with the Devil's Brigade. And you want me out of the way."

"Very astute," said Todd. "I presume it was your involvement with the Nevada Survival Skills operation that led you to think that the Crusade and the Devil's Brigade were connected?"

"Among other things. And also Sarah's comparisons with Hitler's Germany. You invented the Devil's Brigade as a kind of antichrist. A rallying point to give Billy Carstairs and America Awake the credibility it needs. Like the Reichstag fire did for Hitler."

Todd stood up. "You're quite right, of course, there is a connection, and a parallel. But it's not the Reichstag burning. More like *Kristalnacht*, with you playing the role of Herschel Grynszpan."

"I don't get it," said Philip, frowning. He remembered that *Kristalnacht* was the night when the first massive Jewish pogrom began in Germany, but who the hell was Herschel Grynszpan?

"It doesn't matter," said Todd, smiling. "You're in the unfortunate position of not being able to see the forest for the trees. At any rate you'll have to excuse me for a moment."

Todd left the room for a few seconds and when he came back it was with the two bodyguards in tow. Todd had a disposable hypodermic needle in his hand which he proceeded to fill from a small vial he took from his pocket.

"Now let's not be silly about this, Mr. Kirkland. This is nothing more lethal than a drug which induces sleep. Please roll up your sleeve and co-operate."

Philip almost balked, but the deadpan expressions on the faces of Todd's two heavies were easy enough to read. Any trouble and they'd clout him into submission. He did as he was told and winced as Todd slipped the needle expertly into a vein in his arm. A few seconds later things began to get fuzzy, and as he drifted off into unconsciousness he managed one last question for Todd. "Who was ... who ... who was Herschel whatever?" he said groggily.

"A fall guy," said Todd, smiling down at him. "Herschel Grynszpan was a fall guy, Mr. Kirkland."

And then the lights went out.

* * *

She was dead. The smell of mold was thick in her nostrils and her mouth tasted the sweet dankness of earth. She was dead, or buried alive, and the sounds of crawling things and night whispers filled her ears.

Sarah Logan woke up, shivering, her heart thundering and a scream rising in her throat, her wounds throbbing. The darkness was fading, and half-hidden by the veil of moss and vines she could see the forest beyond her hiding place. Her heart slowed, but the shivering grew worse.

She struggled into a crouch, her head brushing the thick mesh of tree roots above her head, then crawled forward and pushed back the protective screen of foliage. She looked and listened, but as far as she could tell there was no one in the immediate vicinity. She held up her wrist and checked the time on her watch. It was 5:30. Almost six hours had passed since the attack on Fox Run. She let out a long, whispering sigh of relief. If they had looked for her at all they would have given up by now. Her head jerked up in horror, slamming into the low roof over her head. Heather! My God, what about Heather? She crawled out of the tiny space hollowed out under the giant tree and stood up, her joints aching. She sneezed, trying to choke it back, in case anyone was nearby. If the cold didn't get her the dew-damp of the early morning was going to give her pneumonia.

She stood on the low hillside above the pond, listening hard. Still nothing. She was alone in the woods, silent except for the faint sounds of birds and small animals.

"Now what?" she muttered to herself. Alone, dressed in clothes that were stained, crumpled and filthy, penniless, twenty miles from anywhere, and catching a cold. She sneezed again, this time letting it go full blast.

She realized she had two choices: she could stay where she was and die of exposure, or she could go back to Fox Run and take it from there. She could take one of the canoes from the boathouse and head across the river to Riverside on the Maryland bank of the Potomac. That was only a couple of miles and she'd done it dozens of times before.

She set off, moving more slowly the closer she got to Fox Run. It took her the best part of an hour to travel the mile through the forest and by the time she reached the sloping clearing the house was built on the sun was a watery low in the sky and the dawn chill was gone from the air.

She traveled the last hundred yards through the thinning trees on her belly, taking extra care just in case the Tenth Crusade had left some kind of guard behind. She needn't have bothered: Fox Run was deserted.

She was surprised to see that the house was still standing. Except for some trailing scorch marks around the shattered windows on the first and second floors there seemed to be very little damage. Best of all, the rental car was exactly where she'd left it, parked in front of the house.

She waited, stomach flat on the ground, and watched the house for a full twenty minutes before she made a move. When she was absolutely satisfied that there was no one around she stood up and cautiously came out of the trees and into the clearing.

She went in through the back door, now off its hinges, and tiptoed across the small rear vestibule to the kitchen, almost afraid of what she'd find. There was no sign of Heather. The knife she'd used had been picked up off the floor and was sitting on the honey wood of the kitchen table, beside her purse. Sarah crossed the room and picked up her purse and the knife, the heaviness of the handle and Swedish steel blade making her feel a little safer. With the knife held at the ready she went through the rest of the house.

Things were worse on the inside than the exterior had indicated. The front hall, her grandfather's library, and the living room had been almost completely destroyed, although, strangely, she saw signs that some kind of foam fire extinguisher had been used to stop the fire before it got too far. She had no idea what the condition of the second floor was; the spiral staircase had been burned through in several places. There was no sign of Heather anywhere. It was probable that the Crusade had her again.

Sarah went into the family room, stepping over the charred remnants of the fire. The room beyond hadn't been affected except for the smell of smoke that permeated everything. She went back into the kitchen and washed the knife wounds and her face and hands. Now at least she was ready to face the world, she thought to herself; the question was, just what was she going to do now that she looked reasonably civilized?

She went out to the car and got in. Sitting down behind the wheel, she felt the tears start to well up. The shock of Fox Run almost in ruins, the shock of Heather coming after her with a knife, was finally beginning to sink in. The implications were terrifying. She grabbed the wheel hard and forced herself to calm down; if she flipped now it could be disastrous; Philip had found something in Todd's computer that had him scared—something that was going to happen today, probably in a few hours' time. She turned the key, ran the car around the drive, and headed down the road. As she hit Highway 3, and headed toward Fredericksburg she let the broth of information, supposition, and hypothesis about her present situation brew.

Guns. Philip had seen them at Ragged Mountain, and they'd been fired on at Pilot Peak. Her father had killed himself with his favorite Purdy, the one that still hung over the mantel at his Watergate apartment. Guns. Violence. Violence at Fox Run. Philip's suspicion that something violent was going to happen today, something connected with the Billy Carstairs rally. What? Assassinating the President? No, they'd dumped that one. Mob violence? A riot? Unlikely, and it wouldn't accomplish anything. The Devil's Brigade? Terrorism. Some kind of terrorist act that would benefit the Crusade. Maybe, but still the question—what?

The Washington. Philip had seen it on the computer repeatedly. But The Washington what? The Washington Monument? The Washington Airport? The Washington Transit

system? The Washington Police Department? The Washington Mall? The Washington Naval Yard? *The Washington Star*? The Washington Coliseum? Cathedral? Hospital Center? The Washington Circle? God, the list was endless. Wait. Maybe not. What if it wasn't part of a phrase, what if The Washington was a noun, nothing after it? Okay, go with that. Whatever is going to happen is going to happen at The Washington. Period. What place was called The Washington, period? Only one that she knew of. The Washington Hotel. All right, now *why*? Why The Washington Hotel? What made it key? What was it known for, why could it possibly be important?

Unbidden, a shard, a phrase from Steve Birnbaum's *U.S. Travel Guide* came into her head, read once, and almost but not quite forgotten. Under "Best in Town," between the Quality Inn and the Tabard, Birnbaum's description of The Washington: "Always comfortable, but great during an inaugural parade. Fifteenth and Pennsylvania Ave."

And that was it. The pieces flew together like charged particles. Everything, from the beginning, fit like a glove. She knew the How, Who, What, Where, When, and Why. Right down to her own involvement, and Philip's as well.

She took a quick look at her watch. Seven-thirty, and she still had at least an hour's drive ahead.

Chapter Twenty-one

The effects of the drug he'd been given wore off slowly, giving Philip Kirkland small broken glimpses of things happening around him. First there was nothing but a deep, velvet blackness and the sound of murmuring voices, far away. Then movement and a suggestion of consciousness. A car? Traffic noises, the thunder of a bus close by, and the thick wash of diesel fuel. A wailing siren, more voices, and a blurred image of large, white buildings. The vehicles stopped, and after hearing a series of familiar clicks and metallic snaps he had the vague impression of a car door opening and he was lifted out. Then he was sitting, head lolling. A memory tickled as consciousness ebbed and flowed. A hospital, why was he thinking of a hospital? Then he remembered the feeling from long ago. Dublin. He'd had his leg broken during a riot. The same feeling. He was in a wheelchair! Why was he in a wheelchair?

"The nurse will take care of everything."

What nurse?

"Certainly, sir. I hope Mr. Kirkland finds things comfortable."

"I'm sure he will."

"The room is on the south side, facing Pennsylvania Avenue, as Mr. Kirkland requested."

"Thank you. I'm sure it will be fine."

Whose voice was that? Male, well modulated, educated. Todd? No. Too young. What the hell was going on?

An elevator. The bright lights of a hall. Key in a door, out of the wheelchair and down into another chair, soft, upholstered. Then a sharp nauseating feeling of vertigo as he shed the last effects of the drug and his eyes opened.

He was obviously in a hotel room, not a hospital. It was large, furnished reasonably with a king-size bed, chest of drawers, coffee table, and armchairs. Early-morning light was sifting in through sheer curtains that were pulled across a large casement window.

He wasn't alone in the room, a man was at the window, looking out through the curtains. Beside him was the wheelchair. The chair had been taken apart, the seat removed. A square, gray metal box sat on the floor beside it. Philip groaned, and the man turned. He was clean shaven and good looking, about thirty-five or so. He grinned when he saw that Philip had regained consciousness.

"You're awake," he said. "Good."

"Who the hell are you?" grunted Philip. The drug had left him with a splitting headache. He tried to bring a hand up to his forehead but he found that he was restrained. He looked down at the arms of the chair. He was handcuffed—two pairs, one for each hand.

"My name is Freeman," said the man. "Not that it matters."

"Freeman?" said Philip.

"Nevada Survival Skills. I talked to your girlfriend, Sarah Logan. That was before you came to Pilot Peak like Captain America."

"You were at Pilot Peak?" mumbled Philip. The pain in his head came in great stunning waves.

"I'm the commander there. I must say, you caused us a great deal of trouble. We underestimated you." Freeman shook his head, smiling. "Poor old Harky. He didn't know what hit him."

Freeman reached into his trouser pocket, took out a key, and knelt beside the gray box. He opened it, flipped back the lid, and began taking out the contents. As Freeman began putting the black metal components together it was obvious that it was a weapon of some kind—tube-stocked, short-barreled, and with a pistol-grip handle. The last piece out of the box was a curved, ribbed metal magazine that Freeman snapped into place just in front of the trigger housing.

"It's a Valmet M62 assault rifle," said Freeman, glancing at Philip. "Finnish. Latest model. Six hundred and fifty rounds a minute with an effective range of eight hundred and seventy-five yards. You'll be shooting from less than half that. Easy target."

"I'm not shooting from any range," said Philip.

Freeman smiled. "Sure you will. At least as far as the criminal investigation people at the FBI are concerned." He reached into the box and brought out another piece for the rifle. A pistol grip identical to the one on the gun. "Nice set of prints on this. We took them while you were knocked out. The pistol grip snaps in and out. Afterwards the one with your prints will be substituted."

"I'm going to shoot with my hands cuffed to this chair?" said Philip. Sweat was breaking out on his forehead, and he could feel his guts doing a spasmodic jig.

"The cuffs will be taken off after you're dead," said Freeman easily, as though he was talking about shifting chess pieces on a board. "It's going to be a double suicide. I have to hand it to Todd, he's planned a very neat operation. No loose ends." He smiled again, and propped the rifle against the window sill. He reached into the box again and brought out a small can of what appeared to be spray paint. He took the cap off the tin and walked over to the bed. Climbing up on the mattress he pressed the button on the can and began writing. The hissing can put out a thin blurred line of scarlet across the patterned wallpaper: DEVIL'S BRIGADE."

"Jesus!" whispered Philip. "This is crazy."

"I think it's brilliant," said Freeman, stepping down from the bed. He capped the can and came to Philip's chair. He took Philip's left hand, squeezed it against the side of the container, and then, holding the container by the rim, took it back to the window. He set it on the sill and left it there. "Nice detail," he said, turning to Philip with another of his woeful smiles. "Your prints on the rifle, your prints on the paint can, your name on the register."

"What about you?" asked Philip. "The desk clerk must have seen you."

"So what?" said Freeman. "I can be the one that got away.

The grassy knoll anomaly. Nothing like a good conspiracy to keep the media people interested."

"You said a double suicide. Who's the other body?" asked Philip. His brain was in a whirl. "And who am I supposed to have killed?"

"I think I'm going to leave you in suspense, " said Freeman. "It would spoil the fun if I told you." He reached into his trouser pocket again and came up with another key. He placed it on the window sill beside the can. "For the handcuffs," he explained. He walked across the room and checked the restraining bands of steel. "Don't want to cut off the circulation," he whispered into Philip's ear. "It might make them curious at the autopsy." He took a roll of surgical tape out of his poplin windbreaker, tore off a piece, and placed the strip across Philip's mouth. "They might notice a bit of adhesive on your face, but I doubt it. There probably won't be much of your face left when this is all over. You've probably heard that the Devil's Brigade tends toward the grotesque." He smiled again and patted Philip on the shoulder. "Well I think that about does it." He checked his watch and nodded to himself. "I've got to be on my way, the meter is running out. In case you're wondering you've got about forty-five minutes to zero hour, Mr. Kirkland."

Freeman grinned, patted Philip on the shoulder again and moved out of sight. A few seconds later there was a small click as the hotel room door gently closed behind him. Philip was alone.

* * *

Sarah came into D.C. on Highway 1, inserting herself into the maze of clover leaf access routes around the Pentagon, fuming at the slow-moving traffic that clogged the expressway. She eventually made it onto Washington Boulevard and, counting the passing minutes, she crossed the Arlington Memorial Bridge along with 100,000 other commuters.

All the way from Fox Run she had examined her theory, looking for flaws, but there were none. It was the only scenario that made sense, even though the sense was in itself the result of insanity. In the beginning she had thought that she was the source of the Crusade's attacks, but now she knew that, if anything, she was the fly in the ointment, the X factor that the Crusade and the other members of the incredible plot had overlooked. Philip, and his relationship with Heather Foxcroft, was the key. With all the facts aligned it wasn't difficult to see how the whole thing had happened.

America Awake, the Crusade, and in fact neo-conservatism in the United States, were all in trouble. After the first flush of glory that had come with the success of Falwell's Moral Majority, Dolan's work, and the phenomenon of the Political Action Committees, things had gone the way of all politics. Reagan and his policies, which had appeared hard hitting at first, became millstones. Reagan's budgets, policies, and personnel were just as flawed as anyone else's, and even though the New Right, America Awake included, quickly disassociated themselves from their once shining knight, the stain was there. On top of that, the laws of inertia came into play; the media simply wasn't interested in the New Right any more, and without widespread publicity, the enthusiasm and the impetus were wearing off.

So, something was needed, not only to spur interest, but also act as a catalyst, and the best kind of catalyst was a martyr. Enter Heather Foxcroft and the Devil's Brigade.

Todd had undoubtedly had Foxcroft on his computer for some time, and whatever he was blackmailing the general with probably had to do with Heather. At any rate, they had him on the hook, and when Heather returned to the United States Todd and the others had seen what kind of use they could make of her and, in consequence, Philip.

He'd said it in San Francisco: things had been too easy. The break-in at Barrington had never been followed up, Philip's entrance and exit from Ragged Mountain had been too easy, and the escape from Pilot Peak had been classic. She was willing to bet that the people chasing them had never intended catching them, and that Harky and his machine-gun had been for show. In the final analysis, Philip had been led around by the nose, every step of the way, taking him deeper and deeper, and piling up evidence against him. The blood on the wall of his loft, the murder of Janet Margolis soon after he'd visited her, the stolen car from Ragged Mountain, and her own involvement—taking Heather to Fox Run: a drugged woman on a plane, carried across State lines. Kidnapping. It wouldn't be hard to paint a picture of violent people with violent intent, especially if you made the connection with the flurry of activity by the Devil's Brigade.

And all of it leading to *right now*. A split second at a hotel window; a carefully laid trail that they'd followed, bringing them to the climax conceived of by Todd and his people. An assassination. Not the President, but, considering the times, something as good, if not better, as far as America Awake was concerned. Todd and his people *needed* the President.

But they didn't need Billy Carstairs. Not alive anyway. Dead, shot down by a terrorist from the Devil's Brigade, Billy would be of tremendous value. A martyr to the cause of Americanism and God. Fence sitter born-again types would come out strongly for a hard-line law-and-order-let's-clean-up-America ticket, and the sudden appearance of the Tenth Crusade as a paramilitary vigilante organization on the streets of Middle America would be welcomed. After all, if a terrorist group could blow up rail lines, transmission lines, rape people and murder them, then *someone* had to look after community safety, and who better than a group of God-fearing Christians who just happened to be well armed and well organized? A grassroots movement with a highly sophisticated group in Washington running interference. If there was any opposition in Congress, "Todd's book" could cut the mavericks out of the herd. Hitler and his Brownshirts had done it in two years, with almost no support and no money. Sarah was willing to bet that Todd's timetable was much shorter.

Sarah swung the car around the brooding bulk of the Lincoln Memorial and headed down the Rock Creek Parkway past the Kennedy Center to Virginia Avenue. She found a spot under the shadow of the huge, curving expanse of the Watergate, parked, and went inside the infamous building.

She went to the flower shop on the lobby floor first and purchased two dozen long stemmed roses in a box. Carrying the roses under her arm she left the shop and crossed the

259

lobby to the elevators. It had been months since she'd been to her father's apartment, but Hugh, the security guard at the desk, still recognized her. She gave him a nod and then stepped into the elevator, pushing the button for the eleventh floor.

Stepping into the apartment was almost too much for her. A cleaning lady still came once a month but the air was musty and old. The scent of death. And every piece of furniture, every painting on the walls was charged with memory.

It was a big place, eleven rooms in all, and her father had joked about its size more than once. A bank of windows ran along the length of the apartment, overlooking the Potomac and Theodore Roosevelt Island. To the left, half-hidden by the curve of the building, you could see the Kennedy Center.

Sarah took a deep breath and let it out. There was no time for memory. No time even to get her wounds properly attended to. She put the roses down on the small Queene Anne table in the living room and crossed the thick Persian carpet to the fireplace. The Purdy hung there, sleek, dark, and menacing, three thousand dollars' worth of firearm.

For an instant she could almost see the gun barrel in her father's mouth, and taste the bitter oil. She banished the thought, stood on her tiptoes, and brought it down. She carried the heavy weapon to the Queene Anne table and opened the box of roses. The gun fit with an inch to spare. She left the box and the gun together, and went into her father's small study, just off the dining room. The box of shells was where it always was, in his desk drawer. She took the shells back to the living room and loaded the gun quickly, sliding four shells into the overhead chamber, and that brought on another wave of memory: at Fox Run, when she was eighteen and trying to impress a friend she'd brought down from Vassar. Sarah had asked her father to show her how to use the shotgun and he'd explained carefully. She'd fired it once, aiming at a deadhead in the river a few dozen yards out from the boathouse, and the recoil had almost knocked her off her feet. Her friend, far from being impressed, had laughed her head off and the bruise had stayed on Sarah's shoulder for a week.

The shotgun loaded, Sarah replaced it in the rose box, retied the ribbon and left the apartment. Three minutes later she was back in her rental and heading down Virginia Avenue. She went through the underpass, came out on the far side, and turned onto E Street.

She doglegged around Rowlin's Park and continued east along E Street. There was a barricade across the section of E Street that ran behind the White House and above the Elipse, and cursing under her breath she hauled the wheel around and went up 17th past the executive offices. She turned east again on Pennsylvania and went past the White House, craning her neck to see if there was any activity.

There was a line of cars parked in front of the portico entrance, and as she went past Sarah thought she caught the burst of a camera flash. Damn! They were leaving; there wasn't much time left. She'd seen at least a dozen limousines but the car that caught her attention was a white Cadillac convertible. That would be Billy's car. She pushed her foot down and cut out in front of a bus, then back in again.

"Calm down, sweetie," she whispered to herself. "Don't get stopped by a cop now."

She reached 15th, turned due south, and looked for a parking spot. She spotted a hydrant almost on the corner and without pausing she turned in, then jumped out of the car, grabbing the now heavy box of roses. She ran down to the corner of Pennsylvania and burst in through the lobby of The Washington, then slowed down, trying to look casual.

She located the house phones and, walking over to one of them, she dialed 0 and, winging it, asked to be connected to Mr. Freeman's room. Almost immediately the operator came back, saying there was no such person registered in The Washington. Sarah thanked the operator and hung up, wondering what to do next. Her theory was logical, but perhaps she'd taken it too far. But if she wasn't wrong? She stood for a moment, planning her next move. Then she took a deep breath and prepared herself for what would have to be sheer improvisation.

She walked confidently to the front desk and engaged the clerk's attention. "Would you tell me Philip Kirkland's room number, please. I have some flowers for him."

The clerk smiled officiously. "I'm sorry, madame, but we are not allowed to give out that information. Why don't you leave them with me. I'll see he gets them. Mr. Kirkland was not feeling well when he arrived, and I doubt he's receiving visitors."

So they *had* got Philip! Sarah's heart began to pound wildly. "I don't really think that's for you to decide, now is it?" she said, in her most imperious tone.

"Very well, madame, if you insist," the clerk said coldly. "Mr. Kirkland is in room four-twelve."

Without another word, and clutching the long white box of roses, Sarah headed straight for the elevators.

*   *   *

The connecting door between rooms 412 and 414 opened and a woman dressed in a crisp white nurse's uniform appeared. She closed the door and turned to face Philip. Through the partially opened window he could hear the faint sounds of a marching band approaching.

"Hello, Philip," said the nurse.

At first he didn't recognize her, distracted by the uniform. Then it sank in.

"Heather!" he whispered, his eyes wide. She was utterly changed. There was no trace of the dead-eyed expression he'd seen in her before. She looked alert and in full possession of her senses, terrifyingly normal.

"Are you so surprised?" She smiled.

"I don't understand."

Heather walked across the room to the window and looked out. Then she picked up the sniper rifle, and checked it carefully, clearly familiar with it. Philip saw for the first time that she was wearing tight fitting surgical gloves.

"We are all instruments of the Lord," she said quietly. "We all have our place in his plan. By following his will we can cleanse ourselves of sin. Rejoice with me, Philip."

The sound of the band was getting louder. Philip swallowed hard, his mouth dry. Heather looked briefly out the window and then came back to the chair. She crouched down in front of Philip, her hands on his thighs.

"I'm so glad it was you they chose," she whispered, smiling up at him. "From the beginning our lives have been joined. I know it was a terrible sin to have loved you the way that I did, but we can pay for our sin together now, redeem ourselves in the end."

"God, Heather! Please! Get me out of these handcuffs. There's still time to stop this thing!"

"No," said Heather, the soft smile still on her face. An angel's face. "I have a duty to God. This is his will."

"Todd's will!" said Philip. "Not God's. The Tenth Crusade's will. They've used you, Heather."

For an instant the smile faded, but then it returned and she shook her head. "Those are not your words, Philip. I have been shown the way, and I know what I have to do." She rose up and leaned forward, her mouth touching his lips softly, almost a caress. She stood back, looking down at him, then turned and went to the window. She picked up the Valmet and slid back the bolt. There was a faint snapping sound as the shell popped up into the chamber.

"You'll be a murderer," said Philip, his eyes locked on the black snout of the Valmet's barrel.

"It's the price I have to pay," murmured Heather. "I'll pay for that sin along with my others, but I shall be redeemed. I shall be saved." The barrel came up, aimed at his chest.

A creeping coldness began to spread over Philip, his heart became a terrible pulsing weight. He knew that he only had a few more seconds to live, and nothing on earth was going to save him.

"Did you know from the beginning?" he asked, teeth clenched. "Did you know it was going to end like this when you called me in New York? When you came into my bed? When I was making love to you, did you know you were going to kill me then?"

"Don't," whispered Heather. She raised the skeleton stock to her shoulder. "Don't make it worse."

"Bitch!" he spit out, lip curling. "That was your job, wasn't it? Make love to him, make him care again. Make him follow you. Set him up. And kill him."

Heather groaned. "I had lost the way," she whispered, her finger tightening on the trigger. "I had lost the way, but they showed me how I could redeem myself."

"I killed for you," said Philip. "Two people are dead now because I thought you were in danger, and all along you were setting me up. A lie. It was all a great big fucking lie!"

"STOP IT!" screamed Heather.

Philip felt a tearing pain in his lower back and then the room exploded around him. Before consciousness faded he saw Heather disintegrate before his eyes, the white uniform suddenly shredding, the bits of cloth mixing with blood and tissue spraying back against the walls as the force of the blasts blew her out through the shattered window, her face a featureless paste of gore, her chest, stomach and groin a single, bloody open wound.

Then, madly, from the band, two bars of "When the Saints," then a final, black silence.

Chapter Twenty-two

It took the various authorities involved almost a week to re-construct the events which had culminated in the carnage of room 412 at The Washington Hotel. The shotgun blast from Sarah Logan's Purdy, which had blown open the hotel room door had also demolished the rear of the chair Philip Kirkland was handcuffed to. Some of the pellets had struck him in the lower back and buttocks, but, according to the doctors at Georgetown Hospital, the wounds were minor and he was able to answer questions the following day.

Over the next few days, impounded files, from Nevada Survival Skills, Todd's residence, and his consulting firm, as well as from Barrington and the Eagle One Institute in Reno, were more than enough to build a chain of evidence connecting them with the Devil's Brigade.

The impounded files showed that the plan to assassinate Carstairs had been established almost a year before, each step having been meticulously planned in minute detail. There were a number of fallback plans in case anyone balked along the way, and if Philip hadn't followed the carefully laid out line of clues, he would have been kidnapped at any point and brought anyway to The Washington Hotel. Nothing had been left to chance. Among the files was a detailed profile of Philip Kirkland's personality, with scenarios describing his probable reactions under various circumstances.

Psychiatrists with the Federal Bureau of Investigation and the Secret Service division of the Treasury Department were beginning to form a picture of techniques used by the Tenth

Crusade to make an assassin out of Heather Foxcroft. Already mentally unstable, and vulnerable after years of isolation within the Sisters of Charity, Heather had been easy prey. By a process of physical and mental humiliation Heather had been made to believe that she really was an instrument of God, and since God's law superseded all others, any moral qualms that might have interfered with her actions were cast aside. Further specific programing—tailored to make her react mechanically to key phrases and signals, such as the single long ring of a telephone at Fox Run—had been easy to lay into her already malleable consciousness. According to the doctors, the same process could have been used on any of hundreds of members of the Tenth Crusade group, but it was assumed that Heather was used because of her prior relationship with Philip, and for the value of having the daughter of a man like General Foxcroft turn out to be a "terrorist" member of a group like the Devil's Brigade.

Unlike the various Manchurian Candidate or Seven Days in May hypotheses, there was no plan to actually take over the Government of the United States; Todd, Snow, Krone, and Keller were wise enough to know that for a totalitarian government to succeed, it must be elected by the population, not forced on it. The purpose of the assassination was to lay the groundwork for an even more complete neo-conservative power base than that which already existed, and that, coupled with a growing acceptance of the Tenth Crusade as a quasi-official police group, would have eventually given that organization the power it needed. The projections set out in the Jericho computer program saw a full "Christian America" within three years.

Not surprisingly, once deprived of its leadership and the complex structure of authority that governed it, the Tenth Crusade would collapse quickly. In much the same way as the early National Socialist Party in Germany and the communists, the Tenth Crusade was built on a "cell" system, with almost no interaction between groups. Isolated, the small cells would simply disband for lack of direction, and out of the simple fear that members would be arrested.

Nevada Survival Skills was shut down, Senator Snow,

Krone, and Todd were on bail pending indictment for charges ranging from conspiracy and kidnapping to murder and blackmail, and Freeman was killed in a gun battle while trying to cross the border into Canada. Billy Carstairs was in seclusion at a friend's home in the Bahamas awaiting the verdict of an Internal Revenue audit on the assets of 21st Century Communications.

Sarah Logan was interrogated, questioned, and interviewed by the District of Columbia police, the FBI, the Secret Service, the New York City police, the Nevada and Colorado State police and the chairman of the Senate Ethics Committee.

When she finally visited Philip in the hospital, he was lying on his side reading a complexly folded newspaper and smoking a cigarette. He was wearing a hospital gown and he had the sheet drawn up to his waist.

"Hi," he said. "Have a seat." He pointed his chin at one of the plain gray chairs beside the bed.

"You look pretty good," said Sarah, seating herself.

Philip lifted his shoulders and grinned. "Not bad for someone who was shot in the bum by a crazy woman with a shotgun."

"Sorry," said Sarah, blushing hotly.

"Forget it. You shot me in the ass but you saved it as well. Not to mention Billy Carstairs'. One of the FBI types who've been grilling me said that the parade was right underneath the window when you fired. Another couple of seconds and Carstairs would have been dead meat."

"Not to mention the vice president," said Sarah. "He was sitting beside Carstairs in the convertible."

"No big loss there."

"Be serious."

"All right, you want serious? They'd been planning the Devil's Brigade-Carstairs thing for quite a while, from what I can gather. They were probably going to use somebody already in the Crusade to do the dirty work, but when Heather came along they jumped at the opportunity. She had no past associations with the Crusade, and neither did I. We were both 'clean.' They already had General Foxcroft on their blackmail list, so it was even easier. The idea was for me to get led around by the nose, piling up criminal evidence against myself, and evidence that I had something against the Crusade. The FBI told me they'd found some stuff in my place in New York that had obviously been planted to tie me to the Devil's Brigade. If things had gone the way Todd and his people had wanted, it would have looked as though I'*d* kidnapped Heather and convinced her that we should kill Carstairs. It sounds pretty thin now with hindsight, but after the fact no one would have questioned it. A nice tidy wrap-up to an assassination. Dead victim, dead assassins, and no loose ends. But you screwed it up. They hadn't counted on me meeting up with you, so they had to run around patching up the leaks when you started making waves. You either had to be accounted for in the scenario, or wiped out. That's why they staged the attack on your grandmother's place. They wanted Heather back and you out of the picture."

"You're giving me a headache," said Sarah.

"I know what you mean. I've been lying here for the better part of a week trying to put all the pieces together. The one thing I can't figure out is how you knew I'd be at The Washington Hotel."

Sarah lifted her shoulders. "I didn't *know*," she said slowly. "It was a long shot. After all, what we were involved in had to mean something, it had to lead somewhere. The Carstairs rally was the only connection I could see, and killing Carstairs would make sense. I took that one step further and it clicked that it would be logical to set you up to be the assassin. The only other thing I could have done was go to the police but I thought by the time I'd convinced them of my story it would have been too late. I wasn't cut out to play at being the U.S. Cavalry coming to the rescue of the wagon train."

"You did just fine, thank God," said Philip. "A female version of James Bond. By the way, did you get what you wanted ... on your father, I mean?"

Sarah nodded. "Yes. It was all there. I've decided not to make a specific issue about it. I read the file. They were blackmailing my father, but they were doing it with fact. I'm going to drop it. According to the Secret Service there are close to seventy-five thousand specific blackmail dossiers.

Enough to put Todd and the others away forever. It's all wrapped up except for Keller. He's jumped bail and disappeared into Europe somewhere."

"So the universe is unfolding as it should," said Philip. He butted his cigarette. "Except for Heather."

There was a long silence that lay like an ocean between them. Finally Sarah spoke up.

"I didn't know, Philip. I didn't know until afterward. It all happened so fast."

"There's no need to be sorry for what you did," said Philip. "You saved my life, and a lot of other people's too."

"But you loved her." Sarah began to cry softly, the tears tracking down her cheeks. "You loved her and I killed her."

"Once upon a time I loved her," said Philip gently. "Having her back again was like dipping into a dream. I thought it was real ... I *wanted* it to be real so badly I believed in it. They showed me the psychological profile Todd had done on me. They *knew* I'd feel that way. But I was wrong. The last time Heather was real for me was when I took that photograph of her at Orly. You didn't kill Heather. You killed someone I didn't know. A stranger." He took a long breath and shook his head. "Shit, that's not much of an epitaph is it?"

"No. Not much."

There was another silence. Brief and thoughtful.

"Come here," said Philip. "Sit on the bed."

Still crying, Sarah did as he asked. "What?"

"Bend down a bit," instructed Philip. He moved up, bracing himself on one elbow. He kissed her lightly on the mouth and then sank down onto the pillow again.

"What was that for?" asked Sarah. "I'm the one supposed to be giving out sympathy, not the other way around."

"I didn't do it for sympathy," said Philip. "Bend down." She did and he kissed her again, firmly.

She felt herself drifting into the kiss and then pulled back, looking at him.

"I could quote poetry, if you like." He smiled. "'Trust no future howe'er pleasant. Let the dead past bury its dead. Act, act in the living present! Heart within and God o'erhead.'"

"Wordsworth?"

"Longfellow," smiled Philip. "The librarian can make mistakes just like the rest of us."

"What's that supposed to mean?" asked Sarah.

"It means," said Philip, raising himself up to kiss her again, "it means how do you feel about coming to Hawaii with me as soon as I can get myself out of here?"